CAPE TOWN COOLIE

RÉSHARD GOOL

HEINEMANN

Heinemann International
a division of Heinemann Educational Books Ltd
Halley Court, Jordan Hill, Oxford OX2 8EJ

Heinemann Educational Books Inc
361 Hanover Street, Portsmouth, New Hampshire, 03801, USA

Heinemann Educational Books (Nigeria) Ltd
PMB 5205, Ibadan
Heinemann Kenya Ltd
PO Box 45314, Nairobi, Kenya
Heinemann Educational Boleswa
PO Box 10103, Village Post Office, Gaborone, Botswana
Heinemann Publishers (Caribbean) Ltd
175 Mountain View Avenue, Kingston 6, Jamaica

LONDON   EDINBURGH   MELBOURNE   SYDNEY
AUCKLAND   SINGAPORE   MADRID
HARARE   ATHENS   BOLOGNA

British Library Cataloguing in Publication Data

Gool, Réshard
Cape Town Coolie
I. Title   II. Series
823 [F]

ISBN 0–435–90568–6

Photoset by Wilmaset, Birkenhead, Wirral
Printed in Great Britain by
Cox & Wyman Ltd, Reading, Berkshire

90 91 92 93 94 95 10 9 8 7 6 5 4 3 2 1

Réshard Gool was born in London in 1931 and died in May 1989. He was educated in Edinburgh and Cape Town, and attended universities in England, Wales and Canada. As an academic he travelled extensively to teach, lecture and pursue his many lines of research as well as to present literary papers and give poetry readings.

Professor Gool had a huge capacity for work and thrived on political and cultural interests. He lived on Prince Edward Island with his artist wife, Hilda Woolnough, and was actively involved in the local politics and culture of the island. He founded Phoenix Galleries and Phoenix Galleries Craft Co-operative, acted as co-ordinator of the Prince Edward Island Summer Festival of Poetry and Music and was one of three poets/writers from the island invited to read at the Cultural Olympics in 1976.

Author and poet, Gool's commitment to literature led him to establish Square Deal Publications in 1970 and he played a major editorial role for the company. He also edited numerous books and magazines for publishers worldwide, whilst maintaining a steady output of articles which ranged across the sphere of politics, art, literature, music and drama. In 1975 he was elected to be a member of the Writers Union of Canada.

Among the many prizes, awards and grants which Gool received were the Norma Epstein Award for his novel *The Price of Admission* in 1970 and the Bronfman Foundation Award for a reworked volume of this work, entitled *Price*, in 1976. *Cape Town Coolie* is based on this successful and popular novel.

To 3 M's: Margaret, Marian and Milt;
to HMW and Georgette; John and Betty;
Bill and Pearl; Andrée; Leon and Karen; Verner Smitheram;
Joan Murray; Lee, Daniel and John;
my students in all the
'Politics and Imagination' courses at UPEI;
and lastly to:
Eva Marliese Held, and her murdered parents:
indeed to all others who have been maimed or destroyed
by gestapo regimes on different faces of the earth:
with love.

. . . treat humanity, whether in your own person or in that of any other,
in every case as an end,
never solely as a means.

Kant

When philosophy paints its grey in grey . . .
The owl of Minerva spreads its wings
only with the falling of dusk.

Hegel *from* Hegel's Philosophy of Right

ACKNOWLEDGEMENTS

The author must thank very particularly Zeena Mascarenhas of Goa, India, for her cheerful, prompt, and fastidious retypings of his final manuscripts; Moyez Vassanji of TSAR, who excerpted earlier versions of this book; Judy Young of the Secretary of State, Ottawa: Ronald Sutherland of the Université de Sherbrooke, and John Smith at UPEI, for their various unrivalled, literary helps; Mario Cabral e Sa who made it possible to finish this and other literary work in Goa; and finally Dr Sarojini Shintri and her colleagues in the English Department who were such gracious hosts during the author's visit to Karnatak University in Dharwad, India, early in 1988, where unpruned excerpts of *Cape Town Coolie* were part of a literary reading.

CHAPTER 1

Even now they desert meaning – as if like their gangster hats and so much else essential to South Africa they belong to a dated Hollywood script – and yet they were my fate.

It was just after eleven o'clock – a beautiful summer morning; and they stood in the foyer outside my Sea Point flat. Both wore suits and standard army-issue ties. Not until the taller man – with the lined forehead and lantern jaw – produced identification, did I unfasten the safety chain.

'CID' he announced; then, perhaps because my face expressed puzzlement, more assuagingly added:

'Just some routine questions . . .' His lips began – I was sure – to shape the word, 'Mister', but he decided instead on '*Mijnheer* Van der Merwe'.

'Come in,' I said unenthusiastically and noticed across the hall – next to the lift – that Elizabeth Milner's door was slightly ajar.

'Just go right in,' I said, pushing past them and pointing back to my living-room. 'I won't be a minute.'

I didn't bother to ring Elizabeth's bell. She wore a floral morning coat and her auburn hair, which framed an ivory neck and cheeks, seemed to gasp in shock when she caught sight of me.

I put a finger to my lips.

'I need a favour,' I whispered, and because suspicion continued to steep her grave amber eyes, I added, 'very badly. Phone my lawyer, AK Blum. Ask him to come here as fast as possible.'

'Blum?' she whispered back, 'the ex-mayor?'

'That's right. He's in the book.'

'Right away,' she said.

'Bless you.'

In my living-room the short fat detective was looking through the balcony windows at the tides which lapped and foamed over the smooth dark rocks of Sea Point. A few holiday-makers were tanning almost nude bodies where the rocks were bare and dry.

'These people,' he said in strong *Platteland* Afrikaans, 'are mad!' – He used the colloquial word, *bedonderd*. – 'They all want to be coloured!' – Once again he used a local word; the word, *kleurling*; which added contempt to his disbelief.

He had taken off his hat which he held loosely between both hands over the seat of his pants. I noticed that his gingerish hair was almost the same colour as his *veldtschoene*.

The other man was taking an inventory of my bookshelves. A group of framed photographs on the central shelf had arrested most of his attention.

'There!' he almost shouted at his colleague, 'there he is – Naidoo!'

'Yes,' the fat man replied, not moving his eyes from the sea front. 'I noticed.'

After a moment, with surprising bitterness, he added:

'I suppose you had your *coolie* friend here to watch the white women taking off their clothes.'

The idea was absurd. I laughed so spontaneously that he turned to evaluate the irreverence. His small eyes were red about blue irises; his lashes were gold flecked, perhaps because he stood in a shaft of strong sunlight.

Still laughing, I said:

'No. As a matter of fact we used to play chess. He disliked the game and played only to humour me.'

'So you admit you knew him well?' the taller detective suggested.

I smiled wryly, remembering both how unfathomable Henry Naidoo could be, and also how my wife, Yvonne, once said that tall lean people, like Henry, tended to bottle up their feelings.

Still smiling I crossed the room and took the photograph of Henry and me off the shelf.

The move worked perfectly: it took the taller man's attention away from the bookshelves where, I had noticed, Henry's notebooks, diaries and other papers occupied a fat legal folder.

I examined the photograph with less surprise than I do now, here in Canada.

'You knew him well?' the tall detective repeated, coming to sit on the sofa opposite my armchair. He took off his hat. His black eyebrows contrasted oddly with his high crew cut which was grey

2

under a top layer of discoloured black. It looked unnatural: as if it had been badly dyed.

'Where is Stewart?' the fat man barked suddenly.

'Stewart?'

'Gordon Stewart.'

'I have no idea.'

'And that Coloured bitch?'

I was about to tell both fools that the 'Coloured bitch' – Katherine Holmes – was one of our best friends but the front doorbell pre-empted a spate of self-indulgent anger.

No sooner did they catch sight of Blum than their faces fell; they seemed to forget the point of their mission and left soon afterwards.

At the door, however, the fat policeman felt compelled to tell me how unco-operative I had been: how I had turned myself into a 'marked' man.

'Us fellows in the force,' he hissed bitterly, 'don't forget, *Mijnheer*.'

'Doctor,' I corrected him, 'Doctor Van der Merwe.'

He shook his plump face with its small, sardonic blue eyes.

'Remember that!' he prophesied, 'we'll fix you one day, doctor or not, my friend.'

As a precaution I asked Blum to take Henry's effects into safe keeping and somehow to get them to my cabin a week later: the day the ship sailed. Until the arrival of these louts, I had twice postponed leaving.

The precaution was intelligent as I discovered the next day when, returning home, I found several items of personal property missing: in particular, my university lecture notes, copies of the British magazine, *Freedom* (to which I had become a subscriber) and some innocuous correspondence from Bertrand Russell.

When I rang police headquarters to report these losses I was told that an investigator would be sent over at three, that afternoon.

'Not,' I said, 'I hope, those two clowns you sent yesterday.'

'Excuse me? . . . Do you want to speak to the desk sergeant?' she asked.

'Never mind. I was just fed up about my Russell letters. Three, you say?'

'Three p.m.,' she confirmed.

'Good enough.'

I was tempted to ask Blum to join us but it was just as well I didn't because the investigator was a welcome surprise.

'Good Lord!' I exclaimed, when I answered the door.

Jan Coetzee – a cousin of my wife – stood in the hall.

'Come in. Come in, man.' I inspected my wrist-watch, 'we've just time for a quick drink. I'm expecting someone from the police.'

He hesitated, then apologised that it was he whom the police had sent. His small head was bent slightly to one side so that, through thick-lensed glasses, his right eye stared at me enormously while the other interviewed aspects of the carpet at my feet. – At primary school the phrase 'cock-eye blue birdie' used to haunt him mercilessly, in spite of the fact that both his eyes were brown, one a shade lighter than the other.

He was stiff at first – barely sipping the sherry I had poured – but after a while he thawed out enough to tell me that his was a political appointment and that the party – his party, the Afrikaaner Nationalists, the HNP – believed I had been associating with 'too many subversive elements'.

The remark evoked in me more surprise than anger.

'Who in particular?' I enquired politely. 'Not Henry Naidoo surely?'

He shook his head.

'Not Naidoo', he said.

'Who then?'

He hesitated.

'It's probably because of Yvonne,' he suggested apologetically, 'isn't it? That's what I told them.'

At the mention of Yvonne I did not explode. I remembered what she used to say when I lost my temper: 'Count, darling, count to ten!' At the same time I remembered another voice from the past: this time an early entry in Henry's diaries in which he advised himself to be *invisible, always courteous to the white man, to keep control and never let him see you as a threat.*

The idea of me, a golden-haired representative of Afrikaaner *Herrenvolk*, behaving as a lesser breed, was an incomparable irony but I remained loyal to Henry's caveat.

For Yvonne I counted silently to ten, then – as cordially as possible – suggested that we could part agreeably if we levelled with one another.

4

His response was disconcerting. One eye fixed on me while the other seemed to explore the heavens.

'Alright,' he said at last, rearranging the foci of his eyes. 'What do you want to know?'

'Shaikh-Moosa,' I went straight for the jackpot, 'has your party bought his Cape Flats deal?' I wanted to confirm what I'd heard from another source.

Coetzee didn't answer at once. After several re-orbitings of his eyes, he said:

'Alright, but this is off the record. I never told you this. Is that agreed?'

I nodded conspiratorially, and continued to do so while he filled me in on the most recent of Shaikh-Moosa's complex and manifold financial plots: in particular with the levels of the HNP with whom the Great Man was dealing.

In return I told him that neither Henry Naidoo nor I had ever had much to do with Gordon Stewart. Neither of us had liked the man, much less shared his ideological positions. Katherine Holmes, I suggested, was a false trail: his people would be wise to stop trying to track her down. More confidentially I explained the relationships she had had with Rycliffe and Stewart – matters I will disclose more fully later. For plausibility I had to implicate Henry, though I didn't want to.

He was remarkably understanding. In his freshly laundered cream tropical suit – a neat, silver key-chain on one wrist twinkling each time he raised the sherry glass – he behaved more assuredly than the graduate law student he had so recently been; first with one eye on me, then the other, he listened intently. Before we parted, nevertheless, he could not resist repeating what had perhaps – throughout our exchanges – lain uppermost in his mind: How could I – coming, as I did, from such eminent *Voortrekker* stock – have 'gotten tangled up' with all these political radicals?

I was tempted to ask him the same question, to remind him that one of my grandfathers had been a founder of one of the country's most progressive institutions – the *Afrikaaner Bond* – but in the end, Yvonne and Henry won the day.

At the door he suddenly lost all reserve, or seemed to. With a firm, self-confident hand he took the limp one I proferred, and told me confidentially that I was in for a pleasant surprise.

'Soon,' he intimated, 'perhaps even as early as tomorrow.'

For a moment, alarmed, I wondered whether his present would be the two goons that had arrived the day before. Because I must have looked unusually apprehensive, he tried to reassure me.

'It's because – as you said,' he explained, 'we levelled with each other. What I'm going to do is a risk, but you keep mum, and I'll do the same. Agreed?'

I couldn't quite manage a thankful smile but the next morning I had no difficulty. By special delivery I received an unstamped parcel filled with my missing documents.

The day I left Cape Town produced a visitor who replaced the relief I was feeling by a sadness that, to this day, often brims over into a sense of desolation, even of tragedy.

Was it for Yvonne or Henry, or the country, or indeed all my own past that I grieved?

For a long time I wondered whether this book was about Henry or about South Africa or really about me, and even when I decided to concentrate on Henry where was the start?

The diaries – and his papers generally – were a deciding corrective. After I had reread them for the umpteenth time, as well as the most recent gaol-sentence correspondence, it became clear that I should plunge *in medias res*; that everything began on that fatal day when he encountered Katherine Holmes.

Two passages in the diaries offer revealing preludes.

One is bizarre. Henry's first year on his own – in private legal practice – continues to be a risk, and he wonders if failure is circumstantial or characteristic. Insecurity is turning him into a 'workaholic'. One evening he stands before the wardrobe of his darkening bedroom and the gaunt image in the looking-glass that stares back belongs to shadow kingdoms.

His prose grows airless:

Circles, like dark areas on damaged fruit, surround the eyes; the complexion has the sallow etiolated look of plants left too long in the dark. And the clothes? The clothes are threadbare. They sag like the ghostly shoulders which make only a bare, pitiful attempt to keep up appearances. God, how I hate

myself and the sterile life I'm leading!
The second passage is less self-indulgent.

Monday, 15th December, 1947.

A few minutes ago Doc barged into my study. He was in dinner togs: dines out a lot these days. For days on end we are independent existences registered only by a few unwashed plates in the sink or a scum line around the bath-tub. I should speak to him about using my toothpaste and towels but I owe a month's rent.

'Tomorrow,' he announced, 'it's Dingaan's Day.' He's closing up shop. I should do likewise.

His habit of barging in is exasperating but – even after five years – his manner and his patter continue to entertain.

'Now look here, ol' chap', he drawls from a small, neat, baby-like face (urbane self-mockery about the mouth), 'you must get organised. Pull yourself together. We absolutely must get a little action around here!'

'We?' I ask.

He hates cross-examinations.

'Pieter,' he attests vaguely, 'some of the others, perhaps.'

Pieter, dearest of all diaries, is Doc's latest protégé. A recent arrival from Holland: clings to Doc pathetically. Sells insurance and has a thing about Coloured girls: always lands up with clinging, insipid girls.

Doc has the whole jamboree planned. We are to meet early afternoon at Trafalgar Baths. Some sort of swimming gala there; school kids mainly. 'But,' Doc promises, smacking together velvet lips, 'big sister always comes.' He laughs immoderately at the double entendre. *'Many, many hotcha-hotcha girls, therefore lots and lots of fun!' He speaks of women succulently as if he were munching grapes.*

If the Baths are no go, he promises other diversions which must mean more succulence: more grapes to munch. We might 'ride out' to Paarl, 'look in on Elizabeth and Frederic just to see what's cooking out there!', later on we might go for a duck. 'Sea bathing, man, tremendous. Wakens the sexual glands!'

Who the devil Frederic and Elizabeth are, I'm tempted to ask, but the phone rings.

It's a new number for the harem. Must be, because he talks at length; the old ones are treated like medical calls, perhaps because they've become ones.

I don't mind his barging in on me but I do object to having my life organised. Funny thing is I'd forgotten it was a holiday tomorrow. In my mind

7

I've planned another day. No need to endure Pieter's fatuous chatter, or the graceless women Doc invariably picks up. In the morning I'll bring my casework up to date, in the afternoon I'll potter about the garden. Might do some reading too.

Needless to say, these plans broke down. By way of self-apology he told me later that, not having been able to sleep, he'd begun work on a brief only to discover suddenly that it was Tuesday; a new day was waking beyond the panes of his bedroom windows. Haggard, yet still wide awake, he went into the garden to watch the sunrise.

Standing there in the cold garden, in pyjamas and dressing-gown – at home, he always worked in pyjamas – face unshaven, he had no augury of special events. It was just another ravishing, Cape summer morning. It was only later that *Dingaan's Day* assumed more dramatic consequence.

What he saw instead was less fatal.

In his diary he reports the morning with characteristic extravagance. The Cape (province and peninsular) was for him a haven – *a golden island of sanity, a prediluvial paradise outside the Iron Curtain of more general South African despotism* – and he salutes Cape Town that morning with a rapture that is almost as poignant as the adulation he later accords to Katherine.

Imagination is not given *carte blanche*: his prose is not yet advertising copy, but it is close.

The day is – he writes – *beginning fair; a cool, white morning. Scent of pinewoods still fresh with dew comes off the misty, upper slopes of Table Mountain, and in the young sunlight over the city, mingles with the richer effluvia of fish, cargoes, seaweed, and warming brine.*

Milk carts will now be rumbling over the cobbles of older parts of the city; but soon those same streets will sink back into brightening emptiness. Then, because it is a holiday, there will be no early hawkers in the Cape Coloured and Malay Quarter of District Six; there, as in the town centre, shops and offices will remain closed all day.

About ten o'clock, in sunshine already quite fierce, a movement of leisurely traffic will spread through the suburbs towards country and seaside resorts.

By noon the city will have the stark, robbed look of a ghost town. Sprawled across the wide maternal lap of the central valley of the mountainside, it will rise in tiers to yield a scene panoramic and mediterranean and filmed in sunlight as dazzling as the white beaches of the rocky shores. It would be low tide, then; sea sucked back into hot blue sky. Perhaps a few grey trawlers might be pinned to a white horizon against Robben Island. Elsewhere, the atmosphere will be hushed and blue.

The day promised delicious, memorable prospects, but Henry's eyelids were seared with prolonged wakefulness, and he knew that unless he had a few hours of sleep, the headache already throbbing at the back of his head would be intolerable.

Much later, when he woke, the room was hot and stuffy. The bedclothes clung to him, but he was strangely light-headed. It was half-past eleven. He washed and had to force down a necessary breakfast. There was a brackish taste in his mouth. A note on the kitchen table asked him to bring Pieter's car, which was parked in the driveway, to Trafalgar Baths. The note was exasperating. It highlighted a fact he didn't wish to face – namely, that he had already wasted a good working morning.

It was a few minutes after twelve when he parked the blue convertible in the large, otherwise empty, open square before the Baths. He shut off the engine and for a few minutes played absent-mindedly with the ring of silver keys.

From behind high white walls rose a chaos of rampant pandemonium – crashing wire baskets, children pitching shrill trebles above a general confusion of speech and splashing water. In the foyer – a hall of cool, pink marble – a small queue of mainly District Six people had formed. Now and then, someone pushed through the glass swing-doors to join the queue.

Unable any longer to bear the pretence of making a rational decision he shut the car door and locked up with the care of someone determined not to be burdened by haste. In the plate glass of the ticket bureau, he eyed himself, casually, scornfully – a tall, upright man, balding prematurely, dressed in sandals, an off-white shirt, and a light-blue summer suit. He noted, too, counting his change, that his fingers were broad, the nails shaped like small, purple spades.

There was a short antiseptic corridor, two steps, then he was standing on an open balcony where the sun again unexpectedly clapped about him a straitjacket of hot, taut light.

Below on a plateau of blazing green was the pool – a hundred yards of sparkling, sunlit *lapis lazuli*, with a concrete border and diving-boards. The lawns were not crowded yet; here and there sprinklers blew up ghostly rainbows of spray and tangled small jewels of dew over the grass.

Doc had already arrived. He sat on a low, concrete pedestal near the tuck-shop. Below him on the grass Pieter was a gawky figure wrapped over his own knees. The others had not materialised.

Henry paused once more to debate whether his choice was wise or self-indulgent. The office in Hanover Street presented a table of incomplete work; a vision of impotence and waste. Taking off his coat and slinging it glumly over one shoulder, he saw himself as a mutinous votary of Pluto entering the underworld and went down the stone staircase, smiling ironically.

He had no sooner completed one flight when someone – a new voice, unfamiliar, a strong Indian accent – called out.

'Henry – hey there! Henry Naidoo!'

The speaker wore a pair of plum-coloured bathing trunks – a Tamilian, perhaps, by the darkness of his complexion. He parted full lips in a rapturous grin.

'Well, I'll be buggered!' he exclaimed, clasping Henry's right hand in both of his and shaking it vehemently.

'How's it, man? *Hoe gaan dit*? Long time, no see!'

He spoke Durban slang in a voice that was quite hoarse, as if years of ingratiating enthusiasm had corroded the larynx.

'Doan you remember me, heh? We was at Crabbe Street School together, remember, both of us, same time? How's your heart, *maartjie?* You remember me! Moodley. John Moodley.'

'John Moodley? Of course.' A cordial smile masked continuing uncertainty. 'How are you, John?'

'Terrific!' Moodley's dark face went ecstatic. 'Hey, hey – what you doing, man?' Enthusiasm leaned him so far forward he was almost spitting into Henry's face. 'On holidays?'

Henry winced imperceptibly. 'Just took the day off,' he said as casually as he could. With a controlled yawn, he said, 'And you?'

The hint didn't penetrate. Moodley seemed to wish to drag out the encounter.

'Me too, man. I'm on holidays too.' He laughed good-naturedly. 'Hey man, this place's t'rrific. How long you been here?'

'A few years,' Henry yawned again.

'Okay, is it?'

A defensive shrug reversed its intent. Moodley began to magnify recent experiences. Henry noticed that Pieter was talking urgently to Doc: probably seeking erotic advice. Doc was also pretending to listen: his eyes were screening all new arrivals – women particularly. With an effort of will Henry moved his attention back to Moodley.

The man was saying he had never visited the Cape before. The climate was 't'rrific! Man, one hundred percent better than Durban!' The scenery, too, deserved lavish accolade – 'so diff'rent, mediterranean, what you think, huh?' Then there were 'the folks – the *hombres* and *sterra* are kinda free, isn't it? The *boks* – the women, 'cepting old Malay *bokkies*, didn't have no *purdah*! There were so many parties and other *jorls* . . . man the place has what it takes.'

The elated monologue was music eight years old. Henry felt the uncontrollable distaste that in-groupers feel towards those without.

Moodley must have sensed the falling interest. He waxed importunate.

'I hear it,' he said, 'you made a name for yourself down here!' Henry shut exasperated eyelids.

'You got a private practice, I hear. What's the score?'

'Oh, not bad. Not too bad. So, so.'

Moodley smacked wet lips together: preface for a juicy disclosure.

'Listen man,' he said, sidling up, as confidential as a racing tipster; he looked over one shoulder to make sure no one overheard. He had caught Henry by the left elbow, and plucked the sleeve whenever he wished to emphasise a point. 'Listen, I'm on holidays – okay?' He jerked at the sleeve, and Henry nodded foolishly. 'Okay now, you know Shaikh-Moosa?' Henry again shut exasperated eyelids. He tried to extricate his arm; but Moodley was persistent. 'Hey, listen, man! This is a red-hot thing. Listen, it's all lined up. Shaikh-Moosa's looking for a lawyer – a Cape Town solicitor. Chance of a lifetime, big deal! Big-big! You know, big-big.'

All at once he noticed the lines of scorn running towards Henry's lips. 'What's a matter? What's wrong with Shaikh-Moosa?' He stood back to meet a challenge to personal honour. 'My father works for Shaikh-Moosa,' he said, his tone that of a child who's been told another child's father is bigger or richer.

'I know,' Henry said. He remembered that Old Man Moodley was one of Shaikh-Moosa's trustiest lieutenants – a bent crock of a man

11

with a cracked owl-like face, superficially innocent, but as vicious, cunning and underhand as his more flamboyant master.

'Well, what's wrong with Shaikh-Moosa?' Moodley repeated.

'Nothing.'

'Nothing was proved about Isipingo . . .'

'Or Cato Manor?' Henry asked. These were two real-estate scandals.

'It's all lies,' Moodley pronounced. 'Dirty lies!'

Henry smiled.

Moodley inspected Henry's threadbare suit ironically.

'I can see you don't need a job!' he exclaimed and laughed sneeringly.

It was not worth a fight. The man was only defending himself.

'Look,' Henry said, 'I'm fine. Don't worry about me. I'm doing quite well, thank you.'

He was annoyed that he had been lured into self-justification; but the situation was also comic. While he regarded Moodley as a huckstering outsider, Moodley thought the opposite. In their different ways they were both showing off.

Henry noticed that Doc was waving to him, and turned slightly to wave back.

'Friend of yours?' Moodley asked.

Henry nodded.

'I seen him at a party,' Moodley explained. 'And the white guy? Who's he?'

'Just a friend.'

'He's a big man for the *boks*. A doctor, isn't he?'

'Who?'

'The guy wh' was waving.'

'Yes,' Henry said, 'he's a doctor.'

There was a long awkward pause.

'Well,' Moodley said at last: the serious tone suggested that he wanted to be forgiven for having poked fun at Henry's appearance. 'I'll tell SM I bumped into you.'

'SM?'

'Shaikh-Moosa.'

'Do you tell him everything?'

Moodley smiled condescendingly.

'What's the address, by the way?'

12

Not to answer would be downright rude.

'It's in the phone book,' Henry said.

'First-rate!'

Feeling now ashamed of himself, and wishing to make his circumstances inescapably plain, Henry thanked Moodley for the courtesy, saying, with a self-effacing smile, 'I'm not ungrateful, but . . . well, it's not really necessary. Very kind of you, though.'

It was a mistake. Moodley eyed him suspiciously, and Henry saw that he was going to take the amends for embarrassed gratitude. To offset the inevitable, Henry said, quite firmly:

'Really, please don't mention me to Shaikh-Moosa.'

Moodley was doubtful again, then he laughed.

'Very good!' he said. 'I would do it myself.'

Henry frowned blankly.

'You want to sell yourself dear – ha! ha! SM would 'ppreciate that!'

They were on such unrelated levels that Henry realised nothing would dislodge the belief that he needed an introduction.

'Well,' he said awkwardly, and offering a hand, 'nice to meet you – again. I must go – my friends are waiting.'

As they parted, Moodley held Henry's hand still, for a moment, then winked one eye. In that moment Henry thought Moodley had gone quite mad; perhaps he had a nervous twitch and couldn't shake hands without winking, but while he was walking away Moodley shot back a sidelong approving look which suggested that a firm link with Shaikh-Moosa had been struck. It was the kind of wink you give to an accomplice; it said that they were now eternally bonded against the rest of the world. With a mental shudder, Henry turned quickly away and hurried across the lawns towards Doc.

It was almost half-past twelve. The December sun glowed in an umbrella of rich blue flame, dumb but awake, like the heart of a blowlamp. The lawns were beginning to fill. The pool had been cleared. Near the high diving-board, a group of officials, wearing bright multicoloured rosettes, were supervising the erection of a trestle-table and microphone apparatus.

Doc was talking assertively to Pieter. His pedestal turned out to be a stone ventilation box. He sat forward, and even in repose, held the short brown stump of his body upright from the hips. He was dressed, as usual, with calculated Bohemian abandon – a mottled red, yellow

13

and black safari jacket, ash-blue slacks which a stream of whirring ventilation continuously ruffled, and black sandals.

Pieter's lanky body was doubled up against his own kneecaps. From this crouching position he was toying, on the grass, with Doc's Leica.

'Well, hello there, Henry!' Doc always threw out greetings like challenges, 'I was just telling ol' Pieter here we might run out and see ol' Frederic and Elizabeth in Paarl. God man! When I think of Frederic surrounded by all those lovely Paarl *bokkies*, oodles of Paarl *lulus* – hell's teeth, man! we must get organised. Activate! This place is just deadleh!'

Henry was about to ask who Frederic and Elizabeth were, when he remembered. Frederic was a composer and taught music for a living. Elizabeth was the elder daughter of Councillor Holmes, a woman reported to be remarkably beautiful, intelligent and charming. One could not live in the Cape without hearing of the Holmeses: they were one of the oldest and most distinguished Coloured families. There was some sort of rumour, too, that Elizabeth's sister, another beauty, had gone to the bad and was now attached to the Rycliffe crowd, a group of left-wing socialists who followed Yussouf Rycliffe, a man even better known than the Holmeses. Rycliffe also came from an upper-class family but preferred, perhaps because of inverted snobbery, to hobnob with the *hoi polloi*. These recollections led Henry, for the first time, to consider visiting Paarl seriously: he had often wanted to meet the Holmeses; his interest was not entirely snobbish; it was more born out of curiosity: the Holmeses represented an uncharted area of experience, he admired Councillor Holmes for all that he had heard of him, and wanted to test his own values against fact and report.

'Vot you tink?' Pieter asked. His large, oafish face was irritating. Henry had not quite recovered from Moodley and had to resist making sport of the question. He was thinking how feudal the Cape was: people belonged to families which were sometimes confusingly interrelated. Though he had decided to join the inevitable visit to Paarl, he stretched himself wearily over the grass.

'Up to you,' he said, shielding eyes with one hand. 'I'd like myself, to watch some of – ' he yawned, ' – of the racing.' He patted his mouth, closed his eyes, and breathed in deeply. The air smelt warm and of freshly-mown turf – voluptuous!

'Okey-doke,' Doc said. 'We'll stick around a bit. But only for a

14

while. We'll have to push on soon. God, man! When I think of all that *dop* brandy in the cellar! And Frederic playing the piano . . . just tinkling away at the keys – man!' He smacked his lips loudly together. 'All those red-hot hotch-hotcha girls – chaps! We must move; we must go out to Paarl . . .'

As he grew older Henry found himself more and more liable to lapse into unaccountable dozes. Doc drifted into a confused babble of other voices. Now that he had fully accorded Doc the role of plotmaker, Henry relaxed and fell into a light sleep in which real words and vague imaginings impinged themselves and were located somewhere in a tumbled sunset upon his retinae. He had a short, intense, disordered dream in which he was shaking hands with a man who seemed to be Councillor Holmes but turned out to be Shaikh-Moosa, and simultaneously Doc and Yussouf Rycliffe were making love to Katherine Holmes who was shrieking with a mixture of horrifying pain and rapture while he, Henry, stood by dumbly; then suddenly he was trying to get into his own bedroom but it was locked and something at once wonderful and frightening was happening behind the door which kept sliding on runners, like the doors of train compartments, to and fro, and in the train corridor (for he was now definitely on a train) a large glass water container was swaying rhythmically and snakes, like eels, were slithering around in the greenish waters winking at him; then the train was about to plunge over a precipice, its whistle piercing his ear-drums . . .

He woke, and found that the racing had begun. It was, in fact, the crack of the starter's pistol that had roused him. Automatically, he inspected his wrist-watch – ten-to-one. He couldn't have slept more than ten or twelve minutes, but he felt alarmingly fresh.

People were thronging the concrete border of the pool, cheering and cat-calling. The microphone, toned down, was happily churning out a recent hit – a piece of incredible American gibberish about a man who refused to leave the jungle.

> O bongo bongo bongo
> I doan wanna leave the jungle
> O no no no, no – oh!
> Bingo, bongo, dingo, dongo
> I'm so happy in the jungle
> I refus' to go – oh . . .

The song was as depressing as the lawns, littered now democratically, with empty ice-cream cartons and other waste.

Henry usually found crowds menacing but this afternoon he felt sociable – perhaps because the short nap had revived his spirits – and while he was drifting along the edge of cheering people, now and then catching a glimpse of ardent competitors, an old man whom he'd never met before doffed his hat with embarrassing humility.

'Mr Naidoo,' he said, touching Henry's arm.

'Yes.'

'You're a friend of . . .' He mentioned a man whom Henry had done some unpaid work for.

'Mr Naidoo, I wonder? Could Mr Naidoo, perhaps, please help, please?'

Henry instantly put a hand into his coat pocket – he had an idiosyncrasy of carrying money in jacket, not trouser, pockets – but the favour was not of that order. Haltingly and still embarrassed, the old man explained that the problem was, if he 'could rightly explain, sort of legal, a little sort of.' He spoke of a widespread rumour that there were going to be mass evictions in District Six. In a neighbourhood where most people led hand-to-mouth existences, where tenancy agreements were seldom honoured and hardly ever set out in correct legal form, such rumours were common. Had he been in a less easy mood, had the old man not looked so desperate, Henry might have fobbed him off. Doc, who had been growing more and more restless, signalled that he and Pieter were leaving and Henry waved them on.

The old man said his name was Parsons and that he had tried to see Councillor Holmes who represented his Ward in the City Council, but 'Uncle Albert' – as Holmes was affectionately called – had been 'very busy, right now'. He had tried several other times, but always the same response. He was worried about relatives – a son who had recently moved, with family, into the district. The rent collector, who came once a month and then could never be traced, had warned quite definitely that they and others in the street would be evicted, but he didn't say when. The people had paid several visits to the real-estates offices of Fylfot Holdings, had pointed out to the agent that their rent payments were not in arrears, but had received no reassurance that the rent collector had been misinformed. The agent had been evasive and recommended that enquiries be directed

16

to head office, but when the address of his head office was sought, the agent had hedged and asked them to come back later. This they had done, several times, only to be given the run-a-round. The old man wondered whether legal action might be taken against the agents. Henry smiled.

'Have you got a rent book?' he asked.

The old man shook his head as if such documents were unheard of.

'Have you anything in writing?'

Again, a shake of the head.

'Could you recognise the rent collector if you saw him again?'

No: the collectors changed every month.

Henry shrugged. 'I'm sorry,' he said, as gently as possible, 'but there's nothing . . .'

Aware that the others were probably waiting, Henry interrupted the charming, long-winded, typically Cape Coloured appeal; he promised to have a word with Councillor Holmes.

'Can I please come and see Mr Naidoo then tomorrow?'

Henry checked an impulse to suggest a later date.

'Yes. Alright,' he said. 'Before lunch.'

Henry did not know then, that he would be meeting Shaikh-Moosa in the morning and that he would have to shorten the encounter on Mr Parson's account, but he was in a hurry. In the morning there would be ample time for a conference with Holmes. Henry still thought of himself as a free agent. He did not realise that this simple tenancy affair underlay issues which would plunge his own life into tragedy, but there was much else, at that time, he did not know. He did not know that he would soon be meeting Madge, Jessie, and Katherine – just to mention a few – and the first meeting was less than ten minutes away.

CHAPTER 2

While Henry did not know he would soon be meeting Katherine, she, for her part, was not without an inkling that he might turn up later that afternoon.

Katherine Margaret Holmes. As I write her name, I am still puzzled. Jacques Maritain says somewhere that, faced with love, with the ineffable, descriptions fail. Katherine was, and still is, an enigma quite as complex as Henry. For Henry she represented all that he saw in the Cape – the strange wild amalgam of grace, intelligence, sensuality, charm, impudent gaiety and tenderness . . . tenderness, in fact, extreme enough to be a fault. In a later diary, when he was visiting Durban on Shaikh-Moosa's behalf, he said that she rose in his imagination . . .

like an emanation, like a pungent whiff of black sea-wet hair flung back, of pale powder and perfume in the car which smells also of petrol and warmed leather upholstery . . . then intoxicating, importunate, seemingly inaccessible – the ripe erotic must of clustered grapes, the sour-sweet rape of this year's Constantia vineyards.

And elsewhere . . .

the faces of clocks are always wrong, the days tick by. She is not just a person, though she is one, and so very, very much, but the tart vanishing frock of every dark-haired girl down every bright city street: and yet she is unique, and more real – like the image of my city at night when bracelets of light decorate the velvet mountainsides, sea-wind and dark fresh sea-place air, a dream as living and mysterious as people, a history . . . an unforgettable promise of a gracious way of life.

Returning Tuesday. Durban has lost its significance.

He could turn on the music when the mood caught. The romanticism is touching and absurd; absurd, perhaps, because it touches too

18

deeply – he loved her as if she were a wound that brought simultaneous happiness and pain. His diary is little help. Perhaps the best approach is a short summary of what she was like before he met her. Perhaps, in this way, some of the ineffable might emerge.

I knew her long before Henry did; long, in fact, before she became associated with Yussouf Rycliffe and his latter-day saints. At this point I should identify myself a little more. I come from the Cape Town branch of the *Stellenbosch Van der Merwes* who, as has already been indicated, had more than a hand in the beginnings of the Great Trek, and later in the formation of the liberal *Afrikaaner Bond*. I am not boasting. I am proud of some of my ancestors, but I really want to explain how my family became associated with the older Coloured and Malay families of the Cape. When I was at Oxford, well-meaning English friends would reproach me for outrages inflicted by my kinsmen upon peoples of colour in South Africa. I remember at first being angry and surprised; then more angry after I had tried, without avail, to explain that it was an error to identify the Dutch of the Cape – more particularly the older families – with all Afrikaaners. I would try to explain that our family had intimate ties with all the different races, and that so-called peoples of colour were frequent – sometimes too frequent – visitors to our household but I was never believed, and I expect to be less believed now that the affairs of my homeland have taken more than one turn for the worse. But I am digressing.

When my father died, mother, because she had more time, would attract a rather fuller house than she used to, and it was at one of these 'little tea parties' – where there was never anything less strong than sherry in generous supply, and seldom fewer than twenty people present – that I first met Katherine Holmes. She had come with her mother, who was then still alive – a woman, like both her daughters, of arresting rather tropical good looks, a well-built woman of above medium build with a full bosom and a very erect back. I always remember Mrs Holmes dressed in blue silk, perhaps because she came most frequently so attired. She had a fine nose, arched cheek-bones and a slim mouth; but her most captivating quality was her eyes, which, like her elder daughter's, Elizabeth's, were green, with perhaps a shade more grey in them. The eyes were set in an olive-brown complexion and against a rich head of black hair streaked with white, and they compelled attention. I did not, when I grew to know her better, like her much. She was a domineering sort, rather prim and fussy, and always inveighing against maid servants whom she suspected of 'plotting to walk off with her knives and forks'. In her defence, however, it must be said that she had taken pains over the upbringing of her daughters. The Holmes 'gels' – as mother liked to say; mother was English – were 'quite the little charmers', prettily-mannered and full of agreeable high spirits. They were high-spirited everywhere but in their mother's presence; and that afternoon Katherine was indeed subdued. She had recently turned sixteen, just matriculated from high school, and seemed to be rather pleased to be out of uniforms and wearing frocks again. I did not pay much attention to her that afternoon; there were many other guests and because I had just celebrated my twenty-first birthday I tended not to find anyone younger than myself very interesting.

Mother had invited Katherine to stay overnight, and, if she cared to, a few days longer. After dinner, when I was about to retire to my den – my bedroom study – one of our maids tapped at the door and, with the giggle of all young women of a certain age, handed me a note 'from the young lady upstairs'.

The note read:

Dear His Nibs,

Why are you so snotty? You ignored me all afternoon, and a person of my infinite charms can ill afford to be thus retired. If you do not wish me more miserable, you will come at once to my room, and apologise on lowered knee (yours, not mine) and tell me – as I must always be told – that in no mirror is there one lovelier in this or any other world.

– and it was signed, *Katherine Margaret Holmes*, with the surname struck out. Overleaf was this postcript: *You look intelligent and kind, and I'm bored stiff*.

The audacity was delightful. I put on my new smoking-jacket – a birthday present that I rather fancied myself in – groomed my hair, and set off, heart galloping, towards her room.

She was already in bed. The small, blue-walled attic was sparsely furnished, but it had lost some of its uninhabited look. Yellow roses stood in a blue vase before the white muslin curtains. An orange towel hung tidily over the chair beside the writing-table next to the bed. Several books with bright covers, cosmetics, and a neat pile of freshly laundered handkerchiefs lay on this desk. A faint odour of talcum powder and strange scent fringed the bed; one window was open, and the reading light was focussed upon the close print of Jane Austen's *Pride and Prejudice* – the book which Katherine, knees drawn up to form a tent of furling blankets, was gravely reading.

Her hair was done up behind in a fillet of blue ribbons: indication, perhaps, that she intended to be awake some time yet. She looked up as I entered – I had knocked, but apparently she had not heard – her gravity abruptly dissolving into a peal of delicate silver laughter. Her expression was pert – dimpled cheeks, high cheekbones, an ironical wrinkling under small, lively, black eyes.

'At last!' she exclaimed, with another of her memorable, twinkling laughs, 'I had quite given you up. That girl promised to see you at once, but apparently she didn't.'

She moved her knees to suggest that I should sit on the edge of the bed.

'Did you get my epistle. Epistle, what a silly word! Of course you did, otherwise you wouldn't have come. I am practising being a young lady. Do you think I am very naughty?'

The speech had been rehearsed and she was out of breath.

I laughed.

'Quite the contrary,' I said gruffly. 'I think you are quite enchanting.'

'Thank you,' she said, with just a trace of awkwardness, 'and now you must tell me I smell wonderful – *nuit d'amour* – straight out of Paris!' She rolled her eyes as she pronounced Paris. 'Ah, gay Parée, city of a thousand sins and loves and ecstasies!'

'You are marvellous!' She really was a good actress. 'And you really do smell wonderful – m-m-m – quite out of this world!'

'Well,' she said, suddenly serious, 'that wasn't hard. Just had a bath. Incidentally, does your lavatory chain always go "fut", or is it because it's the way I pull it?'

I told her that the upstairs lavatory was not supposed to be used.

'I'm glad you told me,' she said, 'I thought something was wrong. I nearly tore my shoulders off yanking it. I used both arms, you know. Anyway, it flushed, so there's another thing mother won't have to hear about.'

She wasn't looking at me, she was speaking as if to herself, but suddenly she did look at me, and said, 'Do you want to kiss me?'

My surprise delighted her.

'Good,' she said, 'then you can kiss me here', and offered a dimpled cheek. Laughing, I kissed her cheek, then drew back, waiting to see what would happen next.

'Thank you,' she said, simply, 'now we can be friends. I thought you might be a boor, like some of the chaps at school, but apparently you're not. Are you a boor?'

'No.'

'Not even the littlest, teeniest, weeniest bit?'

'Well, just the teeniest, weeniest bit.'

'Good, I'm glad. You're honest, too. Do you like recitations?'

I nodded, but fortunately she didn't recite. Instead, she started to ask me what I was doing, and fairly soon we were less whimsically launched.

I cannot now remember in detail what we talked about, but I remember her telling me that she wanted to be an actress, but that whenever she mentioned it, her mother always trotted out a line about the daughter of a certain Mrs Worthington whom Noel Coward implored, on his knees, not to put on the stage. We had many similar long talks in the next few days, and during the course of the next year when she had started going to Hewat Teachers' Training College; then, because I left for England to do my doctorate, we lost touch and when I returned I heard, with chagrin, that she had joined the Rycliffe crowd and was one of Yussouf Rycliffe's many mistresses.

I say chagrin not because I am opposed to men keeping mistresses, but because the position made her miserable. How she came to associate with Rycliffe can be dealt with later; meanwhile, a more recent experience may be of value.

When I got back to South Africa I saw her once or twice, from a distance, and had the impression she was deliberately avoiding me. After several years in Britain I had changed, and felt, in my unsettled state, wounded; English reserve and respect for privacy had rubbed off onto me, and though I thought several times – especially when others said she was no more than a 'cheap, hysterical, promiscuous and scatter-brained tart' – of importunately renewing our old friendship, I held back. Then, one night, by accident, we were face to face again, and the experience still desolates.

22

I have said I had changed, but so had Cape Town. There was a new violence in the atmosphere. There had been a time at a meeting of people of different races when friendliness and propriety had been keynotes; people of an older generation – even my mother who would boil at the slightest suggestion of racialism – confirm the impression. Now the tone was vicious and the incident I am about to relate perfectly represents the alteration.

In Britain I had grown used to a jolly evening pub-crawl but when I returned to South Africa it took me a while to realise that when people drank here it was not out of comradeship or to wash the dinner down. One of my cousins, a painter and therefore more inclined to examine faces, said that he couldn't do portraits anymore: he could no longer add colour and volume to the flat, taut faces he encountered everywhere.

What happened that night was simple. They used to say that at the University of Cape Town farewell parties took place at least seven days a week; someone was always leaving the country for good. Because I had recently begun to lecture I was invited to most parties, but because I had new courses to prepare, I could excuse myself. When, however, the head of my department summoned me to his own final leave-taking, no plea of being behindhand could satisfy.

I arrived late, hoping to make a quick show of face and an equally quick departure, but the house was full and I couldn't find my host and – because when tired I become a wilful intellectual – I allowed myself to be trapped into a fierce argument about historical determinism, the subject of my doctoral thesis. In the meantime, drinks kept being passed round. I was talking too much and was thirsty. Within less than an hour I was quite loaded. It was now after midnight. A rugby player – a huge blond superman – whom I had known in youth and quite liked, suggested that we go to Sea Point, and being in a game mood, remembering England, I fell in with the plan. We did not, however, go to Sea Point, nor did we play rugby. My comrade decided once we had left the house to scout the grounds for mating couples, and while I was pleading that he desist and we were debating this and other matters on the steps of the house, there was a shriek – a vibrant female cry of alarm – that sent us both hotfoot to the point of disaster.

Outside one of a line of parked cars, a brawl was in progress. While the rugby player and I were in furious dispute, one of our party had been running a flashlight over the insides of the line of vehicles parked in the driveway. What the idiot saw, I don't care to think, but what I saw wounded to the quick. A party of men were squabbling beyond the doors of a parked car, one of them, more savage than the rest, without trousers. A woman pulling down her dress, tight-lipped, face smudged, stepped out of the car. Even in disaster, Katherine had dignity. She walked straight through the babbling roulade, but suddenly, my rugby player shouted, 'Get her! There! The Coloured bitch! Let's all --- her!'

Now I raised my voice, and even Katherine turned around.

'Anyone touches her,' I shrieked, 'I'll kill him!'

I have never before felt murderous and I hope I never will again, but I did that night, and I meant it, and strangely enough it worked. I stood between Katherine and the rabble and waited for a single movement, shoulders lowered, like a wrestler, deranged and homicidal. But there were only murmurs, and I turned and took Katherine's shaking arm and led her away.

We were both shaking, and I am not sure how I managed to drive to Woodstock Beach. We didn't say a word, but when I stopped the car, she threw her arms around my neck and said, wildly, 'Thank you, Adrian. Thank you, darling,' and held me so urgently I felt half of her large bosom tight against me, and then she started to cry. I held her for a moment, then pushed her away, and looked at her, but she said, 'Oh, don't look at me like that, not like that!' and threw her arms round my shoulders again, and for no reason at all, perhaps because I, too, was in a state of tension, I began to cry. Then, suddenly, we were laughing and I gave her my handkerchief, and because her sense of humour never failed her, she opened her handbag and gave me hers, and we both wiped our eyes, laughing.

We were silent a long while, staring at bruised faces, then we talked; we talked all night there, in the front seat of the car while clouds like huge blown-up crabs moved sideways across a silver sliver of moon. I told her about England because I wanted to talk about England; because I hadn't talked about England to anyone for a long while – except to mother who didn't understand anyway because her England was bicycling with bloomers tucked up – and because I wanted her to feel that the rest of the world was not quite so beastly, because I didn't want her to feel embarrassed and have to explain her conduct. But she was not a simpleton. She listened, then leant forward and kissed me very gently on one cheek, saying, 'Dear Adrian, dear kind Adrian, you've learnt very well how to act, the English did an excellent job, but I have to do this sort of thing all the time, so I can tell!' I mumbled negative platitudes, but she kept shaking her head, cheeks again smeared with tears, smiling. And now it was my turn to listen. She told me of her mother's death, of how she had met Rycliffe, of how, though they lived together, she and her father were at daggers drawn. She also told me about Gordon Stewart, but that's a matter that can be treated later. We talked, as I have said, for hours, and something of our old fellowship returned. In the dawn, even though the back of my head was thumping with sleeplessness, when I kissed her cheek, she took my hand and looked at me a long while with those liquid black eyes of hers and said, very simply, very quietly, 'Don't think too badly of me. I'm not so bad, you know. Just confused. I'll be better soon. You'll see.' Then, she picked up her skirts and ran across the lawn towards the porch of her father's house, pausing only once when she reached the front door to blow a kiss and wave goodbye.

◇

I now return to Henry; to what followed when he left Old Man Parsons.

When he arrived in the carpark outside the Baths, Doc and Pieter were disputing about who should drive.

'Well,' Henry asked, puffing slightly because he had been running, 'what gives?'

Doc turned to reply, and noticed two young women coming through a nearby turnstile. At once his doleful expression evaporated.

'Am I right?' he asked, eyes gleaming, 'or is life once more deceiving?'

The girls were carrying beach bags. One was on the plumpish side and wore a scarlet dress. The other was dressed in blue – a slim figure, long hair, shy manner.

'Now, just hang on, chaps. Hold everything.' Doc turned to Pieter. 'The camera! Give me the camera!' He was marvellously excited – distracted, breathing heavily, a wild stallion. 'Watch this!' he said, then – to the girls about forty yards away – 'Hello there!'

The girls stopped abruptly and held a short giggling conference;

the buxom girl eyed Doc wetly. She was egging the other girl on. After a moment, she waved back.

'Never fails!' Doc was jubilant. 'She's waving. Aha! Did you see that? She waved back. Lucky, lucky girl. Watch out, I'm coming to get you.' Camera in hand, he hastened towards the turnstile.

'Ter liddle von is nize,' Pieter declared soberly, breaking out of a deep adjudicative trance, and ambling gawkily after Doc.

By the time Henry reached the turnstile, Doc had completed his 'you're so interesting' routine and had the girls posing.

'Back *mes dames* – back!' he was saying, 'Who-a there! Now watch the dicky. Everyone must watch Maurice's dicky. That's the stuff. Now, smile. A beeg, ha-appy smile!'

Everyone, even Pieter, was grinning. The plump girl's pug nose was tilted up so high, she seemed in danger of toppling over backwards. Her companion, all kittenish giggles, nervously screwed a damp white handkerchief between nail-bitten fingers.

The camera no sooner clicked than the plump girl gave a bright, knowing smile.

'*Mes dames*,' she said, 'that's French, isn't it?'

Doc's answer was immediate.

'But, yes,' he said, 'but of course, naturally.'

While the mockery drew low, marvelling snickers, he hissed to Pieter:

'Fetch the car!'

Pieter turned obediently.

At once the plump girl said:

'Where's he going?'

'He forgot something.'

She smiled, again knowingly, and watched Pieter leave, then she turned to Doc, delivering what perhaps most concerned her.

'You're a doctor, aren't you?'

Doc liked to separate medicine from other activities and was momentarily taken aback. Henry chuckled lightly.

'But yes,' Doc said at last, 'but of course, but naturally.' He fully recovered urbanity by adding, 'For you, I'd be anything. Doctor, prime minister, Hindu husband-god.'

'And him?' The girl pointed to Henry.

'Just another Hindu husband-god.'

'That's right,' Henry confessed, gravely, 'Krishna among the milkmaids. No less.'

The joke was out of the girl's range. She gave an uncertain guffaw and glanced at Henry to reassess him. Then she turned towards her companion and announced:

'This is Jessie.'

The slim girl went scarlet.

'Maurice Lambert.' Doc bowed and clicked his heels in the German fashion. 'At your service.'

He bowed and clicked to Jessie, as well. Jessie mantled again.

As Pieter halted the car, Doc said to the plump girl:

'But you haven't told us your name.'

For the first time the girl lost her look of superiority.

'Oh,' she said, abashed, 'I'm Madge. Madge Dietrichs,' she added casually: but Pieter, slamming the car doors, destroyed the dramatic effect of the gesture.

There was a pause.

'How's the car?' Doc asked Pieter.

'Ol ride.'

'There,' Doc told Madge, 'the car's in great shape!'

'Meaning what?'

'Meaning, we're all ready to go.'

Madge guffawed hoarsely.

'Who said anything 'bout going with you'll?'

'Only for a ride.'

'You go. We're going swimming.'

'No.' Doc shook his head. 'That's not the spirit.'

'What you mean? What you mean, not-the-spirit?'

'Well, you promised, you know.'

'Promised? Promised what?'

'Promised you'd come with us.'

'You've got a nerve!'

'Now, look here,' Doc explained gravely. 'A promise is a promise.'

The girls giggled.

'Well, she did say so, didn't she?' With a wink, Doc appealed to Jessie, who giggled again.

Pieter saw that Madge had begun to weigh up the situation.

'Weel tage you home,' he put in and smiled awkwardly.

Misgiving immediately tainted Madge's calculations. Pieter's blue

27

eyes and flaxen hair, most of all his colour and foreign accent, introduced old prejudices and a new unknown. Noticing this, and giving Pieter a withering look, Doc rallied with heartiness. He threw one sturdy prehensile arm around Pieter's back and drew Pieter towards himself. Though short, Doc had amazing strength of limb, and he pulled Pieter in, without turning his torso or eyes away from Madge.

'Don't worry about him,' Doc said and gave Pieter another tough hug. 'He's alright. Aren't you, Pieter boy?'

Pieter, still looking guilty, tried to smile.

'Come on,' Doc said. 'We'll bring you back safely. Don't worry.'

He had gone over to Madge and taken her by the hand, and though she was allowing herself, with only an extended arm of resistance, to be drawn, her face was looking over one shoulder towards Jessie, whose eyes were still lost in frightened indecision.

'Wait a moment.' Madge withdrew her hand from Doc's and went over to Jessie and whispered into her right ear.

Doc had already taken the driver's seat and begun to rev up the engine. Henry went round the bonnet and leaned over the driver's window-sill.

'Are you still going to Paarl?' he asked.

Doc gave an exasperated nod; he sensed an argument might change Madge's mind.

'Well, I'm going home,' Henry said.

Doc hesitated; through the windscreen he saw that Madge's whispered persuasions would take a few more minutes, so he said:

'No. Don't be silly. I told Frederic we were coming.'

Henry frowned angrily.

'Well, why the devil didn't you tell me?'

'For Christ sake, not now!' Doc said. Madge was leading Jessie, who still seemed a trifle doubtful, towards the car.

'Well, where do I sit?' Henry didn't want to join Pieter and Jessie in the back seat, and he saw that Madge would be sitting next to Doc.

'Here!' Doc said, shutting off the engine and giving Henry the keys. 'Open the dickey.' He leaned away, and drew forward the seat-back next to himself so that Pieter and Jessie could get in.

When everyone was seated, Doc started the engine again and shouted:

'Everybody happy?'

28

Pieter and the girls produced a loud cry of agreement.

'Right,' Doc said, and smiling lecherously, moved one hand towards Madge's plump calves. She jumped away at once, eyes furious.

'Not to worry,' Doc said, casting a business-like glance over his shoulders to reverse. 'Not to worry,' he said reassuringly, and patted her on one kneecap. 'Just wanted to release the hand-brake.'

Madge relaxed out of flurried dignity, and half-an-hour later they were cruising through flat, sandy, open countryside.

CHAPTER 3

Pieter's car was parked beyond the front gate of a modest, two-storied house, surrounded on all sides by flower gardens, flagstoned paths leading to statues, rockeries and small orchards.

Henry paused uncertainly at the gate. The house looked so congruously anchored to its surroundings that he wondered whether it belonged to Africans. He had asked to be dropped at the corner of the street, ostensibly to buy cigarettes. Actually his low spirits had returned; he wanted to be alone, and didn't feel quite up to meeting new people, especially Frederic and Elizabeth, and certainly not as a member of Doc's gaudy party. If he was to be evaluated, let it be on his own merits; if they were waiting for him, so much the better: his absence would constitute a gap, his arrival would receive special welcome. The conceit sprang from insecurity.

This was how he had felt when he entered the tea-room, really an old-fashioned *winkel*, at the corner of the tree-flanked street. There was a bench outside and when he came out into the sun-mottled shade, a packet of cigarettes proof of his mission, he sat down on the bench to compose himself.

A Cape cart, clattering rhythmically along the main road drew his attention to the warm, suburban peace. He was on the outskirts of the town. The cart passed an imposing Dutch-gabled mansion and turned a corner out of sight. Presently the trotting grew fainter, as if the horses' hooves were entering a region of cotton wool, and soon Henry was listening to the pulse of his own heart. A quiet contentment began to prevade his being even though, like a traveller at a railway station, he belonged nowhere. He looked about to validate the feeling consciously. Bunches of honeysuckle drifted over gleaming, powder-white walls. There were trees everywhere, leaves pouring tessellated shadows onto pavements. Butterflies fluttered among peach, plum and apricot orchards. Now and then, birds flew off perches on glistening telegraph wires, singing happily in the perfect freedom of open sky.

As he usually did when he felt pointlessly happy, he fell into reverie. Life seemed strange, fortuitous, a miracle. Stones and trees had no consciousness. One day it would stop: the heart he took for granted, then nothing – darkness. He wondered if there was life after death, and thought of his parents: their stopped hearts. It was odd, too, that he should be sitting on the bench, thinking of them, part of nature dying metaphysically like his mind. He thought of a passage in Hegel whom he had been reading recently: a passage about philosophy and death. But because the passage was disturbing he postponed reviewing it.

For a while, he thought nothing, then he began to wonder about the others. Was Madge aware she was Madge Dietrichs, the adult version of the child who used to run about District Six with dirty brooks and unkept hair; a Woodstock factory girl, courted by a doctor, anxious to convey the new status to the other girls? And Jessie, who had so painstakingly ironed her new birthday frock, believing that she needed only white gloves to look more ladylike: Jessie, who didn't want to look foolish, what were her uncertainties? Henry thought about Doc's promiscuity, and pity overwhelmed him. He was ashamed at having cut himself off and, in a stupid way, wanted them alive as he had created them, excited by fresh possibilities, this side of eternity. Then, because he believed the quality of his present joy was incommunicable, he pulled himself together; loneliness had brought on this sentimentality. Slowly and sadly, he began to walk up the street.

A woman in an orange outdoor frock was bending over a multicoloured patch of flowers before the verandah, back towards the gate where Henry stood. A wide straw hat gave the impression of a Chinese peasant weeding a paddy field. Her arms were plump and peach-coloured – was she European? Henry decided eventually to ask directions.

She did not look up until he reached the verandah; then she turned remarkable green eyes upon him and smiled in a calm, friendly, maternal way. Broad cheekbones distinguished her as Coloured. Nevertheless, she spoke without a trace of accent.

'Can I help you?'

'I'm looking for the Peters'.'

'What fun for you.'

The humour was unexpected.

'You're Henry Naidoo,' she smiled at Henry's surprise. 'I'm Elizabeth.'

Henry was back at school, winning prizes; only schoolmasters used a full name. He waited for her to take off her gardening gloves, remembering that it was good manners not to offer his hand first.

'You have a lovely garden,' he said, casting his eyes about.

''Tis rather nice, isn't it? Hard work, though.' Her laughter, however, said that she enjoyed the work.

The house had a silver-coloured tin roof, large windows with clean white casements, and eaves along the upper frame of the main verandah – a wooden, glass-roofed affair which projected from the ground floor and turned a corner to a greenhouse around another wall. The eaves were composed of creepers about a nucleus of vine.

'Let me take you in.' She led him up the main verandah steps where the eaves spread momentary relief of cool shade. Conversation, in full swing, could be heard from one of the rooms off the corridor. Though it was Tuesday, there was a Sunday after-dinner lull within the house. Somewhere, dishes were being washed and rinsed; a faint breath of roast lurked in the corridor, which was long and airy; cool, also, with the clean tranquillity of well-kept country places.

In the corridor, Elizabeth hesitated. 'I wonder . . . would you be a dear and carry in some glasses?'

'Certainly.'

At the end of the corridor she stopped to open a door, but a man's voice hauled her back to the drawing-room. She left her door half-open, called back, 'Coming!' and to Henry said, 'Won't be a tick.'

Henry peeped round the half-open door. The noise of splashing water was louder. Someone was rinsing dishes in the scullery, an alcove of the kitchen. It was a young girl – a slight, slim creature in a blue frock and black, high-heel shoes. She was back to the door and placing crockery, noisily, onto an enamel draining-board. Because of the noise she didn't hear Henry entering the kitchen – a large room with blue walls and modern appointments – and went on with her work; her hair, sleek and raven-black, was in a snood of blue ribbon which bobbed about any time she moved her head.

'Hello!' Henry said, his tone bantering and indulgent, the self-protective tone one adopts towards teenagers.

Katherine turned at once: cheeks dimpled, an elfish twinkling smile; in her small, lively black eyes she retained the shock of having been watched.

For Henry she was a head-on collision, unharnessing sensual excitement so intense he could scarcely breathe. She was not a girl. Her features were clean and fine, almost Persian. In fact, she had the trim, well-balanced figure of women in Persian miniatures: at once elegant and voluptuous. Her fair complexion and self-assurance, however, were Cape Coloured.

'Dear me!' Katherine exclaimed, dimpling again. 'I was in a *dwaal*!' She turned off the tap and started to wipe her hands on her apron, bending her head as she did so.

She had recognised Henry at once, but she saw that he could not place her, so she decided to pretend she didn't know him. The idea amused her so much that she had to lower her head, while wiping her hands, to keep her face straight.

'Just a minute!' she said as he was about to introduce himself with an extended hand. 'I've seen you before – but where?'

Henry withdrew his hand, surprised.

'No. Don't tell me. Let me guess.'

She stroked her chin, made a humming sound.

'Let me see. You're from Johannesburg?'

Henry shook his head.

'Definitely not,' he said.

'You're not. But why definitely?'

'Because I'm definitely not,' he said laughing.

'Ah well, perhaps not then. Try again. Let me see. Let me see. I know: you're from India, from Bombay. All Indians come from Bombay.'

Again Henry shook his head.

'How awful! I'm sure I know you.'

'I've been in the Cape eight years,' Henry announced rather too anxiously.

'Have you,' Katherine said, thoughtfully, 'Now, there's a clue. Wait a minute – I know!'

She gave the impression of having slammed shut an album of photographs.

'You're – '

The man identified had been a colleague of Henry's at University.

'No. He's gone back to Natal. To teach.'

'Ah!' she said. 'Back to Natal. You're from Natal then?'

He nodded foolishly.

'I thought so. Not from Pietermaritzburgh?'

'From Durban.'

'Good Lord. I would never have thought so. From Durban: well, well. Jiminy Johnson, that's the last place I would have thought of. You don't look at all like a business man, not at all.'

'I'm not.'

'Don't tell me. Don't tell me what you are. Let me guess. You're a teacher. You must be. You look like one.'

Henry shook his head and Katherine saw that he was becoming embarrassed.

'Well, then,' she said, dimpling brightly, 'if you're not a teacher, you must be a solicitor, and therefore you must be Henry Naidoo.'

He burst into manic laughter. She laughed too, then frowned: the excess in his laughter disturbed.

From the moment she had turned, it had become urgent to him to signify. He had recognised her at once, not personally, but as a type: shape of body, look of crushed flowers about the eyes, domesticity. She belonged to the special limited category – the few who immediately flushed through him unaccountable sensual and personal excitement. Because she was so luring, because he wanted so wildly not to remain anonymous, his self-assurance deserted, and when it returned, a mad joy and madder fears – of unknown dimly remembered fates – plunged like a spear through him. It was like his first arrival in the Cape – the checked breath, the boat spreading with everlasting slowness the warm blue thighs of Table Bay, and out there on the edge of the world . . . Hesperides . . . brown, silver-rimmed lips of land. There was a quality of expected surprise to her, a false reality yet more real than false, and he was in new territory, vulnerable and shocked.

'I'm sorry,' he said, uneasily. She had retired behind a sealed look.

'No,' she said. 'Not your fault. I should have known.'

'What?'

'I've gotten into bad habits.'

She measured him deliberately.

'It doesn't matter. Nothing. Forget it.'

She was accessible, yet she wasn't.

'No. Please tell me.'

34

'Oh, it's nothing,' she said, and tried to smile again. 'Just the way you laughed. It reminded me of someone.'

Another spear sang through him. He looked thoroughly confounded, and waited.

'Oh dear,' she said at last, 'you really aren't the playful sort. I'm sorry.'

'I still don't understand.'

'Are you religious?'

'Of course not. I'm a Hindu.'

'I thought so. You are religious.'

'If it's not impertinent,' he smiled, 'could you tell me – '

'What we're talking about?'

He nodded.

'Facts. You, mostly.'

'I give up,' he said. 'You win. Go to the top of the class.'

She smiled.

'It's complicated,' she said.

'So?'

She sighed. 'Alright. I'll try to explain. Once upon a time, there was a woman – oh, no. Let me be serious. I met a man once, and he laughed as you did, and then – ' she hesitated, but decided to go on, ' – and then things happened.'

'Was he religious?'

'In a way. I read a book once, which said you can tell when people are religious.'

'How?'

'Because they're grave.'

'Nietzsche' he declared, perhaps too pompously, 'says that the devil is the spirit of gravity.'

'You don't say?'

'No. Not me. Nietzsche.'

'What does Marx say?'

'Marx?' Henry imitated Doc's heartiest manner. 'Marx says: Well, hello there. Hello there, you *femme fatale* What's cookin', good lookin'? What's cookin' on the religious front?'

They were both laughing when Elizabeth returned. 'Ah,' she said, 'bedlam!' which only made them laugh the more. Then they realised they were being rude, and stopped.

'Well,' Elizabeth said, hands on hips, aware of being, with this

35

gesture, the stereotypical housewife, but embarrassed enough not to know what else to say, 'I see you've been introduced.'

The remark brought Henry suddenly back to sanity.

'Actually,' he said, 'we haven't. She knew me, but pretended not to. That's why we're laughing.'

'Liar,' Katherine said. 'It's he who was making me laugh.'

Elizabeth looked from Katherine back to Henry, nonplussed. Katherine had begun to laugh again.

'It's all very complicated,' Henry explained. 'Did you want me to help you with some glasses?'

He was trying hard to be responsible but couldn't restrain a twinkle. Fortunately, Elizabeth laughed too.

'Dear me,' she said, 'I don't know why I'm laughing, but it's dreadfully funny. It's like that awful stage trick when someone comes on, you know, and just begins to laugh, and there's silence, but he goes on, and then – ' she was now holding her belly, ' – and then, for no reason at all, the whole audience starts laughing. Oh, dear, I shall never stop. *Sal volatile*. Good knights and gentle folk, a pause, I pray thee. Prithee, stop!'

'Oh,' Elizabeth said after all three of them had fairly exhausted themselves, 'isn't it fun to be alive? Oh, hell, now I've forgotten what Frederic asked me to get. I know. The sherry. Kath, be a love and get it out of the oven. I keep it in the oven,' she explained to Henry, 'to stop him filching during the day. He's a dreadful filcher, but he never looks in the oven 'cos he got a shock once – 'lectric – touching the stove. Wise, I am. See?'

'Good storage,' Henry said. 'Better than a cellar. Adds bouquet.'

They set about composing a tray of glasses and the sherry. Henry was awarded the duty of carrying in the prize, and the drawing-room greeted him with handsome applause. He met Frederic, an intense man, with clean Slavic features and a mop of rich black hair, who said he was a glass short. As usual, Elizabeth had forgotten to count herself, so Henry went back to the kitchen. In the corridor he passed Katherine who was bringing in another tray, sweetmeats, and smiled at her, but she simply nodded – a crushed vulnerable look, a mixture of characteristic sadness and smears of freckles, again around her eyes.

In the kitchen, Elizabeth was bending over her stove, twiddling knobs.

'Who is she?' Henry urgently asked her, looking over a shoulder in case Katherine returned.

Elizabeth stood up and widened her eyes.

'You really don't know?'

He shook his head.

'Really! Don't have me on!'

'No. Really. I don't.'

'Bless us! I thought you knew. She's Katherine. My sister.'

'Katherine!' Henry was astounded. 'Your sister. But of course. I thought she was a cousin or friend or something.'

'She is fifteen years younger.'

'Katherine. Katherine Holmes. Well, I'm damned!'

He felt obtuse. That blend of self-assurance and intelligence ought to have distinguished her at once; while he had been at University, she had been a steady source of gossip. First she was that 'amazing Hewat girl – a peach!' the ambition of many to take out and some, merely to be seen with, a kind of Zuleika Dobson figure. Later she became counter-claiming dislike: she was 'that Hewat bitch – nothing but a gold-digger' and 'who the hell does she think she is?' These, and similar complaints of slighted concupiscence, and then, when the talk of her association with the Rycliffe crowd became public fact, sour grapes and gratified respectability released torrents of abuse: she was now every description of a slut; indeed she had been a slut all along. Henry was almost indignant that he had not recognised her, for, though he had never met her before, he had seen her twice – once, from the back row of seats in a College performance of O'Neill's *Anna Christie*; a bold restrained interpretation of Anna that brought down the house; and once, after his graduation, when he had had more time to go to parties. In a haze of smoke and music and people he remembered her doing a strange dionysiac version of the jitterbug with a short blond-haired man whose eyes gleamed from a Paul Kruger face.

Elizabeth had bent again over her stove. She wanted Henry out of the kitchen, so she said, with characteristic eccentric geniality:

'Look, would you mind clearing out. I'm trying to get these beastly oven burners going. The sherry must have upset them. They're a great nuisance, these burners – frightful Calvinists, and very sensitive; easily, all too easily intoxicated. Come on, you drunken mules, get going!'

Still confounded, Henry apologised and left her barking at the burners and switching off and on the controls. Re-entering the drawing-room, he remembered that he had forgotten the uncounted glass, but before he had time to react, Frederic had given him the sherry bottle and was saying, 'Hold this a moment', and dashing off to get the opener.

Everyone ruthlessly watched Frederic uncork the bottle – a man of medium stature, hunched shoulders, locks of sleek black hair lolling over a low forehead. He had the bottle between his knees and his concentration had the anguished interest of a small child on the chamber-pot. Henry realised that Katherine wasn't in the room, but he thought nothing of it until Frederic drew his wife aside and asked, in a whisper, 'What the dickens did you say to her? She's all upset again.'

Elizabeth had just re-entered the room; she turned to look for her sister and to see if anyone had overheard. She noticed Henry turning away, and converted an expression of protest into a soothing smile. The others were talking inconsequentially. As he turned away Henry heard her whisper, 'See if you can keep things going. I'll see what I can do.' She touched her husband on one arm and left the room.

Because he was nearest, Frederic asked Henry to help serve the drinks. He seemed not in the least put out by what Henry had just overheard. Henry's own superficial reaction was equally inscrutable, but behind a mask of quiet geniality, several unclear and unanswered questions were eroding a first impression of a calm, domestic household.

In the meantime, when Elizabeth found her sister, Katherine was not packing her bags. She was sitting in an armchair, feet on a footstool, casually smoking a cigarette.

'I'm sorry, Kath,' Elizabeth blurted, after indecisive embarrassment. 'Really, hon. Really, I'm very sorry.'

Katherine refused to look at her. She went on sending out angry clouds of smoke. Elizabeth went on her knees beside the chair and tried to put a hand on her sister's nearest arm, but Katherine withdrew her arm and got up, crushing her half-smoked cigarette into the ashtray. She turned upon her sister still crouching beside the armchair.

'Look: I can do with my own life what I want to, can't I? I don't tell you what to do.'

'But Kath, darling. I didn't mean any harm.'

'That's not what you said!'

'What did I say?'

'Oh, don't come all goody-goody and innocent on me. I know you too well. Good Elizabeth. Why can't you be good like Liz? That's what I've been hearing for years. From mother, from everyone. Well, I'm sick of it. Sick to the teeth with your smugness – your damned suburban smugness – '

'Katherine, that's unfair, and you know it.'

'Is it?'

'Yes. I only said what is quite true.'

'Look. I don't ask you to like my friends, and I don't have to like yours. Now leave me alone.'

'Darling, be fair.' Elizabeth got up and sat on the arm of the chair.

'Oh why the hell don't you leave me alone!'

Katherine's raised voice widened her sister's eyes. Elizabeth went to shut the half-open door. In a less comforting, but still generous tone, she said:

'Look, darling, I apologised. I'm sorry. What more do you want?'

Katherine made no answer.

'Look, we're being horribly rude. A houseful of – '

'I didn't ask to meet them.'

'My God! What mother – '

'Would have said? Well, she's dead. Thank heavens for that!'

'Alright,' said Elizabeth, fetching a sigh. 'Alright. Have it your own way. I agree with you about mother, about so many things, but she was right about being rude. What have those poor people downstairs got to do with what I said?'

'Oh, I see,' replied her sister. 'A new tack! You can't bear to be thought a poor hostess!'

'Oh Kath, darling, you are unfair.'

'Am I? Am I really? What about my pride?'

Elizabeth was about to retort, but desisted.

'Go on,' urged her sister, 'Go on, say it. Say what you said downstairs.'

'No. I'm not going to,' returned Elizabeth with another spurt of generosity. 'I've apologised for that. Kath, let's be friends. I promise I won't say another thing about Rycliffe.'

Katherine examined her sister's face, undecidedly.

'I promise,' Elizabeth repeated. 'Honour bright.'

Katherine restrained a smile. The expression was a relic of childhood, and touched both of them.

'Cross my heart,' Elizabeth drove home the appeal, 'and hope to die. Do you want a forfeit? Shall I stand on my head and sing a carol?'

Katherine giggled.

'No,' she said, 'a hymn. You always sang hymns better.'

'Which hymn?' asked Elizabeth, unable to restrain herself, 'Rycliffe or that excellent man, Naidoo?'

'Oh you are a silly ass!'

'Tch! Tch!' said Elizabeth, 'bad language! Mother wouldn't like it!'

Katherine smiled again. Elizabeth was parodying herself.

'You'd better go down first,' Elizabeth said, 'else someone might – well, you know, notice.'

'Alright,' said Katherine. 'Can I just go and put on some lipstick?'

'That's right,' said her sister, gruffly, mimicking now their father, 'that's my little girl, that's my little girl, that's my bonny little lass. What a nice round bottom she has too!'

Katherine on her way to the bathroom, turned and impudently stuck out her tongue.

Going down the stairs, Elizabeth was reflective. She knew her sister well, and despite Katherine's theatrical reputation, knew that she would withdraw for the rest of the afternoon. She was still a child: she would be well-mannered, but distant: it would be years before Katherine realised that others were not her mother against whom this remote politeness was the only defence. Elizabeth was annoyed with herself. Usually fine Protestant awareness of the importance of privacy stopped her from interfering in the lives of others, but because she knew her sister was unhappy and suspected the cause, maternal instincts and, worse, inveterate woman as matchmaker, had not been excluded. She had not suspected, however, so violent a reaction. She didn't dislike Yussouf Rycliffe; a man of his essential gaiety, courage and tenderness could not be easily disliked; more-over, a woman of her own forgiving good nature could not – though there were savage reasons why she might – condemn the man whose first mistress she had for years secretly been. They had lived together in London, while he was doing medicine at Guy's Hospital, and she, nursing. She had almost married him. Elizabeth stopped on the staircase, indifferent to the sounds coming from the drawing-room and the splash of water in the bathroom where Katherine was, as she usually did after a quarrel, running the cold tap ritualistically over her wrists. There was a far-away look in her eyes, she thought of the strongbox in the vaults of her bank, of the bundle of letters and numerous pieces of cardboard, among other documents, that it contained; twice that year she had resisted a temptation to go to her bank, then she thought of Epsom Downs, and a visit to a certain grimy street in Lambeth. An emotion close to tears welled up in her, but she suppressed it wilfully, breathed in deeply, clutching the rail of the bannister. At last she shook the memories free, and with another deep breath continued down the stairs, firmly resolved not to say another word in favour of that rather nice young man, Henry Naidoo.

Katherine, for her part, was neutral to all but her own immediate discontents; she was neither attracted to the rather nice young man nor positively indifferent. He had a reputation for discipline, stamina, and an intelligence that marked him out as one of the more brilliant law students at Cape Town University. She admired, moreover, the air of candour and detachment that seemed to distinguish his personality. He reminded her of the basement stacks of the public library: he seemed to live in a rich inner world that was quiet and peaceful and safe – but then there was that laugh; it was a crack in one of the walls: it threatened to bring down upper stories and roof. He was more self-reliant than most, but, like others, he fed on social pabulum which could poison, even if it might be longer penetrating the centre. Moreover, whether she had made a conquest was beyond measurement: she had become too much the actress who dispenses charm and cannot discriminate between responses; also, having long been the target of social malice, she had developed armour which sealed out approval no less than condemnation. She had grown distrustful, and had determined, as her sister predicted, but for other reasons, to restrain showing off that afternoon; instead, when she re-entered the drawing-room, she had decided to be quiet and attentive to others, in fact to measure all situations critically.

Her detachment, however, didn't last. Though she did not herself contribute anything, she soon began to take an interest in an argument between Henry and Frederic. Once or twice, however, she had the impression that she was being singled out for special attention, that Henry's arguments were for her particular benefit – he

41

looked in her direction more than once – and this suspicion was strengthened when she caught Doc whispering to Madge that Henry was that afternoon unusually talkative. The comment reinforced her determination to be no more than an attentive onlooker.

This resolve to allow neither alarm nor flattery to dissolve her calm served only to intensify Katherine's mystery in Henry's uncertain senses.

In company, typically Indian self-effacing modesty usually kept him reticent. Mere chatter was boring; when he listened, he realised how little others shared his own preoccupations. To foist, therefore, uninvited convictions upon others was exhibitionism, unmannerly. This afternoon, however, silence was uncomfortable government. He wanted to impress Katherine but at the same time he did not want to voice ideas for any sake but their own; it would be bad taste to monopolise conversation . . . moreover, there was the matter of loyalty. Did Katherine's silence denote disapproval of his friends? He wished to be dissociated from them so as to win her approval, but this was uncharitable: if he spoke up he might throw more attractive light on them.

Katherine had, in effect, sharpened his awareness of the smallest nuance of his environment. When she had come back into the drawing-room, he had noted the impression she made. The girls gave her thorough feminine inspection: Madge became competitively defensive; Jessie, who still seemed afraid to move, was full of admiration. Pieter, who trailed a long right arm along the back of the sofa, seemed more concerned with Jessie, sitting rigidly beside him, to notice Katherine. Doc and Frederic, however, rose: was this more than usual deference?

For a while, platitude was rampant: but soon Frederic started a bristling debate, and Henry needed no incentive to be drawn out of customary reticence.

Frederic began, as he began everything, staccato. Either oblivious or indifferent to the defensive atmosphere, he threw himself into an armchair, cupped hands behind his head – a favourite posture – and said at large:

'My sister-in-law is something of a Marxist.'

'Well, bully for you,' said Doc, turning a gleaming eye upon Katherine. Elizabeth shot an anxious glance at her sister, but though

42

Katherine's face hardened, she remained silent and Elizabeth relaxed once again into her own seat.

Because Elizabeth had introduced Henry as a graduate of Cape Town University – snobbery that annoyed Henry – Frederic turned respectfully to him, and asked:

'How do you University people look at Marx these days?'

Aware Katherine's attention was focussed upon him, yet still not willing to be drawn, Henry muttered vaguely that he had left University several years ago.

There was now an awkward silence.

'In my day,' Frederic said, 'it was after the Popular Front. The God had failed.'

'You were in the music school, were you?' Henry asked.

Frederic refused to be side-tracked.

'It seems to me,' he said, 'that next to Christianity, Marxism is the most pernicious evil of our time!'

Condemnation of Marxism was an offence which even Katherine seemed willing to condone; denigration of Christianity could not fail to provoke a general outburst.

Passion, for its own sake, seemed to please Frederic. He smiled like *Alice's* Cheshire Cat, and defended himself with vigour.

By Christianity, he meant the kind of 'patronising do-goodism' that characterised the more simple-minded brethren, not, as Henry thought, the similarity between Christianity and Marxism as systems of suprapersonal, messianic idealism. Neglect of the present for some insubstantial dream of the future was a doctrine which exasperated Henry. It ran too close to the bone: to his own immediate impasse. He hesitated again before delivering any opinion. How would Katherine countenance views contrary to her own? Had she not been present he might have expressed himself more passionately. Marxism, far more than Christianity, represented; with its impersonal historical theories and denial of natural rights; an immorality: it was bent on the ovethrow of beliefs he deeply cherished. He did not mean what Frederic meant – a group of philistines who had murdered Maxim Gorky and driven Mayakovsky to suicide. The gravamen of his attack was on determinism, Marxist and other eschatologies which always presumed, one way or another, some absence of personal responsibility. In these theories, ends justified means, human beings became faceless ciphers in a suprapersonal conflict of historical forces. A crude form was Afrikaaner Nationalism and the Calvinist doctrine of a Spiritual Elect. Already South Africa was falling into the thrall of class, race, and group politics; every blow, therefore, for self-determination was an act of social deliverance.

Henry sat strangely still, face and hands in a state of deliberate relaxation. He concentrated as much upon his audience as upon what he had to say. The opposition was weak. Ideas exasperated Doc unless they could be recognised as conventional wisdom, and he joined a rather stubborn form of semantic criticism to them. What did Liberalism mean? Why was extreme egalitarianism impractical? Doc consistently missed the central theme and had himself trapped in shallows of grammar. Though Henry knew that ideas meant nothing to Doc, that little or nothing would part him from a code of self-interest, Henry dealt with him patiently, and twice so skilfully that even Doc was forced to see the contradictions of his own objections. As for Frederic, he was on Henry's side and acted as a spur and foil throughout. Katherine seemed genuinely puzzled. Her ideas of liberals were as stereotyped as Frederic's notions of communists and Christians. A liberal was someone like General Smuts, two-faced, professing high ideals and well-intentioned, but eventually without courage to give convictions effect. A liberal, moreover, was a bourgeois, more concerned to lubricate defunct social engines than to proclaim dynamic options. She was quite confounded to discover that there were complex principles behind Liberal-Democratic theory, arguments as intricate, systematic and reasonable as those of Communism. She had been having considerable difficulty absorbing many of the tenets of Marxism, and she was much too sincere to answer uncertainty with a farrago of slogans and dogma. She was a Marxist, less out of conviction than by association, and she was anxious to introduce Henry to the Rycliffes, so as to sort out her own hesitating allegiances. Jessie, on the other extreme, like Pieter, looked as if disputation was irrelevant and seemed gratified whenever Pieter inserted tiresome injunctions like 'In Holland, ower gowerment is verie goot – no Nazis!' and 'Politics is not goot for ewerboty, only politicians.' These platitudes pleased Madge as well; she, too, seemed to think discussion had become too theoretic. Henry soon began to feel he was wasting intelligence upon fools.

It was Elizabeth who seemed to be the most impatient. She continuously circulated bowls of kossiters, mebos, sourfigs and other sweetmeats. More than once, she interrupted with the offer of another glass of sherry or a plate of nuts. She was never overtly hostile; but now and then Henry thought her benevolence overlay deposits of fierce exasperation. He did not know that her distaste for politics sprang from personal bruises; he suspected that, like himself, she disliked speculation that was too abstract. He felt all the more unhappy because – like all shy men – he was afraid of becoming a bore, but also, more importantly, because against so many interruptions and contradictions he was not succeeding in making his ideas clear. He found that he was repeating himself, losing track of previous statements, trying to condense and simplify essentially complex views; and he could not help feeling that what he said was, more often than not, misconstrued. Honesty precluded total answers yet he was aware that, in stressing the tentative nature of his claims, he seemed to fall somewhat in Katherine's estimation. Now and then he wondered whether he wasn't merely using circumspect, therefore discreditable, methods of winning Katherine's approbation; but he remained acute enough to reflect that had he really wished to please that mysterious, exciting, reticent, attentive onlooker he might have delivered more agreeable views.

About five o'clock there was another change of atmosphere. Elizabeth had two boys, and when they came in from play, she excused herself, leaving a gap in the room. Henry used the lull to join Katherine on the window-seat overlooking the back garden. She had been sitting upright, but now leaned sideways, one languid arm on a window-sill. She had meant to make room and to add to his comfort, but her new posture threw entirely out of kilter his self-confidence which the discussion had restored. It sprang, like a flaw of wind across the embers of his senses, unreeled such flaming spools of desire that only by diverting his gaze to a group of small brown birds hopping – beyond one window – about a patch of cabbages and tomatoes, could he master the effect she had on him: the effect of lines flowing from crossed thighs, over an outswung hip, over rounds of full breasts, then across limbs of throat to where an arc of chin sealed the face into so many shifting expressions. She had a droll way of parting her lips so that when she spoke she seemed vulnerable, like a small child. But her body was a woman's, and so desirable that his wits deserted him. The excitement swallowed up thought and speech.

'I'm sorry,' he muttered, bending his head and not daring to look at her, 'I just feel – ' He blinked his eyelids a few times, like an animal having difficulty swallowing. 'I just feel a little dizzy.'

She sat up again. 'Are you quite alright?'

'Yes. Sorry.' he said. 'Silly of me.'

While he shook his head to get rid of the dizziness, he searched for words which might say what both frightened and exalted. Out of the corner of one eye he looked to see if anyone besides Katherine had followed his movement and was alarmed to notice that Doc had risen; the afternoon was almost over, the others, too, were chafing to leave.

Katherine said:

'Tell me something?'

In his eyes, fear had no covering.

She hesitated, changed her mind. She smiled insecurely.

Now he was mystified. Contradictory impulses fought within. Her background gave her such appeal, such a host of improbable excellences that he was flushed by his own daring. Salt rose to his mouth, his pulses raced like immediate drums, a voice that belonged to someone else moved trembling lips.

'Do you . . . do you want a lift . . . a lift to Cape Town?'

Her laughter shot compunction of folly through him. Neck arched back, her face was a jungle of laughter.

'Oh dear,' she said, 'that's very funny!'

He was still incapable of speech.

'I was just going to ask whether you'd like to stay for dinner.'

Joy followed panic sharply; his bewilderment increased.

'I'm sorry. I thought you might be very busy – '

'No,' he mumbled awkwardly, 'I – '

'But what about Thursday? Are you free Thursday afternoon?'

'Thursday?' he repeated, still amazed.

'Yes, there's a party.'

'Thursday afternoon?'

'Sorry, I should have explained. It's a beach party.'

He was about to reply when Doc stood before him.

'Sorry, pal,' Doc said, 'but we have to push on.'

Henry looked at his friend, nonplussed, then he collected himself.

'Just hang on a minute,' he said fiercely, 'I'll be right with you.'

Doc looked from Henry to Katherine.

'What's up?' he asked.

'Nothing,' Henry said, irritably. 'I'll see you in a minute.'

'I see,' Doc said. 'A little secret. Never mind. *Alles sal rectum!*'

Neither Katherine nor Henry found the play on words amusing. Doc consulted his watch professionally.

'Okay. But we gotta push on soon, pal!' The tone suggested that he hadn't liked Henry's brusque response.

When Doc was out of hearing range, Henry apologised for the interruption.

'That's alright,' Katherine said.

'No, he's such a bloody boor sometimes.'

She explained that on Thursday morning an important political meeting was to take place; in the afternoon, she and the others were going to Kalk Bay.

'Do come,' she appealed, 'I want you so much to meet them.'

'You'll be there?' he asked.

'Oh, yes – ' she began, then broke off, realising that his interest was in her, not the Rycliffes. Anxiety swung again, like heavy loops, under her eyes.

'I'd love to come,' Henry said firmly. 'What time?'

Now she seemed unable to speak.

'What is it?' he asked, delicately. There was a far-away, stricken look in her eyes. 'Are you alright?'

She shook herself, and tried bravely to smile.

'Nothing . . . What were you saying?'

The details of the appointment were no sooner completed than Henry wanted to leave, not merely because he feared a reversal of providence, but also because, in an imprecise way, he did not want familiarity to breed contempt. The farewells, which began on the verandah and carried on at the gate, exasperated him. He wanted to leave so as to analyse the implications of the exchange with Katherine, to place meanings across the excitement she aroused. He was never able to impose order on his senses unless he was alone and undistracted. But although he wanted to leave and was unsettled he also had a promonition that futility had at last ended, that he was no longer an outsider but someone with a destiny, like treasure stored up, clearly marked and waiting. The main course had been charted, but what outer stars and winds and currents would direct the steering?

CHAPTER 4

If, leaving Paarl, Henry believed purpose was refreshed – that he was done with inconclusive imaginings, that he was at last within sight of a cherished, tangible goal – it might be appropriate for me to sketch a particular shape ahead.

Underworlds are regions I can do without, and yet what I myself prefer is irrelevant: like Henry, I have no choice, for if I have to depict the web of violence and intrigue in which Shaikh-Moosa, like a huge poisonous spider, was the nucleus, then the word 'underworld' – with all its suggestions of crime and dragon gold and lurking half-creatures – is unavoidable.

How is this gorgeous, and repulsive, figure to be started upon? A few months ago a nervous, pock-faced young man came to my office. He was not a bright student, but eager to please, and from our interview I gathered that he was now in financial trouble, having thrown up a lucrative job to come to University. His name was suggestive, and I racked mental archives to place where I'd heard it before. I had, in fact, that feeling we all do when we encounter people we seem to have met before. Then one day not long afterwards, among the last pages of one of Henry's diaries I came across a reference to 'the young man, Abu' and I had my answer. I called in Abu and asked him point-blank whether he was Shaikh-Moosa's nephew. He hedged at first, stammered, but when he sensed by my manner that acknowledgement would not be held against him, he confirmed my suspicion and upon further questioning provided information which handsomely supplements and confirms certain wild guesses in portions of Henry's last diary; consequently, what I now set forth is little more than a summary of the atmosphere that surrounded the Master, the Great Man, the Black Hat – as he was variously called – on that evening when Henry was returning from Paarl . . .

As you pass through old Malay Quarter, your eye may be attracted to a particular house. The house stands derelict now, its plaster scuffed and part of the roof tumbled in; nevertheless – marooned as it is on barren ground of the mountainside, without relief of trees, higher than other houses, towards Devil's Peak – you cannot resist a second look, for a certain awesome magnificence, perhaps even brutal starkness, still distinguishes it.

On that night of Henry's return, this house – a grand, two-storied relic of the middle Victorian era – alone, above a sprawl of lesser buildings, gained, in the late dusk, ponderous solemnity. The frontispiece, with its overhead balcony supported by massive pillars, overlooked Table Bay to the left; straight below lay old Malay Quarter leading to the city centre and to the right, the dark hulk of Table Mountain, its lower slopes paved with a myriad of lights, a glittering windfall of stars upon mounds of soft black velvet.

All the curtains were drawn – except the inner pair belonging to the French windows of the balcony: a feature which dramatised the seclusion both of the house and of the man; upright in an ancient, carved rocking-chair, a small table with a glass and a whisky decanter beside him; who had been sitting on the balcony for over an hour, motionless as the night before him. Now and then a hand, bearing on the marriage finger a giant blue-white diamond, reached out and firmly grasped the glass upon the small table; now and then muscles of stern jaws rippled with grim thoughtful satisfaction; but otherwise, the man, dressed as formally as if he presided over a board of directors governing the night – a short, well-built man with bandy legs and a dark-brown, weathered face – scarcely altered his dignified, commanding posture.

At nine o'clock in the room behind him the telephone rang. It rang several times before a young man with an anxious, pock-marked face arrived to answer it.

After a short conversation the pock-faced young man crossed the thickly carpeted room, but before opening the French windows, tapped gently a few times on the panes.

'Hassanjee?'

His voice was cautious and respectful.

'Councillor Holmes is there.'

Hassan Shaikh-Moosa did not alter his position.

'He is coming twenty minutes from now.'

There was another short pause, then quite abruptly, Shaikh-

Moosa's square, black-browed face swivelled round. He fixed a hard, intelligent gaze upon his wilting nephew.

'Tell him: soon as he can, he must come!'

'He is going by Senator Goodbrand's first.'

Shaikh-Moosa grunted thoughtfully.

'Did you get that fellow John Moodley's lawyer?'

'No.'

'Bring the phone!'

The nephew disentangled his eyes and recrossed the room. He said a few more words to the caller, then put down the receiver. Bringing back the telephone he stumbled with the lead at the windows and looked up at once, expecting to be sworn at in Zulu, but Shaikh-Moosa's jaw muscles simply twitched.

When the telephone had been placed on the small table, Shaikh-Moosa said:

'Dial the number!'

The nephew shakily obeyed. The answer was almost immediate.

'M-m-mr. N-Naidoo?'

'Yes?'

'Let me talk!' Shaikh-Moosa stretched out his right hand; with his left, he waved his nephew away. When the windows were quite shut, Shaikh-Moosa's expression underwent a dramatic change.

'Mr Naidoo?' His brown eyes narrowed to a twinkling playfulness. 'Shaikh-Moosa here. Good evening.'

'Good evening.'

'John Moodley – you know John Moodley? . . . Hello?'

'Yes?'

'That is Naidoo, the lawyer, speaking?'

'Yes.'

'How are you?'

'Very well, thank you.'

'Good . . . very good. Now look here – you don't mind me coming straight to the point?'

'Please go ahead.'

'The thing is this. I'm having a spot of trouble with a conveyancing deal. Nothing much . . . you must be quite used to this kind o'thing. I wonder if you could help me out?'

'I'm rather busy at the moment.'

'I could make it worth your while.'

50

Shaikh-Moosa paused theatrically.

'Money is no object,' he said. 'I could see you right.'

'Well . . . what . . . what does it entail?'

'Could you come down here?'

'Now?'

'Don't worry. I'll see you right.'

There was a short pause.

'I can't promise anything.'

'No. No. Come and talk. I'll send my driver to pick you up.'

'That's not necessary. I have my own car.'

'No trouble, you know. I could easy send the driver.'

'Please don't. I don't know if I can come yet.'

'Aren't you on holidays?'

'Yes . . . but . . . is your number in the book?'

Shaikh-Moosa dictated the ex-directory number.

'Right.' Henry said, 'I'll phone you back.'

'When?'

'Soon.'

When he replaced the receiver, Henry's first reaction was relief. He had expected the call to be Katherine cancelling Thursday's appointment. The bungalow was empty. For a while he had been sitting on the front verandah, trying restlessly to piece together his feelings, but all he saw were gnats fighting the sunset above the ramshackle garden. Now he returned to the verandah and stood, face against a pillar, experiencing the dewy cool and night freshness cheek to neck. A train was shunting somewhere beyond the trees and houses; it was like the mood of the night – transient, a perishable beauty that would soon pass into suburbs of memory.

Though he knew from experience, that he could not share what he felt, he had a fierce urge to confide in someone. The call from Shaikh-Moosa intensified this mood of impermanence; it registered an industrial wasteland of impersonal machines and neurotic tycoons and faceless toiling millions in whom life had grown as precise as a clock and as bereft of depth as an advertising slogan; in contrast, it fortified isolation – the pleasure of being outside, within another wheel of living where personal choice had not yet vanished. But in this world within world, there was no anchorage for Katherine. Whoever won her would have to offer more security than a fervour for the passing beauty of the universe. While she might not declare for wealth, she could not be indifferent to poverty. Tempted though he was to visit Shaikh-Moosa at once, Henry decided eventually not to: he telephoned to say he would come round the next morning, and having done so, was delighted with himself.

But the restlessness persisted. He could not work. It was too early to go to bed, and he knew he would not get to sleep easily. There were matters he wished to delay thinking about. He ran through people whom he could trust, and eventually – the decision still touches – chose me.

I am touched because I loved him dearly. He was listless and evasive and never quite got to the point that night but the gesture still moves me, and I am even more moved, but with horror, when I recall what happened to him immediately after he left my apartment . . . but this is pain that must be for a moment postponed.

When he drove out to Sea Point he did not know that Shaikh-Moosa's legal problem was not a simple conveyancing deal, that in fact it was part of a master plan which, as I recall it now, evacuates the lungs not so much because of the scale of thought that filled it, but because of the intricate design – a design in which very few contingencies had been omitted. There was only one loose link – the District Six election, an event that may help to explain a few matters.

When Katherine had said she would meet Henry on Thursday afternoon, it was because, in the morning, an important political meeting would be taking place. The meeting was to determine whether the *Flame* group – that is the group of left-wing politicians that surrounded *The Flame* newspaper and Yussouf Rycliffe – should field a candidate in the Municipal Elections, and in particular, whether Rycliffe himself ought to stand. The sitting member for the District Six or Ward Six constituency was Albert Holmes, Katherine's father, but if Rycliffe was to stand, his popularity might unseat Holmes and if he did so then Shaikh-Moosa's scheme might overturn. Shaikh-Moosa had not envisaged such an eventuality, partly because – even if it was possible – it was not incontendable. His network of political intelligence was as yet not quite as widespread as its financial counterpart. Albert Holmes was, as far as the Great Man was concerned, only a pawn and one which would move to any square in the grand design. The Great Man had, however, envisaged the possibility of loss, for Holmes, of European support. In Coloured politics, European support did not count for much, and Holmes tended to exaggerate its addition. Consequently when Senator Goodbrand, who represented the liberal wing of the United Party – the reigning party in the national parliament – refused to commit himself; and therefore the United Party; Holmes was distressed. Shaikh-Moosa, however, had been keen enough to foresee the possibility; in fact, it would have surprised Holmes – poor man, for he was rather simple in so many ways – to have know that it was exactly upon such a possibility that Shaikh-Moosa gambled. Shaikh-Moosa assumed that the entire country was moving away from liberal politics and towards the type of neo-fascist rule advocated by the main opposition, the Afrikaaner Nationalists. The United Party had carried the country through a major World War. General Smuts, the Prime Minister, was bound to be, like Churchill in Britain, associated with the austerities of war, and being concerned with the administration of *de facto* government, had not been able to devote the time the Nationalists had given to theoretical platforms and election machinery. In Shaikh-Moosa's mind it was certain that the Nationalists would win; and if they did, then their nationalistic policies would fit exactly with his own. When, therefore, Holmes arrived to explain that Senator Goodbrand, his 'old friend', a 'true friend of the Coloured People', had been unwilling to speak on his behalf, Shaikh-Moosa had simply smiled and wondered at Holmes's artlessness. Holmes was by turns alarmed, surprised, and eventually puzzled. The news ought to have robbed him of Shaikh-Moosa's support, but it didn't. He accepted the cheque to cover his election expenses like a man in a dream.

Related to the election were the Desai properties which Henry would shortly conveyance. This was another deal that fitted the master plan. John Moodley, Henry's old school friend, had been put in charge; another surface that looked deceptively simple. Involved were several blocks of apartment buildings owned by Ramdas Desai in a European area of Durban. In this area, property values were soaring; but if the Nationalists came to power as Desai, like Shaikh-Moosa, predicted, then Indians who owned these properties would be forced by law to sell well below current market prices. Desai wanted to sell as quickly as possible, but wouldn't indicate why. Shaikh-Moosa of course, knew why and instructed Moodley to contact Desai and find a lawyer who could have the deeds conveyanced as quickly as possible. Moodley, having arranged for Desai to meet Shaikh-Moosa the next morning had, in his report, suggested that because Henry 'looked down-an'-out', his services might be had 'for a song'.

Henry did not have the slightest hint of any of this, and nor had I. I advised him – as I was again later to do, and far more fatally – not to go by ancient prejudices. I suggested that he measure Shaikh-Moosa's proposition maturely and if it seemed above-board, a normal property transaction, why then, what were solicitors largely concerned with, but the legal rights of property? A property was a franchise, I told him, a form of freedom; and though I was not a liberal myself, to help the traffic in private property was to extend private freedom, a view surely that accorded with his principles? I advised him, in short, to have done with nice scruples, to 'get on with being an efficient solicitor!' but he did not take to these recommendations readily and I wish now he had not listened at all. I wish, too, he had not come to see me that night; instead that I had gone to see him, for what took place after he left my apartment is not an incident that throws admirable light on our self-appointed guardians of civilization.

Henry was himself too proud to report the incident directly, but one diary offers a clear account of it.

This form of haggard implacable wakefulness, he writes, *is driving me frantic. It always turns up at critical moments, before examinations especially, when I need to be at my best and need sleep more than ever! I actually wish I could die, so impossible is the prospect of sleep. I've got up twice already, smoked several cigarettes and downed four tumblers of Doc's whisky. I've tried all the familiar devices – counting sheep, persuading myself that I'm fortunate to be in a warm cosy bed, safe from black winds outside, mathematical riddles – but still my heart beats as if my chest is on fire, and my mind is dry and wide awake!*

What launched me to visit Adrian? Sympathy? Advice? Because I was excited and needed a confidant? I only told him about Shaikh-Moosa. I couldn't talk about Katherine: that was too sacrosanct. Adrian is very kind and sympathetic, but he advises the impossible – normal behaviour! How does one, in these circumstances, act with detachment? Every time I think of Katherine, knees go weak. I tell Adrian I am in love, not with whom!

It is two hours at least since I left him, and still I don't know what to do. Thoughts keep running back to Katherine and that madman in Sea Point.

The diary now offers a report of the incident, which I shorten.

He says I live in a block of modern flats in what Capetonians call a 'select area'. Frankly I had never thought of Sea Point that way; it has always seemed to me a rather dull middle-class suburb with only one advantage – proximity to a good swimming beach.

After he left my flat, he says, he was going down the stairway which smelt of floor polish when a large drunken man and two women bristling with cheap costume jewellery, came into the lobby downstairs. He no sooner heard them than he expected trouble; but rather than let alarm paralyse his wits, he collected himself with a will, and attempted to pass unobtrusively on the stairs.

He passed, then sensed the man was turning on the arms of the protesting women.

'Hey, you!'

Pride shut off retreat: Henry turned.

'Yes you, *coolie* boy! I'm – tawkingg!'

The accent sounded Transvaal, only the women seemed abashed.

'Whar are yew du-ing heer?'

Henry made no answer. The women looked foolish and likely to perjure themselves in court. This meant that self-defence would become assault and battery – a sentence, in a South African court of little less than ten years. A few more trumped-up charges – interference with European women, exposure, and perhaps abusive language, would lengthen the sentence. Henry had no witnesses. Though he decided to ignore the man, he did not move. The man sprawled forward, gabbling in *Platteland* Afrikaans, and grabbed the lapels of Henry's coat. Henry allowed himself to be shaken a few times, looking, all the while, with sullen patience into the man's inflamed eyes. Then he tried to avert his face, but the open palm caught him across one cheek. The effort reeled the man, he tumbled forward, and as the women ran to his rescue, Henry detached himself and went swiftly down the remaining stairs.

When he reached his car he realised his hands were trembling. They shook so violently that he had trouble guiding the steering-wheel. Strange warm liquid trickled out of one corner of his mouth where the flesh was numb. It took him a few moments to recognise the taste of blood.

In the centre of town, he stopped the car. In the driving-mirror his eyes were angry and bewildered. Apart from a fine path of blood along his left jaw, his face did not look abnormal. His reactions, however, were unco-ordinated; his mind, a curious shocked blank, was unable to control the tremor of his hands.

What should he have done? As he lay in bed, he recalled the scene again and again. That the man was thinking how he had put another '*coolie*' in his place was infuriating. He ought to have hit back, regardless of consequences, and he grew angry with himself for not having done so. But in the next moment he pictured the court room – a European judge, sneering police officers, the scales tipped to show he, not the man, had started the trouble. He ought to return to Sea Point and kill the man. But if one fought to the death, it should not be like bullfighting – a test of personal courage, life over death – but over some principle, some concern that would make living better and wider. All the same, impotence was maddening. At this point, he recollected the salty taste of his blood, and his left hand automatically rose to find out whether the swelling was still painful. How happy he had been during the afternoon! Now, how lost, hopeless! He ought never to have gone to a European area. Here was the folly – hubris: professional, middle-class status was no protection in South Africa. How idiotic to think that ordinary behaviour was possible in this country. But self-pity was no solution; race relations must be improved; violence would merely foster more violence; someone had to accept the abuse. The man was ignorant. If one turned the other cheek, one was likely to be struck harder; moreover, this was to accept inferiority, to change nothing. 'Yet, for his sake,' Henry thought, 'for his own peace of mind, I mustn't bear a grudge. I must forgive.' He remembered his mother talking in her soft gentle way about the Buddha. 'Only out of compassion,' she used to say, repeating a saying handed down verbally through the generations, 'only in this token of knowledge wilt thou see the flower of rebirth.' And against his will, he felt his eyes filling with tears. 'Yes,' he thought, 'that calls for greater courage – forgiveness. Forgiveness to everyone.' And while he cried, tenderness assuaged in him the anger and the pain, he became suddenly again aware of the brevity and beauty of life, suddenly inspired with a boundless love for everything in the world.

He slept thinly: consciousness a membrane so taut that manifold

56

pressures beat against it with tireless argument. About to drop off, he became conscious of the act of going to sleep and was back at Sea Point, or Paarl, or at an earlier point of life in which a small child played by itself in dense, green canefields. Katherine's behaviour was unfathomable; she was sacred and over-exciting and unavoidable thought; yet he wanted to be purged of her. He longed for Thursday to be over, that it was Thursday night already, that he was in bed, that Katherine requited his interest, that sleep was again possible; but a new fear raised lids of consciousness – he had neither income nor position to offer her the life which was his ambition. At once he remembered Shaikh-Moosa's proposition, and at once a sentimentality like that of Charles Bovary assailed. He would be a well-known moderately successful lawyer commuting from a country home to a city office; in the evenings, he and Katherine would exchange accounts of the day's events, they would plan holidays abroad, tend carefully to the needs of their children, cultivate their garden; now and then he would publish a book on jurisprudence. If only life could be like that!

When, eventually, he did manage to fall asleep, he was not conscious of having done so; he was aware, in the next moment – so it seemed – of bells, then he remembered the telephone ringing, it had to be answered, and yet, like someone having to go at night to a distant lavatory, he went on putting off the journey. Composite fears pounced. He seemed to know in advance, not only who the caller was, but – to very nuances of tone and meaning – what would be proposed. Then he was lifting the receiver; eyes half shut, the ringing still re-echoing in his ears; and pyjamas clung to his body dreadfully cold and wet with sweat.

'Mr Naidoo? Shaikh-Moosa here. See here now – I have this one job for you – legitimate it is . . . ten thousand somewhat pound transaction. Come way this side, straight way. You know the place?'

Quite calmly Henry acquiesced.

In his office, Shaikh-Moosa said:

'First, one thing I want to know. Are you game?'

Henry nodded vehemently.

'There's no backing out!'

Henry was determined.

Satisfied, Shaikh-Moosa elaborated the scheme. In place of John Moodley, Henry was to attend a shareholders' meeting in Durban.

As Shaikh-Moosa arrived at the end of explanation, John Moodley, wearing a dazzling, hand-painted tie, appeared.

'The plane is booked,' he said.

'And the papers?'

John flashed a sheaf of copyscript which Shaikh-Moosa studied for a moment then slapped into Henry's welcoming hands.

'Here is!' the Great Man said. 'It's all written down here. Every word I was saying. Study it carefully. My native driver, Alfred, will be waiting for you at Durban airport.'

As the 'plane took off, Henry discovered he was the only passenger. It was intensely agreeable to have a specially chartered aircraft all to oneself. Luggage, money, briefcase . . . these were intact. Below the clear unbreakable portholes the Cape Peninsula sank steadily into a gorgeous brilliance of two oceans – a vanishing blur of land that gradually assumed Katherine's face, the fine gold of her complexion, the smell of her hair, her sad and lively eyes, cheeks dimpling . . . and she was lost, lost irrecoverably, a dream that had inspired total belief, now the sickening, unavoidable triumph of a nightmare.

The camouflaged hangars on the broad level green of Durban aerodrome were submerged in depths of subtropical heat. Alfred waited with Shaikh-Moosa's old 1946 Buick outside the golf course opposite the airport exits. When Henry had passed through the wire gates, Alfred refused to acknowledge him. This was infuriating.

'Now, look here,' Henry ranted, 'stop playing ducks and drakes.'

'Duckes and drak-es?'

'Yes. Playing the idiot.'

Alfred checked indignation with difficulty.

'I'm a ver' sorry,' he returned, 'but I don't know you at all!'

'Whose car is that then?'

Henry pointed furiously at the Buick.

'That is my car!' Alfred announced with dignity. 'I am a pro-letariat.' The word 'proletariat' gave him fatuous pleasure.

'You're mad!'

Henry found himself laughing crazily.

'Now look,' he said, 'be a good chap and take me to town.'

'Don't you a-patronise me.' Wrath violently contorted Alfred's placid face. 'Ask pro-per-ly! Say, "please".'

'Alright,' Henry said, thinking the man had perhaps been smoking dagga, '-please.'

'I don't like the way you are a saying "please".'

'Please.'

'Again?'

'Please.'

'Alright,' he said good-humouredly, 'get in then.'

'You wait,' Henry thought, as they rode through Stamford Hill, past avenues of Dutch-apple trees, 'you haven't heard the last of this!' He sat in front, inwardly fuming, but managing to give an impression of inscrutable calm. When they reached Greyville, Alfred suddenly thrust Henry out of the car.

'I'm a ver' sorry but I can take you no further!'

Henry straightened his tumbling body.

'I'll have you sacked!' he shrieked, aghast with fury. But the car, its opened door still ajar, was already moving off. A tap on one shoulder spun Henry face to face with a wiry, small man. The protuberant eyes, nose, and teeth were vaguely familiar: a face as in a distorting mirror.

''Ow's it, *ou maartjie*? 'Ow's it, man?' The man poked aggressively at Henry's chest and through pan-reddened teeth sent out a spray of foetid spit.

'Doan you remumber me? We was at Crabbe Street School together, both of us, same time. Come on, you remumber me. I was an old *maart* of yours. We ooze to go fishing, ourselve – Maydon Wharf!'

Henry glared at the fellow disdainfully; he turned to leave but found the man clinging to a corner of his jacket.

'Ey! Where you going, pal?' the man yelped, spitting rammish anger over Henry's face.

Henry passed a hand over his own face, and though he made no further attempt to leave, the man did not release the hold on his jacket.

'I 'eard it you living in the Cape now,' the man proceeded, bringing snapping teeth closer. ''Ow's all those Coloured *bokkies*? 'Ow's all those Cape Town *steakies*? You looking like a Cape-jie already, boy. 'Ow's it if I make a move and pay you a visit sometime? You could fix me up with some Malay *goosie*? Okay. Sweet. Now, shoot!'

'Will you stop spitting in my face!' Henry was apoplectic with rage.

The man looked offended and drew back. With his free hand he took out a filthy handkerchief and proceeded to smear it affectionately over Henry's withdrawing and horrified face.

'Ey! 'Ow's your 'eart, *maartjie*? You forgetting your old mates. I could still boot you, *maartjie*-blue! Watch out! You know 'ow I ooze to come out in the rush! You want to shape it out?'

Henry was quite silenced.

'*Mus u ny negah! Don't make smogoh!*' The threat was less fierce now. 'Anytime you want to put up your *dooks*, call me. You 'ear? Arright, arright. Don't get scared. I was just pulling your legs. Take it easy. Sweet. You got a *skayf*?'

Henry shook his head.

'Okay, *maart*. I 'ave to cut a line now. I'll give you a look-up when I hit the Cape, you 'ear?'

He smacked Henry fiercely on the rump; then, one arm waving, eyes glinting 'remumber me, remumber me' he sauntered off.

A line of tramcars went ting-a-linging towards First Avenue. Outside a new balconied villa opposite, a car with curtained windows drew up.

Several women, heads bowed and obscured by bright silk veils, hurried across the pavement. The door of the villa opened to them automatically as if worked within by a hidden switch.

The villa was a puzzle until Henry remembered that on its site had once been a large household furnishing company.

As the women crossed the pavement, two Africans passed behind Henry.

'Indian woman!' said one to the other.

'The Indian peeple nevah let the woman out. I have wuked for Indian peeple. The woman are kep' in the house luk a jewelry.'

'O, these Indian people – too crazy peeple!'

Pandemonium at once sent fire-engines hurtling up First Avenue, followed by people, crowds of people, rioters and brandishing firebrands. Henry leapt into the air. The pavement had become a sheet of reddish-blue flames. Fire-bells rang. People and splashing buckets of water converged upon Henry. Church bells jangled hysterically. Nearby, a religious ceremony was taking place. A circle – Indians and Africans mostly – stood round a flaming bier, topped by thorny flowers and the figure of a woman with black hair and closed, blue-veined eyelids. A man, wearing a black fez, was reading Koranic scriptures to the small congregation. The man was Shaikh-

Moosa; the woman, Katherine. Henry's mouth opened, unable to emit sound; his feet would not move; flames leapt around his legs; the shops, houses, multicoloured shapes of the world whirled round . . . round and round . . . bells were ringing, millions of bells . . . bells everywhere . . . crazy, changing bells . . .

Scalded cold with sweat, Henry shrieked, and woke – and across the shuddering luke-darkness of the bedroom the nightmare shrilled metallically back at him. He let it ring, holding his breath. At last he crossed the room, but even now fear almost paralysed his hand on the receiver.

'Hello? Mr Naidoo? Shaikh-Moosa here . . . '

The voice was appallingly the same. The bedroom momentarily blurred.

'Hello? . . . hello? . . . are you there?'

Was the alteration a plan to make him believe he was still asleep? Not even Shaikh-Moosa could be satanically omniscient – or could he?

'Y-yes?'

'Something small. Could you come an hour earlier?'

The appointment had been for eleven o'clock. Henry consulted the travelling clock on the mantelpiece. It was ten past eight. The action was as rational and business-like as his next reply.

'Yes. Alright.' But no sooner had he put down the receiver than the atmosphere of the nightmare brought back a flurry of doubt. Had he begun the morning in the right mood? Might he not continue to misjudge situations? When he went to shave he was still unsettled. The nightmare was an omen, surely; a warning not to be involved in high finance, in Shaikh-Moosa's bizarre underworld. His rational self argued that omens were no more than coincidences: fears dressed with significance.

By the time he reached Shaikh-Moosa's residence, self-assurance had replaced superstition; he was now eager to meet Shaikh-Moosa, to let reality speak for itself.

In the broad light of midmorning the residence had shed its aura of solemnity. It was a monumental, functional blank. In surroundings innocent of vegetation, a stony waste which older Malays would have explained as land cursed, grandeur had thawed to impressive loneliness. Henry studied the structure of the house – the monstrous pillars, the gaunt large windows masked by curtains of thick rep, the pregnant balcony – did it resemble the owner's character? It was powerful, certainly, the paintwork rich and fresh, but it was dull, rather like a large piece of Victorian furniture.

A pock-faced young man greeted Henry at the front door, and led him into a grand, richly carpeted room. Behind a huge, stinkwood desk, splashed with papers, hung a cracked owl-like face. Its owner, an old man, sat forward, both arms on the desk, heavy-lidded owl eyes patiently watching an event opposite that was being swallowed up by an enormous armchair.

' – why, why must be?' The event was protesting in a thin, anxious voice, 'Searchers, eberything you have. Only to sign now. Pibe hundred and piberty thousand pound – Uropin area, remumber it . . . is sumthing little . . . is nuthing to ask!'

A pudgy hand, twisting then disappearing in a frivolous arc above the armchair, indicated how footling was the amount – over half a million pounds! As if the gesture or his English could not quite establish cogency of meaning, the speaker burst into demotic Gujarati.

'You offered five hundred and fifty thousand,' he agitated.

'You have the vendor's titles and all other material – there! – on your desk. Now you claim that these flats – '

The owl-faced man put up a hand.

'Just one minute, Mr Desai,' he said, 'one moment, please. Our lawyer is here. We can straighten out everything in one minute.'

Desai, a small tubby man in a rumpled brown suit and no tie between his gold-studded collar, bounced out of concealment, and when he was satisfied that the lawyer was neither rich nor European, bounced back again.

'My son tol' me about you,' the owl-faced man leaned forward a deferential hand.

'Mr Moodley?'

Mr Moodley nodded.

'Happy to make your acquaintance. You know Mr. Desai – Desai Fancy Goods of Johannesburg?'

Hennry nodded curtly at the seated, tubby man.

'Mr Henry Naidoo,' Moodley went on, 'originally of Durban, if I may say so? Please accept a seat, Mr Naidoo.'

While he explained that Shaikh-Moosa was in Port Elizabeth, Moodley sorted the papers on his desk into two files. Behind him, on the wall, hung an excellent portrait of the Indian fascist, Subhas Bose.

'This lot,' Moodley hastened to say, 'is Mr Desai's property – the title deeds, clauses and so on, for some blocks of flats in Durban. Just please quickly check if everything is checked, legal and everything. Price and terms is left out for filling in. Otherwise everything should be right. Mr Reynauds, our Durban lawyer, saw everything right, but he's . . . he's gone away to holiday at Lourenco Marques. This papers – ' he flapped the pile in his right hand, then reconsidered, 'no, this is something else', and he stuck them hurriedly into a folder and, writing 'FOR POSSIBLE AUCTION' on the cover, pushed the folder into the top drawer of the desk.

Henry took the papers and looked around. There was a desk next to a door across the room. Henry paused before it.

'Shall I sit here, or leave?' He nodded towards the door.

Quietly, but swiftly, Moodley came over and led Henry away from the door. The hand on Henry's arm was trembling slightly – a sign of age, Henry thought.

'The desk is quite safe,' Moodley said, confidentially. 'We don't use that room.'

While Henry went through the documents, the bargaining continued. He had almost finished when the telephone rang.

'Moodley senior spekin' . . . yes, very good . . . yes – '

To listen undistracted by the quiet, Moodley plugged his right ear with his right index finger. Suddenly he removed his finger, switched the receiver round to his left ear and held it there, propped up by one shoulder. On a piece of blotting paper he made rapid pencil jottings, grunting now and then, affirmatively, into the handless mouthpiece.

'Well, Mr Desai,' he said, laying down the receiver and looking up, 'some important matters I have coming up. Before I make my final offer I want to tell you something. Something you should know by now. I'm not a two-year-old in this business.' He made an open, expansive gesture. 'Very well I know the next government will be Nationalist. The Smuts Government by the Pegging Act made Indians owning property in European areas a bad thing – very, very bad, Mr Desai – '

Desai protested.

'But the Cape Town Agreement – '

'Oh, now, Mr Desai!' Moodley's expression mixed geniality with mock pain. 'Now you are really taking me for a fool. Better than me even, you know the Cape Town Agreement is a joke. You know that, Mr Desai. Why ask? Nothing happened since 1926. Next year – tomorrow even – your property won't be worth the bricks and mortar. What would happen, I ask you now, if you put it up in open sale? Let me tell you what! It wouldn't fetch the market price!'

'What you offering?'

Moodley, before answering, consulted the oracular jottings on the blotting paper.

'Four hundred thousand in shares.'

'Shares? Shares what . . . what shares?'

'Uralco shares,' answered Moodley, casually.

Desai was silent, face sullenly contemplative. At last he said: 'I use your phone, yas?'

'Help yourself.'

When he reached his number Desai said:

'Ello? . . . Ramdas Desai here . . . that's right – oh, yas, good morning. Can you explain me this, plis? What price Ooralco shares? Yes, that's it. Oor-al-co . . . yas, that is it . . . good, I'll be waiting – '

Moodley, his movements as casual as the expression on his face, crossed the room towards Henry.

'Are the deeds alright?'

Henry's attention was divided.

'Well . . . er, there is this.' He explained that the surveyor's reports were not fresh. Desai's lawyers were in Durban and their relations with representatives in Cape Town were not clear; certain documents were in conflict. To clarify matters a visit to Durban was necessary. Moodley seemed to be only half-listening; although he stared at the factory rooftops near Table Bay, his real attention seemed to be focussed upon Desai's smallest reactions.

'When did Mr Shaikh-Moosa leave?' Henry asked conversationally.

At the drop of the name, Desai glanced quickly at Moodley who yawned and blinked.

'What did you say?'

Henry repeated the question.

'Yesterday. Some time yesterday.'

Henry was about to protest, but seeing that Moodley wished the subject closed, he returned to the papers.

The silence persisted until Desai had received his information and made a few quick calculations in a small black notebook. Then he turned – a small chubby face, twitching impatiently with greed.

'You getting it for nuthing,' he said.

'Good,' said Moodley, and, with Henry's help, they went through what the law required.

Shortly after Desai's satisfied face had left, the door next to Henry's desk opened, and Shaikh-Moosa appeared.

Henry's surprise seemed to delight the Great Man. He was dressed in a black suit, narrow-toed shoes, and the collar of his shirt – which was silk and striped – was starched and glazed in the manner of Edwardian collars.

'Well, Mr Naidoo,' he proclaimed in a deep, wooing voice. 'Nice to see you at last. How are you?'

As he offered a hairy right hand, his left, which had a huge blue-white diamond on the marriage finger, floated up to pet a gold tie-chain; replicating the shape of South Africa and cross-initialled SM; which hung across his tie – a crimson tie with a small, neat English knot. A gold watch, under a white sleeve, glittered among glittering gold cuff-links, and seemed to match its owner's brilliant self-assurance.

'I thought you were in Port Elizabeth?'

Shaikh-Moosa produced one of his gold-bright smiles. His marriage finger flashed in the air as if the matter were of small consequence.

'I knew your father,' he announced grandly. 'Very fine man, if you don't mind me saying so. One of the finest of men. I always speak frank, always the truth you'll hear from me. Never a word of lie. Never!' He frowned reminiscently. 'When did I see him last, when was it? Let me see now. Something like fifteen years ago. Before the war it was. That's right. I remember passing him in my car – I had a Dodge then, colour of red if I remember rightly. A red Dodge, wasn't it, Mr Moodley?'

Mr Moodley nodded sheepishly.

'It was a red Dodge, Mr Shaikh-Moosa.'

'That's right!' The indestructible reminiscence brightened Shaikh-Moosa's dark face. He licked a purple tongue over his nether lip, sucked it back as if straight through his teeth (two canines were solid gold) and then elaborated.

'I remember the day exactly. I have a good memory for these things. I remember I told my driver, "drive me to the Indian Market, I must get a white carnation" – always a white carnation I used to wear in the buttonhole: a silver vase I had, silver-rimmed with a little bit of platinum. The vase my father had given me. The driver was Alfred, wasn't it, Mr Moodley?'

'It was Alfred before the war,' Moodley agreed.

'All my drivers I call Alfred,' Shaikh-Moosa explained ''cepting this fellow's name *was* Alfred.'

'Why was that?' asked Moodley, the only person closely following this senseless rigmarole.

'Don't ask me.' Shaikh-Moosa waved the problem away. 'His mother or something must have called him Alfred. I got used to him, but he let me down, badly.'

'How?' Henry asked, remembering a contrary account.

'That fellow was a rogue!' Shaikh-Moosa suddenly started to rave. 'A dirty, low-down rogue. I told you at the time, Mr Moodley. I said from the first, "Alfred is a r-rogue." All these Kaffirs are rogues. I told you at the time: "I may be speaking out of turn just now but let me tell you a thing or two about that fellow which you have there! He's nothing but a wholesale humbug, r-rogue all over." Spur of the moment, I'll say this, I just have to see him straight in the eyes. You may not think so, but I was watching him – carefully. A man who wouldn't see you straight in the eyes is a r-rogue, a bloody rogue, Mr Moodley.'

Looking straight into Shaikh-Moosa's eyes was a strain: Henry blinked. The tirade seemed quite pointless.

' – a man like that!' the Great Man continued, 'humph! One thing he would speak front of you: something else behind your back. Such a man you should never trust. If I didn't look sharp he would steal the trousers from off my backside. Like this – off! So!'

A phantom adroitly stripped off phantom trousers, leaving Shaikh-Moosa aghast, open-mouthed, hands exclaiming the hideous, painful theft.

'Then what?' he pleaded. He paused to take sober cognisance of his denuded legs. 'I couldn't walk the streets naked, could I, Mr Moodley?'

Moodley giggled.

'No, no. Jokes aside, Mr Moodley. What that fellow wanted was a

damn good horsewhip. Futtock! Futtock! Straightway the broomstick you must give him. No talk. Broomstick. I may not be the man I
was twenty years ago, but . . . when I give him one with this – '

His right hand was compressed into a minatory fist with two
knuckles dented: genuine scars of combat.

Moodley said: 'Yes?'

'One: So!'

The invisible, unreliable r-rogue toppled.

'Just one. No hanky-panky. And he wouldn't wake up again – not
in a month of Sundays. Don't think I'm too old, Mr Moodley. Never
think that! You should know me by now. I'm a man like this. We may
be speaking here. All of us having some quiet conversation. But let
something happen. Then you would see! I would just tell Mr Naidoo
here, "Fetch the voo-voo from back of my car." (I always keep two
voo-voos, sometimes a stick, too, back of my car.) Then you'd see
fire!' He thrashed his fingers. 'Stars like sparks, Mr Moodley. Then
ashes! Everywhere ashes!'

He focussed upon Henry a sudden, cunning enquiry.

'You would fetch the voo-voo for me, Mr Naidoo?'

Henry, struggling to contain amusement, nodded.

'You won't leave me waiting?'

Henry shook his head decisively.

'There's a fellow I like. You see, Mr Moodley, He'll fetch the voo-
voo for me. There is! Anything I ask, he'll do it. Money. Money can
make the *kashoom-bah*! What more you want?'

'Oh, no. Just a minute,' Henry said. 'I said I'll get your voo-voo. I
didn't say anything.'

Surprised to be contradicted, Shaikh-Moosa pretended disappointment. He seated himself grandly in one of the Rexine armchairs
against the panelled wall.

'Then money is no good?' he enquired, and laughed.

'Useless,' Henry confirmed.

'God be merciful!'

With a saturnine smile, Henry said:

'Wasn't Alfred to testify in the Cato Manor affair?'

Like the Isipingo scandal, the Cato Manor affair concerned several
hillsides of Indian market gardeners suddenly served notices to quit
their smallholdings. Shaikh-Moosa was said to have headed the land
development company which had made the take-over. The affair had

been walled up in secrecy, and quashed soon after the first land commission enquiries. There had been rumours of the chief rebels having been bought off. The affair nevertheless achieved considerable notoriety. Several public-spirited people had wished to have Shaikh-Moosa prosecuted for fraudulent speculation. But prosecution had depended upon, as the phrase went, a bird that never sang, that is, upon Shaikh-Moosa's African chauffeur – the chief witness who disappeared rather mysteriously soon after investigations started. In one account, the chauffeur had been bought off; in another, his body had been found washed up off the shores of Cape Point. Henry remembered Alfred from a photograph in the Indian newspaper, *The Leader*, and the caption, 'Native driver may clear up alleged land scandal!'

The question immediately changed Shaikh-Moosa's expression. He inspected Henry shrewdly, wondering perhaps whether escape lay behind a spate of bombast. At last he decided to plead ignorance.

'I can't remember,' he admitted, 'it was a long time back. Small things like that, you forget.'

Henry studied Shaikh-Moosa inscrutably. He consulted his watch: he had promised to see Mr Parsons before luncheon, and he was hungry.

'Well,' he said, curtly, 'as I explained, these flats need a little more sorting out. Mr Moodley will have to come to my office.'

That the mountain should have to go to Mohammed nettled Moodley, who might have protested if Shaikh-Moosa hadn't, almost imperceptibly, blinked his eyes.

'Same thing I was about to suggest, Mr Naidoo,' Moodley quickly about faced.

Shaikh-Moosa smiled happily. 'Is that right, Mr Moodley? You were going to suggest that? Same thing in your place I would do. What a first-rate brain you have, Mr Moodley! First-rate! Without you, Mr Moodley, I would be lost! Lost! There is!' His tone was serious and enthusiastic in an impassive face. 'What a good brain you have, Mr Moodley. I envy you. I am living among Peers.'

The irony, delivered so generously, escaped Moodley who seemed ridiculously pleased.

'Oh, but I'm an old man,' Moodley joked to fill in his master's contented pause. 'I'm getting on in years!'

The idea animated Shaikh-Moosa: he threw up his hands in mock disbelief.

'Old man?' he cried, almost alarmed. 'Old man? You, Mr Moodley? No! Just let one of the District Six *narghiles* stand front of you without what it is they wear underneath. What is it they wear underneath? You know, Mr Moodley?'

'Panties? Bloomers? What is it?'

'No! No! Knickers!'

'Is that it? Is that all?'

'Sometimes nuthing, too.' Clearing his throat, Shaikh-Moosa recounted a pornographic story of a *narghile* who wore 'nuthing'. Moodley giggled callously, like an adolescent.

'No, no. My girls always wear something,' Moodley earnestly confessed, 'something nice.'

'There is!' Shaikh-Moosa attested. 'Something underneath. To whet the appetite. And straightaway all this old-man business is forgotten. *Ghalas*! Old man is gone away, and new man is come-way place of him!'

'True,' agreed Mr Moodley, his expression aged and dead pan, corrupt and zany.

Shaikh-Moosa coughed with laughter.

'Too good, too good. What a witty man you are, Mr Moodley . . . too good . . . *Tho-ba*! *Tho-ba*!'

The locker-room heartiness wearied Henry; he spoke pointedly to Moodley.

'Shall I send you the account?'

Showered with acclaim, Moodley almost answered, but his master sharply took command.

'No, no,' the Great Man said, 'send it care of me. I'll pay you now, if you like.'

Henry smiled with brisk, business-like detachment.

'No hurry,' he said, 'I can always take you to court.'

Shaikh-Moosa's laugh only partly acknowledged Henry's worth; it ended in a snort.

'No fear of that, Mr Naidoo,' he said with adroit cordiality. 'I'll see you right.'

'Very kind of you,' Henry said crisply. 'Good morning. Good morning, Mr Moodley.'

Moodley was startled out of his daze, and mumbled. He seemed quite amazed that his master should receive such careless, impudent address.

When Henry reached the door, Shaikh-Moosa rose.

'Mr Naidoo,' he said. One hand went into a trouser pocket; he bent and straightened his knees – face innocent – to ease money-entangled genitals.

Henry waited.

'I think . . . let me be quite frank – that is my nature . . . I think you're a man I can trust.'

Fundamental indifference joined positive contempt to keep Henry's impassivity and to suppress laughter.

'That's very kind of you to say that.' Henry replied, coldly.

'I just thought I'd tell you.'

Henry smiled politely, shook hands again – Shaikh-Moosa continuing to weigh him up doubtfully – then he hurried off to the other pre-luncheon appointment.

CHAPTER 5

Mr Parsons was waiting outside Henry's office. He took off his hat as soon as he saw Henry and waited to be asked in, head bent like a mourner at a funeral.

In the office he sat forward in his chair, hat on knees, a hangdog look in the eyes. He belonged to that growing race of old men who fend punctiliously for themselves – who repair and wash their own clothes and live lives of blameless probity – obdurate, principled, yet dependent as are all old men who have lost their wives.

Henry felt guilty and found himself wanting to recover the old man's trust: to provide tangible proof that his faith was not misplaced. He explained why he had been unable so far to see Councillor Holmes but promised when he had done so, he would at once get in touch with Mr Parsons.

'Just leave it to me,' Henry said, after Mr Parsons had scribbled down his address, 'I'll get hold of you at once.'

Mr Parsons looked doubtful. Henry assuaged him with another guilty smile and ushered him out.

When he was alone, Henry re-examined Desai's file, and was making notes when a knock brought Doc into the office.

'Ah!' Doc said. 'At last. You're in at last! How about a little spot of lunch? I have a problem – a proposition, pal.'

Henry looked tiredly at the papers. 'Okay,' he said, 'Let's have a bite.'

Over luncheon Doc explained the problem. He had rented a bungalow above a beautiful inlet along the Simonstown coast. He intended to holiday in this bungalow. It would mean 'camping out – virtually pigging it for a while': and he invited Henry to share it with him.

The prospect of two peaceful weeks at the seaside was tempting. Froggy Pond was within striking distance of town so Henry could 'commute if anything vital cropped up'. Doc had 'laid in stocks of the old booze'. The rent between the two of them would be negligible – 'a song, Henry boy, less than a quid a week!'

With characteristic caution, Henry refused to commit himself.

'I'd like to look it over,' he said.

'Excellent. Go out tomorrow!'

Henry was about to mention his appointment with Katherine but reconsidered.

'I might at that,' he said, thoughtfully.

Doc explained where the bungalow and the keys were; then insinuated that he had already spent a night there. Henry knew what this meant and scarcely listened; he was not interested in salacious details of the private lives of others. He had plans of his own. If he invited Katherine to Newlands she might demur; to invite her to Froggy Pond would be quite respectable. It was like an invitation to luncheon at a public restaurant; motive could not be questioned, nor would being turned down or accepted embarrass. He did want to be alone with her. Of course, if Doc was going to spend most of his time at the bungalow, Newlands would be empty. Henry wondered whether his own thinking, under Shaikh-Moosa's influence, was becoming a trifle too devious.

Back at the office he glanced at the papers on the desk, but instead of beginning to work on them, he picked up the telephone directory and after a flush of excitement and hesitation, rang Katherine's father.

He had half-expected – even hoped – to be told that Councillor Holmes was not available and was faintly alarmed, being unprepared, to be put straight through.

He managed, however, after giving credentials, to secure an appointment later in the afternoon, and immediately wondered whether he ought to go home and change into more presentable attire. The amount of work on the desk, however, spoke against such extravagance; moreover, any alteration of appearance might make him more self-conscious than he already was; it might introduce possible delays, gain acknowledgement by dubious counterfeit. He returned to Desai's papers and had fairly mastered them when the alarm clock sang out; it was time to set out for Claremont.

On the telephone Holmes had sounded courteous, impersonal, mild. Henry had little beyond rumour to go by. His absurd adulation of established families blended with equally romantic political ideas;

72

he cast Holmes in a role that did not admit blemish. Holmes was a responsible citizen: a blameless family man, an active and loyal public servant. Above all, his mind was pre-eminently practical, not turned upon nice, pure, metaphysical specualtions; it was noble – it was devoted to holding in equilibrium manifold diversities of interest that were the essential, intrinsic, unalterable condition of the human sensibility. This was what Henry thought as he drove towards Claremont. Fact utterly crippled expectation. Within seconds it was clear that Holmes was little more than an agreeable fool. His entire reputation had been assembled by error and default. He had become a city councillor at a time when candidates of good family had been scarce, and when family counted for more than competence, and he had been kept in office largely by habitual voting. He had a quiet, unassuming manner, which was mistaken for depth; a weak will, which was mistaken for political shrewdness; and an affable naivety, which was mistaken for deliberate charm. Whatever determination had once invested his manner had been an adjunct of his wife and had died with her. He was now a shell echoing stale ideas.

Henry had passed Holmes's offices often. They were set back, off the main Claremont Road, down a side-street – a shabby, two-storied building with a timber yard in front. (Holmes was a builder's merchant). The offices were on the ground floor; the upper floor was a warehouse for building materials.

There were two typists in the outer office – a large drab room with equipment of the type too often found in long-established family businesses.

Henry was led straight through to the inner office which had more modern and comfortable appointments. In a moment it was clear to him that the calm, faintly pompous, middle-aged man, dressed in a brown suit and waistcoat, who hesitantly took his hand, was either a masquerade of simplicity or its epitome. Henry found himself at once asserting his own opinions with rather more than usual force. He had good reason to believe, he said, that rents in a large part of District Six were on the point of being raised; attempts had been made to gain information from Fylfot Holdings – the company supposed to be responsible – without success; did Holmes think, because he would shortly have to go to the electorate, that he could afford to be indifferent?

Holmes, who had nodded distractedly throughout this short

speech, became inscrutably grave; he seemed quite put out by the possibility that a Tenant's Association might be formed. Though Henry had suggested this last idea in passing, when he saw its effect, he began to think beyond mere possibilities.

Holmes was about to reply when a knock brought one of the typists, with a sheaf of papers, to the door.

'Not now, please, Miss Arendse,' Holmes muttered uncomfortably.

The woman said two clients were waiting.

'They're the new contract, sir.'

Holmes smiled unhappily, understanding her anxiety.

'Could you fetch them some tea, Miss Arendse?' he asked, his tone appeasing.

Miss Arendse, who had clearly arranged the appointment, looked dissatisfied, and shot Henry a glance of impatience.

When she closed the door, Holmes rose from his chair and began to pace the floor self-importantly.

'Yes,' he said, glancing at Henry and then away again as if he was incapable of looking him straight in the eye, 'Yes. I've heard these rumours, too. You think it's worth investigating?'

The man's hesitation exasperated Henry.

'There could be hell to pay!'

'True. True enough,' Holmes again paced the floor.

There was a long awkward pause. Henry had a sudden suspicion that the man was hedging; either he was a vacillating man by nature or else an ineffectual actor; his manner suggested that he was privy to more than he wished to disclose.

Henry looked at his own watch.

'Well,' he said at last, not wishing to watch Holmes pace the floor the rest of the afternoon, 'I wonder if you'd like to look into the matter, Councillor. Perhaps, I can phone you in a day or so.'

The notion of action seemed to alarm Holmes, and brought his to-and-fro pacings to a sudden halt.

'Wait! Don't let's rush things. We must go into everything quietly. No need for anyone to be upset, don't you think?'

Henry, who had already determined to see Mr Parsons and recommend that a Tenant's Association be formed, rose and said tartly:

'If rumour is true, then lots of people will be upset!'

The interview threw Henry into such high dudgeon that when he

74

returned to his office he could not resume work immediately. He was unusually brusque with Mr Moodley, whom he arranged to meet after supper, and he sent a small boy with a note to Mr Parsons, which asked the old man to come to the office the next morning. Then he remembered how tired he was and decided to take a nap on the office couch, but he could not fall asleep at once. He kept recalling Katherine's father: the dismay of false promise; he had a sense of events having begun to occur too fast for proper assimilation. The entry in his diary for Thursday represents an aspect of this impression.

> *Too many events happening at once: a sensation that I had as a child when, for experiment, I released the hand-brake of a car and the vehicle started to run uncontrollably downhill. Panic: spring; green effervescence in the bones; an expanding tide of happiness; adventure; intense awareness of being carried towards the unknown, towards some kind of natural miracle in which the landmarks of routine shrivel as if they were markings on a reality being discarded . . . I am afraid and happy; this is what the prospect of meeting Katherine means. I care nothing for Shaikh-Moosa, or Moodley, or Holmes, or even – sad to say – Mr Parsons. Katherine enlarges particular responses, as if she has accelerated rhythms of the heart.*

The diary records several more mundane events.

> *Thursday. December, 18th*
>
> *Saw Moodley again this morning. Explained that things will take a day or two with Desai's solicitors, but someone must check Durban. He suggested that I go to Durban. I was alarmed at first, then I realised that it would only be for a day or so at the utmost, so I agreed. He was at once effusively grateful.*
>
> *Saw Parsons too. He came with two other men, a talkative young fellow and another man who didn't say a word. Together they seemed like a kind of male trinity – father, son and holy ghost. The young man wanted me to come round to see the threatened properties, also the other problem – the squatters, who have set up pondokkies or tin shacks on vacant land, and who would also have to move. I suggested that a meeting be called so as to set up a Tenant's Association, and they seemed vastly pleased, feeling that at last some responsible action was in sight. I promised to talk at the meeting.*
>
> *Last night when I got home, Pieter was in the sitting-room. A surprise. He*

was drunk: wallowing in an armchair. He seemed extravagantly pleased to see me, and at once began to unload. I was feeling washed out, quite bushed, but I remembered how the day before I had wanted to talk to someone, so I heard him out. He hadn't been to work. Instead he had made a desperate pilgrimage through District Six, hoping to bump into Jessie. Why hadn't he made a date with her? He'd been too shy, he explained. I didn't believe this. I suspect that she was scared of being with a white man on her own. But I didn't tell him this. Anyway, he didn't see her, so he spent the afternoon in a cinema. Didn't want to return to District Six because of Malay footpads. He's quite right, too. Petty crime is on the increase in the district. The other day a man from out of town was held up by skollies at gun point. The skollies are more active in the afternoon. It's okay if they know you. Fortunately, like doctors and nurses, I enjoy a kind of Red Cross immunity. This is because I stood up for a few of the Globe gang in court.

Pieter wanted me to see Jessie on his behalf. He knows I don't like him; therefore, feels a need to legitimise his application. The situation became embarrassing. I've come across this sort of thing before, with people who throw themselves upon your bounty, become guilty, then want to prove the opposite: that they are not really destitute and down on their luck. It has to do with pride. Perhaps, because he was drunk, self-justification took a clumsy turn. He said he had no prejudices about Coloured people which made it clear that he had. He began to talk about the way the Dutch had behaved towards Jewish refugees during the war; this was alright; but what was irritating was the cock-and-bull story of how he had fallen in love with an Indonesian girl captured in Paris during the Nazi occupation. All attempts to rescue her had been unsuccessful and she had died after brutal interrogation. Jessie, Pieter said, reminded him of this girl. The story was a bad revamp of a popular novel Doc had been reading. The elaborate fiction was sad. I had promised to see Jessie and didn't want to welsh on him, so I repeated the promise, and that bucked him up.

By accident late Thursday morning, Henry met Jessie in the street. She was standing outside the fish market just as he was about to drive off for lunch. In one hand, she was holding a small shopping net. She was wearing a white blouse with frills, a ballerina skirt, and ballet shoes – an outfit that was the latest in popular fashion. She looked like a high school girl out of uniform, doing the morning shopping, and she blushed as soon as she saw Henry.

She blushed more deeply when she heard what he proposed, and listened, intensely, like a girl receiving hockey instruction: a mixture of doubt and demure, searching attention. Henry realised that she was the type who would not act on her own initiative, so he made an appointment for her to meet Pieter on Sunday afternoon. Eventually, when she had agreed and they were about to part, she gave Henry a piece of information that, as he puts it in a diary, really shook him.

Jessie suddenly asked, he writes, *whether I had been in Salt River yesterday, and when I told her I hadn't she said she'd seen Katherine there last night. She had greeted Katherine, but Katherine seemed to be in a hurry to get somewhere and seemed vastly upset. Her hands were shaking and she looked as if she had been crying. I don't quite know why, but this information really shook me. Not so much the mystery, but another feeling, a kind of premonition. I can't explain it, but Katherine has given me this feeling twice before: a feeling of senseless disaster at once unknown and known, and, because known, expected. I could not have a proper lunch; the feeling sat in the pit of my stomach like acid crystals dissolving every now and then into flurries of the most unaccountable pain. Only when I began to drive out to Kalk Bay did it melt, but then it left a residue, a ghost of itself, so that I did not feel myself. It is as if there are things happening to Katherine, as if she is a victim of something that she can do nothing about. She seems to be bleeding inside. This is what I sense. It's unaccountable and pains.*

Henry was right. Katherine did have, as he puts it elsewhere in a diary, *blood across the eyes*, but what troubled her is not quite so easy to explain. In fact it is again rather like trying to unfold the ineffable. Perhaps it is best to start at the period before she came into contact with Yussouf Rycliffe and even more disastrously, with Gordon Stewart; perhaps in this way also a certain style of politics can be gleaned.

As an infant, Katherine had been the delight of elders; as a girl, a mischievous baggage; at school she was universal dismay. Her imagination and intelligence were lively, but she lacked perserverance. Her background had never pressed upon her the need for steady application. When therefore she passed out of Training College with a teacher's certificate, she felt, with misgiving and native fairness, that congratulation was quite unwarranted.

Because she was good-looking and high-spirited, she never lacked admirers. She was courted and proposed to frequently, and twice she imagined herself in love. Parties, dances, amateur theatricals and some sport, composed the bulk of her leisure, and to these affairs she applied herself without much constraint.

When, however, she began to earn her own living, the cheerful years ended. It had once been possible for those of her station and upbringing to work in slum schools without feeling out of place. Here and there, eccentrics had abandoned comfort to devote themselves to the underdog; but, in the main, the well-to-do and underprivileged had tended to share, with medieval conviction, unaltering traditions of degree. Industrialisation, Western egalitarianism, the war in Europe, and other agencies, had, within a remarkably short space of time, undermined this outlook. Not to have been affected, Katherine would have had to have been insentient.

At school many colleagues were active ideologues. She soon found herself, after school hours, in the swim of study circles, seminars, and political conferences. She was asked to contribute regular dramatic criticism to a weekly called *The Flame* and soon came into contact with the Rycliffe crowd.

At this time Yussouf Rycliffe was, as he would say, 'an old hand' – but 'at my peak, my friends, at the zenith of my intellectual powers!' He was a revolutionary of the Trotskyite variety, a fervent Marxist and left-wing Communist.

'My dear friends,' he would proclaim to an accompaniment of many grand mannerisms (he was a big man, over six feet tall, with a rich store of dramatic gestures), 'I was baptised in the Amritsar riots. A little boy I was, only a child, and those damned stooges of British Imperialism took pot shots at me – look!' At once a right calf would be uncovered to disclose the trophies – several bullet scars. 'I was in the British General Strike. I knew Maxton and all the ILP Boys – never get mixed up with the British Labour Movement. They're a lily-livered bunch, reformists every man Jack of 'em!' A Cambridge graduate, he was a weird amalgam of *fin de siècle* dandy – gloves, hat and gold-topped walking-stick – an unyielding Bolshevik. He liked to imagine descent from a line of Whig aristocrats – 'the English love that sort of thing, and I do it to amuse them!' In fact, his great grandfather had been an Arab slave-trader, operating with a group of equally shabby Indian merchants along the East Coast of Africa, with headquarters in Madagascar. The next generation, after setting up a trading-station at Cape Town and marrying Malay, had settled

78

amid much feudal pomp in a magnificent establishment above old Malay Quarter. The Rycliffes became a sort of Malay aristocracy; they lived in large, feudal homes, kept strings of racehorses, and married, in Moslem fashion, several wives. The eldest son was educated abroad in Cairo and Paris; when his turn came, Yussouf was sent to India and afterwards to Cambridge.

'Cricket's my game,' Rycliffe would announce, 'had Varsity colours at eighteen. I remember Pataudi, the Nawab, you know, said to me, "Rycliffe you get in there . . . !" ' Like many men in ripe middle age, Rycliffe had already begun to live a fanciful past.

A spell of locum medicine in Brixton had introduced him to left-wing politics. On return to South Africa, he was within a few weeks before the courts for organising a two-day waterfront strike against traffic in arms to Abyssinia. International Socialists at first, the Rycliffe crowd gradually emerged as a popular force. 'You don't talk Socialism to peasants', Rycliffe would asseverate, 'they don't cotton on. National liberation, that's the ticket over here, old chap, democratic rights. First things first. Democracy, then the social revolution!'

But it was not liberal democracy; it was Bolshevik alcohol in new bottles, and it quickly intoxicated ignorant, restless, and idealistic youth.

At fifty, Yussouf Rycliffe was already a legend. Though twice divorced and recently married a third time – to a woman much younger than himself – monogamy, for reasons hereditary and ideological, seemed to him an odious institution. 'In everything,' he would declare, playing with words, 'one should go the whole hog: better to end up a pig than a Moslem.'

But life in South Africa was growing more intolerable. The political utopias of young manhood were daily receding. His private sunset was near. He already claimed he was 'not played out': that the frequent defeats of his movement were really 'great moral victories'. Sophisticated bitterness was replacing discrimination; in his medical bag, a bottle of whisky had become an indispensible passenger.

Rycliffe was not yet pitiable. To the young, the mocking detachment of a *roué* was fascinating. Katherine was young. There was glamour and flattery in an experienced lover; the incomprehensible challenged understanding; the ability to manipulate emotions with *sang-froid* betokened an essential refusal to acknowledge a person whose chief immediate interests were personal recognition. Katherine failed to see him as an ageing man fighting desperately to re-establish self-confidence, to recover the powers of lost and diminishing virility. Drawing her close, aware that he acted and no longer felt, that he was living on reserves, Rycliffe would declare, 'Young man, older woman; older man, young girl – the son and the mother, the daughter and the father . . . the Greeks, my dear, were great psychologists!' So, for a long while, exhilarated by the magnitude of her revolt, sheltered by Rycliffe's social renown, Katherine was happy.

Gradually she became aware of his essential disinterest. The shadows of his philandering grew palpable, her vanity was wounded, she began to make desperate moves to win him back. But in self-defence, and with an emotional coldness also part of his complex nature, Rycliffe became cruel. 'This silly bitch,' he would proclaim to a heartless, tittering room, 'thinks she can possess me – me! – what a laugh!' Against such mirth, Katherine was defenceless. Emotion gagged her. Sensual abandon spawned guilt and fear; the treachery was horrifying; pride forced her to accept the crucifixion and to bleed in private. The humiliations shattered self-confidence; she thought frequently of suicide. Yet she could not free herself from Rycliffe: his world remained the only one in which she retained a modicum of social acceptance. Rycliffe had taught her to scorn more desolate, taboo-ridden formalities of the middle and lower classes; his society offered the only freedom, the only area of adventure, but she was still not indoctrinated enough to accept people as mere vehicles for the play of inevitable social forces, least of all, herself. It was at this phase, when she was preparing to renounce individuality, that she met Gordon Stewart, that paradox of violent, impersonal individualism, and now she was on the road to Calvary.

Henry instinctively loathed Gordon. I cannot feel quite the same. If anything, I find Gordon's political attitudes less disagreeable than Rycliffe's but then Henry rather liked Rycliffe. Human relations are complex. Since I have been scornful of Rycliffe's neo-Bolshevism, it is only fair that I should declare my own political allegiances. I am an Anarchist of the pacifist type. This means that, unlike Gordon, I prefer Kropotkin to Bakunin, that I advocate mutual aid. Unlike Henry, also an individualist, but of another tradition, I make no compromise with the nation-state. Nations disgust me; only city-states, as Rousseau saw, can be truly democratic. Unlike Gordon, however, I do not believe in achieving the anarchist millennium by romantic violence, by direct action. I believe rather that Communism, which merely means people living together and making their own laws, must come peacefully, when people at last recover the Greek and Renaissance respect for human dignity. At the same time, I am sympathetic to Henry's Democratic Liberalism, since it also attempts to balance equality with freedom, and moreover belongs to the tradition of natural rights which I find far more acceptable than Rycliffe's glorification of the State, and of the inevitable processes of history. But let me return to Gordon Stewart.

Gordon Stewart was a South African at once typical and uncharacteristic. His parentage was almost as intricate as his character. His father had been an Inspector of Schools, a Scotsman of fine Edinburgh traditions: 'a canny man and muckle tough', intelligent, practical, and civilised. He had come to South Africa before the turn of the century, and having found among Afrikaaners some of the qualities he most admired in the Scots – notably, their blunt refusal to be bullied by the hated Sassenachs – he had sided with them in their War of Independence (or Boer War, as the English called it) and had married into a distinguished *Voortrekker* family. Gordon's mother – the soft, ample, dreamy-eyed woman of the photographs – had been wounded in an English reprisal, and had died not long after her son's birth, of an overdose of morphine.

From his father, Gordon inherited a taste for learning, a rebellious pugnacity and turbulent, fearless, Celtic mind; from his mother – perhaps, more from her absence – a countryboy wistfulness, that inner uncertainty which stamps the dogmatic philosopher. At Wits – the University of Witwatersrand – where he took honours in Classics and Philosophy, he acquired a reputation for unstable genius. At twenty-seven he became senior lecturer in Logic, and might have risen to higher academic glory if his restless passionate temperament had not intervened. It was discovered that his leisure was spent carousing in African townships and preaching extreme political and social doctrines. African trade unions were illegal; nevertheless, Gordon not only formed several unions, but brought his men out on a half-successful strike. After several unheeded warnings, he was dismissed from his university post, and, in his own language, 'forced into a period of agreeable incubation'. For a living he worked as a taxi-driver and seemed to enjoy the restless, shady atmosphere of that vocation; in his spare time, he devoured books with a voracity characteristic of a person who believes that providence is fashioning him for a special historic destiny. When the war broke out he was among the first volunteers. 'Several reasons for that,' he would explain. 'George Orwell was one. Then there was the Jewish set-up. Friends of mine, dammit: the only people who ever helped me when I was in the shits! Also, and what – what? I wanted to get the hell out of South Africa. The country was giving me the screaming shits! But we went to the Western Desert and that was no castle. Piss, flies, shit, parades, and stinking food, and a Commander-in-Chief like Montgomery! You can't get worse. When I got back I was a hero. Of course. Wits took me back – *merde! merde alors!* What a shitty, crackpot, mad society!'

But his war experiences were not altogether valueless. He developed an interest in mathematics – a preoccupation which rapidly became an obsession and indirectly, for some time, kept him out of politics. In the meantime the Rycliffe crowd had created an organisation in Johannesburg which tried to capture some of the members of the Anarcho-Syndicalists, and since Gordon was to attend a winter philosophical conference at Cape Town, he was asked to make a thorough reconnaissance of enemy headquarters.

When he arrived, he put up at Rycliffe's but though he and Rycliffe sat up drinking wine and coffee, arguing late into the night, though they played cricket and chess together, though they reached a stage in which personal intimacies might be exchanged, Gordon failed to penetrate the final veils of the Doctor's guard.

The situation was actually a black comedy because there was little about the Rycliffe group that Gordon did not already know. In fact, he knew more about the background of the group than many of its newer adherents. He knew, for example, that Rycliffe had only recently become the leader, that his leadership was constantly being challenged by Benjamin Michaels – a Coloured school teacher of rather ascetic and calculating appearance and manner – that the group had been formed in the early thirties by an old Bolshevik of the Left Opposition, a man called Gromeko, that Gromeko had sent Trotsky a document called *The Agrarian Thesis* which set out the essential views of the group, and that this thesis had received the Old Man's whole-hearted approval. Gordon had even read a transcript of this secret document. It followed classical Marxist lines. The main idea arose from the Marxist view of history, namely, that the history of all societies is the history of class struggles, and that the nature of these struggles is materialistically (that is, economically) determined. Gromeko had argued that South Africa was a backward, essentially agrarian country, and that the Africans – 'the driving force of the mass revolutionary movement' – were still peasant in outlook even though 'large numbers of them might be urbanised'. In consequence, 'the task before the movement was continuous pressure for democratic rights . . . the usual liberties of bourgeois democracy' – this was the 'minimum' programme, which 'in South African terms, would have the force and effect of nothing short of revolution, since the slightest alteration in the political fabric of the State would precipitate the widest social and economic repercussions'. To prevent the movement from 'being taken over by counter-revolutionary forces to ensure eventual success' and in keeping with the tenets of Leninism, a close confraternity of full-time 'revolutionary activists' was to be created, the familiar Bolshevik 'cadres', or 'elite corps of the people's revolutionary army'. The Leninist view that social change could not occur peacefully was also assumed: force was the 'midwife of history' and indeed 'every ruling class from the dawn of history has understood the use of violence and coercion, the very instruments of the state!'

Gordon knew that Gromeko, now in his seventies, had, since the war began, passed out of active politics: he knew too, who had replaced him as the new 'old guard of leadership'; but whenever he broached these and kindred matters he confronted a wall of silence. It was not merely that Rycliffe felt pledged to his colleagues – 'the necessary revolutionary precaution against agents provocateurs' – but also that he enjoyed the sense of power which mystery ordained. Whenever there was a risk of imprudent disclosure, his eyes would light up with pleasure and superiority, he would toss back his head in a lavish, characteristic gesture and make clear to Gordon that he was a man in whom sacred trust had been enshrined and that only he and a few others were in the know.

'One day we'll discuss these things, Professor!' he would declare. The implication was that before any mysteries could be unveiled, Gordon had to pass a prolonged initiation. 'Bags of time for that, my friend. I make it a rule never to rush things. Good principle, don't you think, old fellow – what?'

Katherine, at this time, was a frequent visitor, and Rycliffe in one of his less civilised moods, happened to intimate that though he was 'quite finished with her', she was 'a peach' (he kissed his fingers) 'a marvel, my dear fellow, in the bedroom!'

Upon Gordon, who anyway found Katherine attractive, these observations were not wasted. He was a restless brute, and had not quite settled down in Cape Town; for a multitude of reasons, he decided to seduce Katherine. There was plain lechery, her vulnerability, and his glamorous self-assurance; there was revenge upon Rycliffe; there was also his belief in 'free love'. If Rycliffe's sexual morals were tasteless, Gordon's were at least logical. All forms of property came under his absolute ban: marriage, to him, was merely a property relation, dishonest and despicable, an obstacle according to his notion of liberty; the sooner it broke down the sooner the millenium arrived. He had only contempt for Rycliffe's indecisive, butterfly flickerings in and out of 'bourgeois morality'. Rycliffe's uninterrupted teasing irritated him; his intellectual arrogance was wounded. He decided to sweep Katherine off her feet.

The task was not difficult. Gordon had an ability of inviting immediate rapport. Unlike Rycliffe, he was not polished and circumspect and devious: he was primitive and direct. He gave her the immediate recognition she had so long sought; he bluntly unveiled mysteries, he declared his feelings without subterfuge. In her insecurity and discontent, in her own desire to inspire jealousy, Katherine was a willing victim. She became his mistress, but now events began to move on a new level. Because both she and Gordon were in frenetic states of mind, their affair, begun so casually, took on an air of desperation; suddenly, Katherine lost control. She and Stewart had begun to find one another irresistible. Their affair lasted as long as he remained in the Cape. Then he left; but recently he had returned, and it was for this reason, partly, that she had sought sanctuary with her sister. The affair was insane; it promised only pain and desolation. She was bewildered and frightened, and she knew, also, that like Rycliffe, Gordon did not care for her, but there was one fact, a single, vital fact that could not be cancelled, a fact which stopped her from breaking off relations. Her pride was magnificent; and suffering, in consequence, unmitigated. In effect, she was no longer aware of what she was doing. When she invited Henry to Kalk Bay, it had been to set a buffer and measure between herself and Rycliffe and Stewart. She was rationalising the last throw of fate's dice. Vaguely, she sensed that Henry might answer her crucifixions; but she was too muddled to be sure. As a result, she had quarrelled with the sister she worshipped, and had unwittingly given Henry the pain that his diaries record. Just as much as he did, she looked forward to what would happen at Kalk Bay, but the suspense froze her. Her response to the fact that the morning's secret meeting had chosen Rycliffe as a candidate for the forthcoming District Six Election was cold; she was so vulnerable that she had to erect the most icy barriers she could between herself and the world.

CHAPTER 6

If Kalk Bay inspired in Katherine uncertainty, in Henry it installed plain panic. Just the thought of inviting Katherine to Froggy Pond intoxicated him. When he arrived at Kalk Bay he deliberately pretended that the future held nothing unusual in store. A ludicrous fear possessed him: the more he wished to see Katherine the more an impersonal mysterious force declaring his unworthiness would draw her, like Eurydice, away. He was afraid that he had already lost his wits over this girl. There seemed only one corrective: he had to want the opposite of what he wanted. In this way if the original desire was gratified he would be delightfully surprised, and if it wasn't, then he would be spared all the sorrows of disappointment.

It was a brilliant afternoon – one of those climatic marvels of the Cape when magical sunlight spills through the golden hole of the sky and rinses the air to an immaculate clarity, raising a tawny spectrum of colour out of the rocks and foliage of the mountain-side and changing, frequently, the moods of the sea.

Kalk Bay was a small, tiered settlement, interspersed by quaint stone stairways on the lower slope of the mountain-side. The houses, halted at the black bar of the Main Road, presented here a curving facade of hotels, cafés, boarding-houses and shops of the seaside variety. The railway station, with its old-fashioned rafters and outdated platforms stood opposite on a permanent way, and below it and beyond, was a short strip of sandy beach.

Henry gathered up the roll of his bathing gear and crossed the main road. The tar had been softened by sunshine and was now embedded by the sand wakes of motor vehicles. Under the station were several arched tunnels, and one had to stoop slightly going through them to reach the beach. When trains poured along the tracks overhead, they emitted a shallow, echoing roar.

Beyond the arches was a strip of corrugated yard with beach-huts and a tea-room which obscured the prospect of the small, deep bay. Henry found the Rycliffe party at once. They were a group of eight –

three men, two women, and three children. Except for them and a tramp curled about an empty sherry bottle next to one of the steel-net refuse baskets, the beach was deserted.

The group was collected about a tartan rug that had been spread over the sand. On the rug, littered with baskets and articles for beach use, sat Mrs Rycliffe, a baby with a large white bonnet, and a short, sturdy, blond-haired man wearing a sports jacket with brilliant wefts of green, bathing-trunks, and open-toed sandals. Standing behind them were Katherine and two men: a short, compact African, and a Coloured man who held himself defensively upright, a pair of rimless sunglasses bridging his aquiline nose, and whom Henry recognised as Benjamin Michaels. Katherine was wearing a two-piece bathing-suit; her hair was composed into a pony-tail, and her eyes seemed to be listening to the men but, every now and then, were directed towards a pair of others swimming near some boats anchored to the mole of the bay.

When she caught sight of Henry, she waved. Michaels and the African glanced momentarily in his direction, and returned to their discussion. Mrs Rycliffe, a cold, beautiful woman, hair done up in a crown of braids, blinked superciliously, but the blond-haired man, who was sitting on his haunches, tracked Henry's approach rather as a hunter might follow the progress of important game.

Katherine hesitated, then came to meet him.

'I was about to give you up.'

'How are you?' Henry swallowed hard and held himself tensely erect. Again her mere presence raided him: whirred up excitement and fear; vulnerability; again control seeping away.

'Shall I introduce you?' she asked. 'Or do you want to change?'

Her expression was one of careful gravity.

'Are you in a religious mood?' he asked.

The remark failed to penetrate.

'Why?'

'Nothing. You look so serious.'

She brightened – a wan smile – but only momentarily.

'Yes. Perhaps I'd better get it over with,' he said, still slightly uncomfortable.

Mrs Rycliffe smiled coldly. The blond-haired man, whom Henry recollected having seen somewhere before, nodded quizzically; Michaels and the African said hello briefly and returned to their argument. They were discussing means and ends and the morality of using, in particular, violence for political ends.

Henry put down his jacket and Katherine showed him to the public changing rooms.

'We've just hired a bungalow,' he told her, 'at Froggy Pond. I have to look it over. Would you like to come?'

She looked as if she had a dozen other things to do first.

'I'd love to. Here we are!' She pointed to the changing rooms. 'You pay a *tiekkie* for a basket.'

When Henry returned, Dr Rycliffe and his sister-in-law – an erect, lean, beady-eyed woman in a white bathing-cap and a brilliantly mottled bikini – had come out of the sea.

The Doctor sat on a broad orange-coloured towel, his back leaning against the random stones of an arch, a panama flopped siesta-like over his face. The blond-haired man, whose name Henry had failed to catch, was talking at Rycliffe, a massive-bowled, long-stemmed pipe in one hand. To stress a point, he occasionally jabbed at the air with the pipe stem.

He was doing exactly this when Henry drew up.

' – so he threw the book at me. So what? So heart, lungs, x-rays, everything hunky-dory,' the blond-haired man was saying. 'So he said, you haven't had a finer constitution, he says to me. So I said, fine, chum. I said fine. By me, that's fine. Now I can hop back and do some work. In a flash I was back at the *Kritik der reinen Vernunft* reading like blazes. And now, only after a few *meshugenah* breakdowns, I think I can make out with Kant. Something. Not very much; but something – '

He looked up, cross at first, then his face warmed with a bright, secretive smile. He moved aside slightly, so that Dr Rycliffe could be introduced.

The Doctor lifted the brim of his panama and, through dark glasses, professionally examined Henry.

'Too many carbohydrates, young man!' he pronounced in an orotund voice. 'You want to eat more protein, more fruit and vegetables – less of those rich curries and biryanis.'

The observation was so surprising that Henry's wits took a moment to recover.

'Don't pay any attention, chum,' Stewart thrust in. 'Eat as much as you can hold. When you're sick, track down a good doctor. Get well. Then go eat some more.'

Dr Rycliffe gave a long Rabelaisian laugh.

'My friend,' he began, talking with many gestures, the corners of his mouth horned in. Though he took off the panama, he was still incognito under the dark glasses.

' – you listen to me,' he continued, 'don't listen to these Jo'burg boys. For twenty years I've been tending the weak and the halt. For twenty solid years, professor. No flash in the pan. Year in, year out: all the black calendar days! It doesn't mean a thing, not two hoots – ' he clicked the fingers of one hand, ' – not a bloody thing professor, if, for one day, just for an afternoon, I come out to Kalk Bay. A little bit of relief – huh? eh? what? Just a little relief. A few healthy energetic movements in the water. A few breathfuls of sea air,' – he inhaled deeply, drawing in and patting his diaphragm – 'and all the accumulated tensions, the nervous disorders of weeks, disappear! Just like that!' – again he clicked his fingers – 'that doesn't cancel my ability as the best *medico* in the Peninsula, does it? I ask you, my friend? Honestly now? Be honest for once in your life!'

The question was so obviously rhetorical, no one answered.

' – But even so, I'm tops when I'm fagged. I can see the world at close quarters! I can get up on my hind legs and roar, my friend! Roar like an injured spavined bull!

'Funny little chaps come to me. Funny little chaps with growing moustaches. Little bits of fluff over the chin. Little chaps just beginning to wet their navels – intellectual navels, of course! Silly little chaps, you know the sort? Come, Naidoo, you're a man of the world?'

'I think,' Henry said, quietly, 'you've given me a rough idea.'

The reply surprised Rycliffe. He re-evaluated Henry and smiled approvingly.

'But seriously though,' he went on, 'chaps say, look Yussouf, the Blacks are oppressed, the folks need schools, houses, food. Folks need immediate things. Where's your social conscience, man? Don't sit about on the beaches, in arm-chairs, on the race-tracks. Do something about it!' He shook his head sadly. 'No, chaps, I say to them. No. I mean t' say. Open your eyes. Look at the matter historically. Don't froth at the mouth for action. Get an idea – an idea of the workings of society. Isn't it bloody obvious that all this reformist stuff, a few houses here and there, a dish of thin gruel, a few cheap clothes, patches on a moribund society are by-the-by – concessions, sops to Cerberus, when a whole continent hasn't got the simplest means of sustenance, when the last – the very last franchise is the Coloured Vote and the Cape Municipal Franchise! Don't be so emotional, chaps. Lie low for a while. Cogitate. All in good time. Come back in five years' time, and we'll discuss things – real things, real ideas! But you see the rational insincerity of these petty bourgeois scions. They don't want to think. They want others to do their dirty work for them – dirty work? – Clean work! Beautiful work! To think is a dialectical feast. To think, is to realise, that in one fell swoop, one stroke, my friends; one collective stroke; we can wipe out all the accumulated rubbish of the ages – '

A train whistled as it left Kalk Bay Station. Picking up speed, it went at a clip overhead, clattering in a black roar of air and dust.

Out of the thinning noise, the vacuum, the Doctor resumed.

'No individual, no romantic stuff. No piddling little individual heroics – effective as damp squibs. In one powerful stroke, we can feed and clothe a whole nation – one stroke – full democratic rights, the real McCoy, no half jobs, no romantic nonsense! Give us time, my friends, time – '

'Time!' interrupted Stewart, who had been chuckling sarcastically. 'Time for the Western Man! Mechanical time. Jesus Christ, Yussouf, don't talk such crap. In the first place, you haven't the smallest inkling of what an idea is, else you wouldn't shoot such rambling cock about nothing. Time, indeed. All this chiliastic, Messianic blah, when you sit on your arse talking like a constipated lunatic. What are the facts? Facts are this. There isn't time! It's now. Here. You can't see the contradiction in this Messianic guff. What happens? Here? Now? Don't mix me up with your funny little monkeys, your compromisers! I want an immediate, expedient correction of wrongs. As for compromise you're a fine one to talk. What in King Buggery's name d'you think you're doing now? You've got a guilty conscience about it already. Don't forget you're the bright eyed cookie who's standing in the City Council elections, not me.'

'You're standing?' Henry asked, interested, for the first time, in what seemed little more than an exchange of gaseous rhetoric.

Stewart looked annoyed that he had been interrupted.

'That's right,' he snapped. 'That's right, chum. This is the twit that's standing. That's individual romantic stuff – that's not full democratic rights. That's a bloody, loaded, blanket vote. Twenty years! By Christ, you haven't learnt a thing in twenty years. Give me ten good strong blokes and some dynamite – blow up a few mines. That'll wake up those fat smug bastards on the Stock Exchange. That'll give them the screaming shits. That'll make these slobs come begging at your doorstep, asking to turn on the brakes. Terrorism, brute force, that's all those miserable pompous shits with their fat untaxed incomes and bridge evenings will listen to. And you prattle about ideas!'

'And what?' Henry demanded, checking anger with difficulty, 'what happens afterwards? What about the lives involved? The police reprisals? The hundreds of innocents shot down in revenge?'

'Human life!' Stewart pulled a contemptuous expression, mainly about the mouth. 'Do those smug bastards give a damn about people dying everyday in Sophiatown – the malnutrition, the disease, the over-crowding, the children with pot-bellies because they eat "fuck-all" but mealy-meal and polluted water?'

'Violence,' Henry rapped back, 'simply breeds more violence.'

'What d'you mean?'

'Just that,' replied Henry, furiously, 'just what I said. Nothing more, nothing less! I never heard of terror doing anything but creating worse despotism. What did Lord Acton say? – '

'Power corrupts, and absolute power corrupts absolutely' Stewart sneered, 'And look what God the Absolute made of this fucking world. And Acton, a nineteenth century Catholic Whig, to boot. Okay for him – a member of the British ruling class! That fine lapidary style, my arsehole!'

'I'm sorry,' Henry said, relenting, but still firm, 'I disagree. Acton was a fine historian. But that's beside the point. The point is – '

'That you like this bloody social system,' Stewart cut in.

'Nothing of the sort,' Henry answered, 'but I don't see that swearing helps. Or violence.'

'Ah,' Stewart said, 'passive resistance! Gandhi! Do you know what Gandhi said that the Jews should do in Hitler's Third Reich?'

'Yes,' replied Henry, hopelessly, 'they should all commit suicide.'

'That's right!' Stewart almost shouted, 'and where's the high moral tone of that? No, chum. Hit back. Give me the Old Testament – an eye for an eye! There's more guts to it!'

91

'Violence, huh,' said Rycliffe, thoughtfully. 'More guts, you think?' He stood up and put on his panama.

'Why not?' asked Stewart, abruptly suspicious. 'What are you going to do?'

He sensed that Rycliffe had resolved a political problem.

'Do?' asked the Doctor, with enigmatic impassivity, 'do what, my friend?'

'Something's brewing. I know.'

Rycliffe's face remained inscrutable.

'I'm going to do nothing,' he said, pleased with the effect of his small drama. 'I'm going for another swim. Coming, Mistress Holmes?'

Katherine hesitated. Henry looked beyond himself for the first time: he saw that Katherine's face was tense; he felt immediately guilty, but did not know what he could do. Katherine accepted the invitation uncheerfully, as if it was a hopeless solution: she was not even amused when Rycliffe swam off to the mole, still wearing his panama and dark glasses.

Henry watched them go into the water. Pieces of blackish bladder-wrack and alluvion, whitened with scum bubbles, swayed upon the water's edge: indication of the weight of the small bay. A few fishing boats were moored to the breakwater; now and then, barnacles and seaweed, clinging to the corroded pillars of the jetty, foamed into view. Henry concentrated on details of his surroundings so as not to have to talk to Stewart. He noticed that Michaels and the African were now walking back and forth across a strip of rough sand at the end of the breakwater – distant figures, still arguing with emphatic gestures. He wondered whether Rycliffe could make the Tenant's Association an election issue. Mrs Rycliffe and her sister were playing with the baby on the rug, rolling it over so that it gurgled. The other children were building sand-castles and occasionally squabbling.

After a long, unsatisfactory silence, Henry turned to Stewart who was staring, sullenly, at a small yacht dawdling on the darker offing beyond the breakwater.

'I'm sorry I lost my temper,' he said. 'It really isn't as simple as one sometimes makes it out.'

Stewart avoided his eyes.

'That's alright, chum,' he forced himself to speak. 'Forget it!'

'No. I'm really very sorry. I can't bear to think I might have upset you.'

Stewart glanced up, suspiciously. Meeting Henry's eyes, he looked away again, touched but embarrassed.

After a moment, in an unusually candid and quiet tone, he said:

'Fact is – sometimes I think you're right.'

'Opposites,' Henry suggested. 'An old problem in Hindu metaphysics. You are always aware of antitheses.'

Stewart became enthusiastic.

'That's it!' he said. 'There's a basic similarity between anarchists and conservatives. Both believe in the individual and say balls to an urban society. I bet you're a peasant at heart – a traditionalist.'

Henry failed to follow the logic; but because it was the first time they weren't violently disagreed, he was discreet.

'No,' he allowed, with a mild chuckle. 'Peasants are okay, but cities are civilised.'

'But rootless . . . impersonal . . . restless!'

'They needn't be.'

'Ah!'

'There's every reason for hoping they can become sociable, quieter, better mannered.'

'What about peasant ignorance, superstition, cruelty, the miserliness of peasants in Southern Italy, for example?'

'Yes, that's true,' Henry agreed, 'but cities are like that, too. Filthy holes in which everything is money: no culture. A few writers, painters and musicians, but otherwise supermarkets, advertising . . . empty nothingness!'

'Not cities,' said Stewart, 'but city-states. Cities are mobs, anonymous crowds. That's why anarchists advocate syndicates.'

'They may be right,' Henry said.

'Rycliffe's view is full of holes.'

'Everyone's is,' Henry agreed, 'that's why we ought to be tolerant.'

'And what happens if some are intolerant?'

'That's the extreme case. General intolerance can't create general tolerance.'

'Quite!' said Stewart, not really agreeing, but following an earlier line of thought. 'That's Rycliffe's trouble. He can't see the contradictions. Theory and practice. You must have ideals, but these become dogmas: contradiction between the individual and society, group leadership and leaderless spontaneity, feelings and intellect – choice between the apparent and the real.'

Henry saw the conversation as one of those endless altercations between basically incompatible people who tug wilfully at the ends of futility and call failure begging to differ. With others, he could build a delicate fabric of thought and crown the edifice with truth, but here no creativity lit up the abstractions. He sighed.

'Yes,' he said, 'I always hope to sit down one day and work it all out. I never do. Laziness, I suppose.'

Stewart laughed, harshly, as if he appreciated the thought. It was now his turn to make a gesture, but it only angered Henry. Katherine was standing, disconsolately, on the mole, and he nodded towards her.

'Are you interested in that trick?'

Henry's expression hardened.

'One ace in the hole, and you can make it, kid. She's a push-over.'

Rather than smash the man across the face, Henry stood up and said, with passionate self-control:

'Excuse me. I think I'll go for tea.'

In the tea-room, looking morosely out of the windows, he felt personally inadequate. He wondered what aroused in him such a storm of hostility towards Stewart. Perhaps he was himself insufficiently humble? Stewart went beyond decorum into obscenities in which no rapport could exist, except that of master and slave. He was furious at having lost his own temper, humiliated. He could not bring himself to any sympathy with Stewart. Perhaps there just were people one couldn't get on with. 'Well,' he thought, 'I must try to be polite. I'm not old enough to get cantankerous.'

When he came out of the tea-room, Katherine was still on the mole. She was sitting on the concrete edge, looking unhappily into green depths, and rhythmically swinging one crossed leg.

Before going to join her, he looked round to see if he was being watched, and was again annoyed with himself. Was his antagonism an answering criticism? Rycliffe was preferable to Stewart. Despite extravagance and demagogy, he seemed open-hearted and courageous: a character. But Stewart was too egotistic, too demonic. If it hadn't been for Katherine, Henry would not have associated with these people. They treated others as ideas, as means rather than ends; they wanted to dominate. Was this insufficiency? Was dislike of domination a desire to dominate oneself? Criticism of others was self-criticism. But one ought to tolerate weaknesses. Henry's own self-assurance was disturbed; problems which might have had easy answers now led back to his own deficiencies.

These thoughts, and others, plucked at his curiosity, but because he became aware of the act of swimming, of the depth and refreshing cool of the water, and particularly of the castration fear which always assailed in deep, unknown salt water – was it sharks? or simply castration? – he did what he frequently did: he postponed solutions until problems could be given more careful, less hurried, consideration.

Katherine was still bemused when he came into her line of vision.

'Is it holy orders?' he asked pleasantly, doing a dog-paddle beneath her, 'or suicide?'

'Oh, hello,' she said.

He climbed onto the pier beside her.

'How many beats to the bar?' he asked.

She stopped kicking her leg at once.

'I'm sorry,' he said. She was still morose. 'Did I do something wrong?'

'You?' she suddenly smiled, generously. 'You're sweet.'

'Can I do anything?'

She smiled again, but weakly.

'Oh, it's nothing. Nothing. Isn't it a lovely afternoon?'

'I'm sorry I was so rude to your friends.'

'Do shut up,' she said. 'It's nothing to do with you.'

'Well, what is it, then?'

'Do you really want to know?' Again she regarded him frankly.

'Yes.'

She hesitated.

'Oh hell,' she said, 'it's a bore. Tell me about you.'

'Okay. What d'you want to know?'

'Everything. The works!'

'I'm not very interesting.' He wanted to equal her courtesy. 'You tell me about you.'

'You're not really interested.'

'On the contrary,' he replied, trying to impose gravity upon the superficial. 'I'm fascinated.'

'That's fighting talk, Mr Naidoo.'

'Henry's the name.'

'Alright.' She sighed, then brightened. 'I'll tell you. Do you want to hear?'

'Absolutely must. Now.'

'Okay. Listen carefully. I'm wonderful. Quite magnificent. The most marvellous, heavenly, out-of-this-world person alive. So. So, being marvellous, heavenly, etc., etc., all I want is what I rightly deserve. Birthrights. What is owed, as 't were. And what is owed is very simple. I want furs and jewels and fast cars . . . lots and lots of the same. Also, I want fame and affection. Also, I want – '

'And I thought you were a simple, country girl. Child of the soil.'

'Oh, but I am, I am. How could you doubt?'

'Seriously?'

'Absolutely. A land girl. Tractors and fertility rites and copulation in cornfields.'

'A spear of panic passed instantly through his soft Hindu chest,' Henry muttered *sotto voce*, then less histrionically, he added, 'No. Really. What do you really want?'

She remained frivolous and parodied Rycliffe, but with an edge of bitterness.

'Full democratic rights!' she announced with pontifical gravity. 'No half-measures – the Real McCoy! Full and total citizenship!'

He chuckled briefly, sadly.

'Shall I tell you what I want?'

'Do,' she said, still facetious. 'I'm impatient to hear.'

'Well,' he said, quietly, wiping his forehead which was dripping, 'nothing much. Just a home, and a good job, children . . . and – ' there was a catch in his throat ' – someone like you.'

She tried to laugh.

'No. I'm serious,' he said, urgently.

She looked at him again, and seemed about to cry.

'You are sweet. You really are.'

'You think I'm joking?'

Again she regarded him, eyes miserable, curious.

'You're mad. You don't even know me. I'm not very nice. There are things – '

He shook his head gravely.

'I don't care,' he said. But realising that to continue might be embarrassing, he took refuge in facetiousness. 'I'll take you as you are – all the dark, impenetrable, immoderate vices, for better or worse.'

She laughed.

'Is that a proposal?'

He shrugged diffidently.

'I should,' he asserted gravely, 'find out if your parents will sell you.'

'Sell me. Lord! My father's always wanted to give me away.'

'Well,' he summed up, after an awkward pause, 'at least we've got that sorted out.'

There was another awkward pause. Facetiousness had begun to pall. Keyed up, he was afraid of losing rapport within clumsy indiscretion. He was also aware that, on the beach, she would become a social being. Under a blue bathing cap, her face was small, the features distinct; the tight sheath of a white costume pronounced the swell of her breasts and width of her hips; her thighs were reddish-gold, rough with patterns of drying brine. She was again, ruminatively, swinging one leg. It took him a moment to suppress the excitement her live presence released; he felt as he had in Paarl, tongue-tied, humbled by her desirability.

'Are you doing anything,' he asked anxiously, 'this afternoon?'

She looked up, still ruminative, but not inaccessible.

'Would you like to come – ' he tried hard to smile ' – out to Froggy Pond?'

'That's where you've got the bungalow?'

'Yes,' he said, then hastened to add, 'the others will be there.'

'That's an idea. Yes. I'd like to.'

His jubilance surprised her.

'What about supper?' she asked.

'We could get some sandwiches – or even cook something.'

The idea of cooking quickened her interest.

'Oh, marvellous! It'll be like camping . . . a picnic!'

'That's right.'

'Wonderful!'

While they were discussing what to buy, a small trawler drew up on the other side of the jetty, laden mostly with small *snoek* and *kappeljou*.

One of the fishermen was a big bronzed fellow with several scars on his face and hands; he had a ship tattooed across his chest and was naked to the waist and barefoot; now and then he directed unloading operations. Katherine's questions seemed to amuse him.

'Why aren't you working?' he asked, in the racy, sing-song Afrikaans, peculiar to Malay fishermen. When she explained that she was a school-teacher, he was impressed and began to call her *mevrou*. It had been Henry's idea that they buy some fish.

'Give for *mevrou* one from that *hottentot*,' the fisherman said. 'No, not that one, not – that looks ugly, just like an old Boer – the other one, now, there! on the top, the nice big little one!'

Katherine protested that the fish was too large. The fisherman seemed to imagine she and Henry were married.

'But how goes it with the children?' he asked, thinking in the Malay way of families.

'Couldn't we have the little old, little one?'

'If *mevrou* wishes.'

He refused payment, and talked, for a while, of the sardine season, of the large catch last year.

'Well . . . that is how it lies!' he said eventually. 'I must away go, now.'

They thanked him profusely.

'Never worry not,' he said, 'us folks must each other help now. Things will be bad soon – the world of politics, you shall see. Things will right mad be.'

When they returned to the beach, the sun – a disc of fiery orange – had begun to dip over the roof of the overlooking mountain-side. It would be light several hours yet, but there was already a nippiness in the air. The tide was rising. Trains were more frequent and there was more activity on the shadowed beach – seagulls arriving for feeding time, men loitering with dogs, couples on evening strolls, groups of tanned athletic men – sedulous after-work – swimmers to whom swimming, as exercise, was work extended. Henry and Katherine went to separate booths to change.

The African and Michaels had left. Rycliffe and his sister-in-law were playing beach cricket with some local youngsters. Mrs Rycliffe was bottle-feeding the fat baby.

When Henry returned to the beach, Katherine and Stewart were talking together. He could not hear what they were saying, but he noticed that Stewart seemed rather angry and was arguing with heated exasperation. Katherine shook her head, stubbornly, several times, and when, eventually, she came away she looked tense and upset.

'Is something the matter?' Henry asked, and returned a good-bye wave from Rycliffe.

Katherine paused under the arches.

'No. It's nothing.' She looked distraught.

Outside the car, she paused again, one hand on the doorknob.

'Alright?' Henry asked, a second time.

'Sorry,' she said and smiled, surprised at herself.

They bought light provisions at a grocery store, then set out on the Simonstown road for Froggy Pond.

The bungalow stood on a secluded shelf of the mountain-side, a few yards off the main road, overlooking a small private rock-enclosed beach. It was a tin affair with three rooms, a patio, and rock garden, and a long, narrow glass-panelled verandah which opened onto a small concrete yard that ended in rubble and a footpath which wound past short, silver-leaf trees and sourfig grass to the beach.

They spent an excited quarter of an hour exploring the bungalow, testing beds, opening mildewed cupboards and windows and laughing pointlessly like people who have come into a windfall. In the kitchen, which was at the far end of the verandah, was an old-fashioned oil-stove and a coke-lined icebox which Doc had already loaded with various bottles of alcohol. Several prehistoric cooking utensils hung against the walls. Beaded curtains separated one bedroom from the small living-room; the other bedroom had a wooden door, and in it, the bed was ruffled with signs of recent occupancy.

'Does Doc live here now?' Katherine asked. 'Isn't it a marvellous place – a dream?'

Henry, looking pleased, shrugged. They went on to the verandah with drinks and cigarettes.

The bungalow had a feel of sad and magical seclusion as if it was propped on the loneliest verge of earth; the tranquillity seemed to absorb them, so for a while, they sat quietly with no more identity than ears listening to the soft rhythmic crashes of waves among boulders, eyes watching thick warm water bubbling over tops of red-brown polyps.

'Isn't it lovely here?' said Katherine, sipping the white Muscatel.

'Sorry. What did you say?'

'I feel I could live here forever. It's so peaceful.'

'Yes,' he mused. 'It reminds me of when I was a child. One is alone and safe, somehow.'

'Tell me about your childhood. Were you happy?'

He wanted to ask her what it was that had upset her at Kalk Bay, but decided, again, that it would be indiscreet. He was alone with her for the first time and wanted to acquit himself judiciously. She was wearing a sky-blue dress, and had taken off the red scarf which had covered her hair in the car; the blue of the dress heightened and clarified the peach-gold of her complexion. It was strange, now that he was alone with her, he was happy and without desire.

'Don't you want to talk about it?' she asked.

'Not really.' He looked puzzled.

'What are you thinking then?'

He gave a short, ironical laugh.

'What is it?' she asked again.

'It's nothing, it's just amazing.'

'What?'

'Well . . . I don't know how to explain. It's silly, really.'

'Tell me. Please tell me.'

'It's just that . . . well, I feel I've known you a long time . . . like an old friend . . . and, well, I'm just happy – '

He explained that he had been carrying her in his head for several days, that he had imagined various ways of being alone with her, but had not expected this peace.

'Are you in love with me?' she asked simply.

He nodded, looked up at her; the question in his eyes received a disappointing answer.

'It's sad,' she admitted, for a moment. 'Sad because – '

'I know. You feel nothing.'

'I'm glad.'

She shook her head bitterly.

'Oh, and yet everything is such a mess – such a terrible terrible mess.'

'Don't tell me,' he said, 'it's your business. But I meant what I said at Kalk Bay.'

'You want to marry me?' she looked desolate.

'Yes.'

'But why?'

'I know. I just know.'

She examined him carefully, doubtfully, full of wonder.

'But you haven't even made love to me.'

'Is that important?'

Now she was puzzled, silent.

'But you might not even like me.'

'You don't understand?'

'Do you want to make love to me?'

He considered her quietly.

'Yes and no.'

'No; because you're afraid.'

He nodded.

'Yes,' he said, 'because I don't want anythinng to change.'

He was sitting on a *rachitic* sofa, an anti-macassar along the top.

'Come here,' he said, 'come and sit next to me.'

She rose and sat down very obediently.

'Now put your arms about my neck and let me look at you.'

For a long intense few minutes they looked at each other gravely, yet partly smiling.

'Kiss me,' he said, suddenly experiencing within, the first statement of desire. For a while he held her in a tight despairing, incredulous embrace; then, he said, drawing away:

'No. Let's make love. Properly.'

She considered him with equal intense quiet.

'Do you really want to?' she asked.

'Yes.'

'Do you love me?'

'Very much.'

'Good.'

In the doored bedroom, while they undressed, she said, suddenly decorous:

'What if anyone comes?'

'Don't worry,' he rose and locked the door, then he got under the sheets watching with approval the rest of her undressing. He was glad she had no false modesty, and yet she was shy and covered her bosom with her arms and looked away when she got into the bed.

'Brr!' she said, 'It's cold. The sheets are cold.'

He moved the pillow so that he could put one arm under her neck, then he stroked her hair for a long time, feeling the flesh of her belly and loins against his, pleased with the look of questioning quiet in her black eyes.

'Do you really love me?' she asked.

'Shush,' he said, 'No explanations. One should never talk.'

She smiled beautifully. She kissed him very gently and slowly on the lips, and he felt again the earlier memory of her body touching his, wetness of pubic hair against his caressing palm, arms closed over his back, rounds of breasts pressing, strangely, against his chest.

'Gently, darling,' she said, shutting her eyes, and holding him with just a trace of anxiety in the cheeks.

'Oh, I do love you,' he said; so earnestly, so quietly, he felt he could cry.

'Just hold me,' she said when he had entered. 'Hold me tight. Hold me. Keep your arms round me. Don't move. Let me feel you here. Close. Just hold me. Oh darling, darling. Isn't it wonderful?'

'Yes,' he said, 'I do love you. You are beautiful. So beautiful. Let me look at you.'

Again their eyes met, smiling.

'Like a poem,' he said.

'John Donne! Lord, I am undone!'

They laughed, clutching each other.

'Nature copying art,' he said, and they laughed again, moving loins, laughing, embracing one another; lost and happy for a while.

Afterwards, the old-fashioned oil-lamp flickered whenever wind passed the sealed windows, creating once again a sense of seclusion, as if the bungalow were in a remote region of sky with no tangible link with land.

Katherine lay on her back, exhausted, too comfortable to move. The sheets had been twisted into a corner, so that only the counterpane – purfled with a design of pre-Raphaelite roses and peacocks – covered their naked, sweating bodies. The bed was hard and narrow. Now and then Henry touched her forehead, stroking away a curl of black hair, and kissed her with a warmth and gratitude which made her relax. She felt, though, that he too had retreated. She was surprised that she had no sense of impending chaos; instead the future seemed to spread quiet as countryside, halcyon and tranquil. She was glad that she had for a while broken familiar patterns. It was like a prodigal home-coming; no reproof. She thought about Henry, how, in contrast to Stewart and Rycliffe, surprisingly considerate he was. He cared for her not only before love-making. He constantly asked if she was comfortable or needed anything. She could not help wondering whether this vague contentment would last.

'Shall I make some tea?' she asked.

'Do you want some?'

'No. Do you?'

'I'll go.'

He attempted to rise, but she was determined not to be found selfish.

'Please,' she said, 'my turn . . . '

She had wanted to use the word darling; earlier it had suited; now, like his naked body, it was faintly embarrassing.

'Alright,' he said, suppressing tenderness, 'make me feel like a louse.'

'Well, let's go and make it together.'

'That's very egalitarian of you.'

In the kitchen, she found herself singing and stopped abruptly, surprised. 'How foolish!' she thought, 'it can't last.'

Henry had gone to fetch water; when he returned, she insisted upon being kissed.

'Let me fill the kettle first.'

'No. Now.' she said. 'On the tip of my nose.'

She felt so childishly happy she thought perhaps she was in love.

After tea, they prepared a complicated fish dish which, like their relationship, was still too experimental, too fraught with care to be a success. There was an Italian film in Kalk Bay; foreign films were rare, therefore pleasurable, and Henry proposed they went to see it. It was a comedy, light but realistic, a sympathetic portrait of lower class Roman life. They had to sit upstairs because the cinema segregated audiences, Europeans having the dubious privilege of being able to occupy pit and stalls. Later, they went swimming in the moonlight, without costumes, and after making love on the beach, spent the night at Froggy Pond.

The next four days were a strange mingling of hectic activity and long spare hours of calm. They were among the happiest Henry spent in his life. They lived either at Froggy Pond or at Newlands, depending on which bungalow was occupied. Since Katherine was on holiday, she had more time to relax, and Henry would leave her with books and records while he made short business-like forays upon the work piling up in his office. They made afternoon excursions to Buffels Bay, picnicked at Cape Point, basked for hours among the sand dunes of Hout Bay, watching seagulls and porpoises and browning themselves almost raw in the white mid-summer heat. Friday evening was spent in a faintly embarrassing but agreeable visit to Paarl, and the next morning they were woken late by the arrival of Doc, Pieter, Jessie and Madge. Doc hired a rowing boat in Simonstown and took Pieter fishing with him. Katherine discovered that Madge also wanted to visit the hairdresser's, so Henry was left at the bungalow with Jessie and some papers that needed final drafting before he set off for his twice postponed trip to Durban.

While Henry was employed upon his papers, Jessie set about tidying up the kitchen and sweeping the rooms. She completed this work with such unobtrusive quiet that Henry, who had earlier undertaken to do it himself, only discovered what had happened when she came rather shyly to his table on the verandah with a tray of tea and biscuits. Her manner had such disarming sweetness that he took a few minutes off to talk with her. He ticked her off for having tidied up the kitchen, but approvingly, and won a gentle engaging smile. Later, when he had finished his work, he joined her on the beach where she was making sad patterns with bits of seaweed and odd pebbles. He had first imagined that she was insipid, but soon found traits that wanted only a little warmth and informality to rise from characteristic shyness. She was concerned about the Tenant's Association which was to be formed that afternoon; her uncle, Mr Parsons, had said that Henry was to chair the founding; the house of her own parents was among those threatened. Henry, occupied hitherto with his affair with Katherine, had begun to feel the Tenant's Association a burden, but listening to Jessie's stories about the hardship involved among, not so much her family, but the squatters in their overcrowded *pondokkies*, changed his mind. She spoke of the squalor, of the lack of sanitation, of the single tap which served polluted water to several dozen families, of women giving birth to healthy, well-formed infants who died within hours, unable to survive coal and oil fumes of stoves that had, for warmth and cooking, to be lit; she told also of the courage of people who went on trying to live in spite of these adversities. They lied and stole, were drunken, fought brutally, but they were also capable of sacrifice and such common fellowship in unequal distress that they showed deeper and more frequent humanity than was evident among people blessed with more comfortable surroundings. A man met with an accident at work; at once the hat was taken round for the widow and children; a woman was ill, others came round, partly from nosiness, but also to help out. They were country folk mostly, simple and ignorant, but they had been driven, jobless, off the land. Were they responsible if, no matter how hard they tried, they could not find work or a chance to improve or change their conditions? Jessie spoke impartially, but with the compassion of someone, unlike Rycliffe and Stewart, unrhetorically aware of the details of human misery. She was, she said, saving up to do nursing at Somerset General Hospital, so that she could eventually work among the squatters. When Henry left in the afternoon to attend the meeting, he was determined to do his utmost to make the new Association work.

In the evening, there was a small party at Froggy Pond; some friends of Doc turned up with guitars and there was a musical *braaivleis* on the beach. Henry and Katherine left early because he wanted to have a long rest before setting off for Durban the next day, and it was only later that he heard that Doc and Madge had quarrelled so fiercely that they had come to blows and the party had ended in a general fracas.

'This sort of thing really exasperates me,' Henry told Katherine, 'I can't stand people like Madge and Doc. They're promiscuous and insensitive and have no moral scruples.'

'Madge is not to blame,' Katherine answered, quietly. 'I had a long chat with her this morning. Poor thing, she's got lots of problems.'

Henry was tired and moody with the insecurity of the unsettled whereabouts; he did not want to leave for Durban, and was unusually intolerant of disorder.

'No,' he said, 'one can make excuses for everything. Some forms of conduct are really unforgiveable!'

Though the conversation was intimate there was still a reserve to their relationship; a barrier which Henry believed was necessary in all relations with others; it implied recognition of the integrity of others and preserved freedom. Though he was still troubled by Katherine's occasional bouts of melancholy, he felt that to probe her would be an infringement of liberty and permitted himself only the most delicate unobtrusive attempts to cheer her up.

Boarding the aeroplane in the afternoon was agony. When he arrived in Durban, he could not eat; reacquaintance with once familiar and pleasant sights brought neither joy nor relief. His work was straightforward, but freighted by nostalgia for the Cape. The smaller associations were hardest to bear. He would get into a car, sunlight pouring over the empty seats, and the smell of burnt plastic would bring Katherine back. She would be sitting next to him – unhappy, silent, a tired head rolling trustfully onto his shoulder as they drove back from Paarl; he would see her face distinctly: the dimpled smile, the gay red scarf that knotted her hair, the mole on her left breast which glistened with sweat when they made love. He adored her. Whenever he was alone, he would torture himself with a particular entry in his diaries in which she had turned up, quite unexpected, at his office, with a large brown paper bag filled with Hanepoort grapes, laughing gaily and saying that she had brought him the present because it was her birthday.

There was also another entry which he constantly returned to:

Froggy Pond. Thursday, December, 18th.

A cool, wet night. Wind clouds across a white arc of moon – across a sky, ink-

black, grotesque, and phantasmal: an El Greco *scene. The sea buffets rocks and cliffs; washes whitened strips of beach with a splashing, hissing sound.*

Katherine, in her blue dress, mouth slightly opened, has fallen asleep on one of the camp beds. A tuft of hair curls over her right ear; she is sleeping on one hand. Her silk stockings are creased. A shoe lies, inert, at one of her ankles. Every now and then the position of her body shifts. People are loveable when they're asleep – innocent, unaware, vulnerable, like small babies.

I think of her when she makes love – her special glad-eyed look of wonder, tenderness, generosity; the grace and assurance which accompanies movements of her body; I have to curb a passionate urge to embrace her again with gratitude, with joy.

We are in the sitting-room. The oil-lamp on my table throws eldritch shadows upon the chintz curtains. The bungalow has an atmosphere all its own. The furnishings belong to different periods; they combine to make an atmosphere of the turn of the century. One bedroom is papered with old-fashioned sailing-ships. Either this paper or the linen upholstery gives off a musty smell. It reminds me of a room in my childhood and wakens an emotion close to pain. The smell engages you the moment you enter the place. You forget the mechanical, speed-haunted, commodity-ridden present; are conscious of safety, of evanescent regret, of tradition. People, you are aware, have lived here, in this small bungalow, their presences linger in the furniture . . . how can one describe it? . . . they are dead, yet more alive than so much in our artificial modern world; the bungalow is like an old tree, a living organic presence, which has absorbed and integrated the living of these dead inhabitants who arouse warmth. There is nothing here of theatre, nothing of antiseptic supermarkets, of museums or art galleries; no contrivances, just identity.

I feel calm and happy; yet, paradoxically, my mind is fecund, restless. Dostoyevsky writes somewhere of loving people at a distance. That is how I feel. It is a detached, quiet state, brimming, now and then, at an image, compassion only a few seconds away from tears. Reveries – snatches of forgotten music, books, films, people drift like disconnected tableaux *across the black eager theatre of the mind. How strange that one can think, remember, participate in such complex actions! Thinking thematically is difficult.*

Katherine has been talking about a film that recently came to the Star bioscope. We have both seen it. It is about Belsen. During my showing, and hers, too, everyone – even the ruffians – was quiet. Katherine said that she cried. I just felt a desire to get behind a machine-gun. On the way from Kalk Bay, we discussed the pacifist dilemma – would you kill to save whom you love?

The thought of six million Jewish people butchered so carelessly, with so little compassion chokes. What sympathy is possible? Six million! The figure boggles. Horror tabulated, multiplied, analysed, loses cogency. One image haunts: a mother with five small children behind, head down, along a corridor of barbed wire and mud. Winter. Trees and buildings stark. The woman and the children are dressed heavily, in the clumsy rags of Central European peasants. The woman has a scarf over her head and the children follow, keeping close like chicks following the plump mother hen. They seem aware of impending doom, but their faces retain that uncomprehending, trustful candour which all human young have. The youngest is barely two-and-a-half, and keeps falling behind and running to catch up. A group of SS sit in a gun-turret, looking on, faces like the winter landscape, bare of feeling. They do not use guns. Resistance has long been crushed out of the prisoners. Life has come to mean nothing, like the gas chamber at the end of it. Perhaps the woman hopes now that she and her little ones should die quickly, without too much pain.

One should never be rich or powerful. It kills sensibility. I remember once at University taking round a tin for victims of famine and being told by an erudite Professor of Theology that he had made two sixpenny donations already. Some of the charwomen, however, who earned less than two shillings an hour, gave ten shilling notes. Only the poor really understand what it is to be hungry.

Sometimes, even I hope for someone like the Buddha to simplify everything. Like Rycliffe and the others I am growing obsessive, driven by circumstances from my precious immediacy into a cold circle of absolutes. The abyss of emotion, of the irrational, of the breakdown of lucid thought gets more and more unforgettably close. It is easy to see why so many Non-European (and European) intellectuals break up in South Africa. It is Dostoyevsky terrain – a land of wonderful saints and depraved sensualists, without any in-between: the ivory-towered monastery or the brothel!

My only hope now, is the liberal spirit of the Cape: Katherine.

CHAPTER 7

When Henry returned to Cape Town, he went at once to see Shaikh-Moosa and handed over the deeds of Desai's properties which now assured complete legal rights to the new owner. Shaikh-Moosa was polite, but not enthusiastically grateful, and Henry did not then know that this response was due to his own involvement with Mr Parsons' Tenant's Association; he was tired, handed in his bill indifferently, and put Shaikh-Moosa's coolness down to the casuality that attended all undertakings of high finance. Though exhilarated by the prospect of seeing Katherine again, he had no difficulty resting a few hours before setting out for Muir Street. He was so grey with fatigue that he was almost late for the appointment.

Driving out to District Six was an excruciating test for self-control, but at last, in the small crowded annexe, a woman wore a white frock and green earrings, and it was really she. She was so tangible she was unbelievable. But for a passionate effort of self-restraint, Henry would have thrown his arms around her in an embrace of crushing relief.

The noise and press of people allowed no more than glad smiles and glad incoherent words. She took his right hand and pressed it tightly, looking into his face as if to find in it her own uncertainty of delight. She explained why she hadn't been able to meet him at the airport; the concert, which they were about to attend, was being put on by the children of her school, and she had been asked to help in the rehearsals.

She was not quite able to complete these explanations because the doors of the church hall opened and a noisy surge of people bore them past an old man who took their tickets, smiled, and gave out hand-printed programmes. It wasn't until it was too late to return the greeting that Henry recognised the old man as Mr Parsons. The old man was lost behind a moving sea of excited people.

Rows of wooden chairs stood in a spaciousness redolent of scrubbed floors and hygienic holiness. On the small proscenium stage, two men (one in gymnastic costume) were erecting a microphone. Behind them were properties of an act – swings, hurdles, ropes and horses.

Their seats were near the front. Katherine scanned the programme. With his surroundings continuously moving, and not quite sure that he had returned to the Cape, Henry felt disinclined to talk. He looked about the hall to orientate himself, but couldn't recognise anyone. The audience seemed to be mostly made up of parents and teachers. He expected performances to be thin, but he liked the atmosphere. A spirit of communal self-entertainment prevailed, and Henry thought of New Year's Day when the Coons and String-bands would march and prance through crowded streets. There would be multicoloured costumes, *tiekkie-draai*, *goema* drums, laughing painted faces – an atmosphere of spontaneous fellowship that joined the Cape to other Latin civilisations – religious processions and fiestas of Spain and Mexico, the Cannes Battle of Flowers, Mardi Gras of New Orleans, Trinidad's flamboyant Calypso Carnival.

Now and then, children and grown-ups, pausing along the aisles and greeting Katherine, examined Henry as if they were memorising a cartoon with the caption, 'So that's Miss Holmes' new *beau*', but Henry felt pleased, even proud, to be publicly attached to Katherine. To join any polity one had to pay a price.

The hall had filled and the audience was exasperated by delays. One of the men on the stage hopped over the footlights and ran down an aisle. When he reached the back of the hall, he shouted:

'Right!'

His colleague chanted:

'Monday . . . Tuesday . . . Wednesday . . . '

'Thursday!' someone suggested.

The audience chuckled.

'. . . testing, testing . . . one . . . two . . . three . . . '

'Four!' shouted the audience in unison.

The curtains closed. The compère came out and the concert started.

Performances were amateurish, but entertaining . . . Henry enjoyed best a display of jiving by two children, a boy and a girl, each hardly more than nine years old. Their dancing joined concentration to fun; they were very self-assured and would not have been out of place in professional *vaudeville*. The audience applauded warmly.

Other items included a gymnastic display, appalling recitations from Sir Henry Newbolt, a few unimpressive, obvious sketches, a ballet sequence – 'Has to be culture,' Katherine explained, 'or people'll get the idea the Head isn't doing his job. Isn't it ghastly?' – and several dismal arias from Madame Butterfly.

It was four o'clock when they came blinking into the broad light of the street. Again, Henry felt glad he had come and spent a few minutes making pleasant chit-chat with Katherine's Headmaster: a small dapper man who seemed unable to stand still and constantly cast an eye over one shoulder, like the cinema villain who has to see if the police are dutifully following.

They had arranged to spend the rest of the afternoon swimming, and after a light supper, to go to the Christmas Eve fund-raising party at the Rycliffes'.

When Katherine at last managed to disengage from school associates, they set out for Froggy Pond.

Before his departure, their affair had reached that stage when just a touch of fingers became electric invitation to make love. Now they were unsure strangers again, glad and excited, yet alienated by separate identities.

The bungalow was locked; in it were the remains of a party – bottles and unwashed dishes and floors littered with stale cigarette butts. Katherine at once set about cleaning and tidying up. The offices were located in the patio, and when Henry went to fetch broom and pans he received the first shock of the day.

He had opened the lavatory door and was about to enter when a live apparition, uttering a horrifying shriek, hurled itself at him. In self-defence, Henry stood back, fists ready to counter-attack, only to find that he, not his assailant, was the object of terror. An African – wearing a pair of tattered jeans – lay cowering in the dusty yard, grime-streaked hands raised protectively in front of red, panic-shot eyes.

The disturbance – a flying pail – brought Katherine to the patio door and she stood there, surprised, quite as alarmed as Henry.

'E . . . please! . . . Pleas! . . . don't e-hit me, no! my baas!' the man repeated and it took Henry a moment to realise that the man expected to be struck. His chest was corrugated by hideous suppurations and he looked on the point of collapse.

For a few moments the three of them scarcely breathed; then the

110

African, with a profound sudden movement, lifted himself, took a few gasping steps and fell again, this time at Katherine's feet. He quivered a moment, coughed, then lay quite still. The movement had been so unexpected that, again, it was another moment before Henry realised the man had fainted. He was breathing faintly, with hoarse lungs – a pitiful sound, like a mine shaft wheezing rustily deep into oblivion, into spiralling bowels of the earth. Between refts in the legs of his perished jeans, his skin was snake-like – tight and shiny; his beard was a growth of several weeks. He must have been in the lavatory for hours: it exuded the fuggish, unhealthy smell which clung to his person. In one corner of the lavatory lay a small, dirty bundle attached to a knobkerrie which identified him at once as a vagrant. Examining his bony, undernourished face, Henry remembered the story of Shaikh-Moosa's African chauffeur having been washed up at Cape Point, but the man did not look remotely like Alfred: in his expression was a kind of hungry pride.

'Well, we can't leave him here!' Katherine said, still not quite recovered from the shock.

'Or turn him in,' Henry added, remembering South African pass laws. The scars on the man's face testified to more than vagrancy: he was obviously on the run.

'Poor fellow,' Henry said.

'What d'you think?'

Henry considered the body, the yard littered with small heaps of leaves, the bungalow with its open door.

'Get a hold of his feet,' he said, 'we'd better take him inside.'

The body was heavy, as if waterlogged; carried, the head rolled backwards with an open mouth – frightening them. When they had deposited him on a bed, they held another conference, whispering as if it was important not to disturb the man. His heart was beating; his eyelids fluttered occasionally without opening; his breathing was difficult.

'I think I'd better get Doc,' Henry eventually decided.

There was a tea-room about five hundred yards away on the road to Sea Point. It was bound to have a telephone.

'Don't worry about me,' Katherine said, answering an indecisive look on Henry's face.

In case the tea-room did not have a telephone, Henry went by car. The tea-room was closed and he knocked at the front door. The

111

proprietress, a fat woman wearing an apron, a cigarette drooling from her lips, and carrying an ugly Pekinese which barked idiotically, came to the door and pulled a face the moment she saw Henry.

'Go round the back!' she ordered in an English accent. She was obviously an immigrant, poor thing, who had just discovered the privileges of colour.

'There's a man dying,' Henry said with surprise.

'Quiet Josephine! There's a good doggie!' She patted the brute's little head, without removing the pluming cigarette which made her squint like a smoker considering a bridge hand. 'Quiet, luv. Mummy says, quiet.' In another voice to Henry, she said, 'We can't have you people using the front.'

'Wouldn't have your arse-hole, either,' Henry thought, but curbed his contempt to say, politely, 'I beg your pardon. Sorry I troubled you.'

He didn't wait for her reaction; returning to the car, he swung it round on the road towards Simonstown.

When he returned to the bungalow, the African had not come round and his breathing was fainter. Half-an-hour later before Doc arrived, he was dead.

After a quick examination, Doc shook his head.

'Nothing anyone could have done,' he said when Henry began to rebuke himself for not having called earlier. 'Double pneumonia, exposure, pleurisy – the works! Better get the cops and let them sort out the rest. I'll 'phone them. I know the routine.'

The dead man's bundle, which Katherine had opened, disclosed little. It contained a dirty pen-knife, bits of string, a small tin of stale snuff, cigarette butts, and, wrapped in a rubber band, an out-of-date pass which suggested, from the name, that the man came from an East African tribe, and that he had been employed in a quick succession of jobs – the mines, a clothing factory, a builder's and carpenter's hand, and lastly, domestic service. He hadn't worked for over a year; his last registered address was Cato Manor, Durban.

When the police arrived they asked routine questions and dumped the body in the back of their Maria as if it was a carcass.

Doc was in a hurry to return to Cape Town. He had promised to take a party of women to Rycliffe's *shindy*, and wanted to dress.

Katherine had made tea and they sat on the terrace which overlooked the sea, unable to make polite conversation. When Doc left, they spoke vaguely of joining him later and lapsed into long, discontented silence.

The translation of a Zulu poem, which he had recently read, kept recurring in Henry's mind; it spoke of parents who came eventually to the City of Gold, Johannesburg, where finding their daughter, who had becom a prostitute, they thought of her childhood days.

Some woman, Henry later thought in his diaries, *had given birth on a Christmas evening like this one, and had watched her child grow to manhood, then had it wrenched from her, aborted into another world. A body with the magic of life beating through a complex miracle of veins and arteries – a person that can think and feel, just like me, with hopes and desires; suddenly, inexplicably out – like light in a switched-off bulb . . . only, it doesn't switch on again. Strange. How can one go on living in a world like this? Death so commonplace? The poor bastard . . .* mon semblable, mon frere!

While Henry and Katherine were pondering, on the terrace, the transience of human life, they were unaware that during the course of the day, Yussouf Rycliffe, mainly under the influence of Gordon Stewart, had reached a decision which crucially moved the open network of the past onto a level of more limited possibilities: a level on which their own destinies were at stake.

Having won approval, within his group, as a candidate in the forthcoming Council Elections, and being a political realist, Rycliffe had been long aware that his success might be chequered by more powerful forces, and had, at Kalk Bay, determined to insure himself against such a likelihood. Today, rising late, he had taken steps to guarantee his decision.

At about eleven o'clock in the morning, while Henry was on the point of leaving Durban, he had brought his car to a halt in Caledon Street, and having shut off the engine, sat quietly at the wheel, listening to a *skollie* strumming a guitar on the steps of a certain, well-known tenement house.

> Katie said
> 'Meet me at the tree,
> Meet me at the tree.'
> But she didn't say what tree.

> I went to the oak tree . . . the fig tree,
> I even went to the lavatory;
> But I couldn't find my Katie anywhere!

The *skollie*, who sang, was an angular man with a cunning, mischievous face. In his three-quarter length trousers and cowboy shirt, a thick brass-studded belt about the waist, a round-topped hat cocked at a clownish angle, he looked juvenile; but precise fingers plucked the guitar strings, and occasional deft gestures for the benefit of his companions indicated a grown man.

Four other *skollies* – one, a boy – sat around him on the steps. On the opposite pavement, outside 'number ten' – a famous brothel – children were playing kennikie, tag, and a grim, intricate, District Six version of hopscotch. Now and then a dowdy woman, hair in curlers and petticoat showing, would come out of 'number ten' and scream at the children and they would pay no attention.

It was barely eleven o'clock, but the sky was already a rich cerulean blue; a few cross-hatched clouds hovered uncertainly about the brink of Table Mountain; the light in the street was so dazzling that the two whores, sitting indolently on the brothel balcony, preening themselves and paging through film star magazines, had to blink every time they moved out of the shade. At one corner of the street, an Indian shopkeeper, wearing a greasy fez, came onto the spittle-stained doorstep of his wooden-shuttered shop and began to eat sourfigs spitting uneaten ends into the gutter.

One of the *skollies* was a boy of about thirteen, and during the singing, he played with a dirty packet of condoms. At the end of each tune, he would pull out a condom and offer it, gravely, to his indifferent colleagues, saying in District Six Afrikaans – 'there, old uncle, go make auntie happy.'

The *skollie* with the guitar had a remarkable repertoire. Most of the songs were vulgar, but also original and witty. Complex words and rhymes appeared in untranslatable contexts. Once he sang a love lyric so fetchingly that even the whores on the balcony opposite sat forward to listen. The structure of the lyric was complex, each stanza disclosing a new attribute of the heroine who was gentle as wine, quiet as the moon, tender as blades of morning grass; the lyric worked towards chorus lines which were suspended inversions, in various ways bemoaning adultery. At the end of the lyric, the

114

heroine's identity was revealed: she was the wife of the singer who turned out to be the Mayor of Cape Town.

Rycliffe waited for the song to end, and while the *skollie* was rolling a fiver, he stepped onto the pavement, wearing tweeds and a smart grey Homburg.

'Where stays Wollenhoven?'

'What says the uncle?' the young *skollie* asked the others.

He put away the condoms and impudently asked Rycliffe for a cigarette.

'Go and sit down, you silly child!' Rycliffe said, and he repeated his original question. 'Know you of Wollenhoven?' He addressed the *skollie* with the guitar because he seemed to be the leader.

'Ya, Doctor.'

'Good. Where stays he?'

The *skollie* nodded towards the brothel.

'Not there?' asked Rycliffe, pointing to the house on whose steps they were sitting.

The *skollie* shook his head. 'He sleeps just here. He works now.'

'What does he?'

'*Hulle dovel – daar, in die kombuis.*'

'*Baie tremakassie.*'

Without locking his car, Rycliffe crossed the street. He was no sooner out of hearing than the boy suggested that his car should be rifled. The *skollie* with the guitar spat on the pavement and said that if anything of the Doctor's was touched – personal or other property – he would himself castrate the offender, a threat that was serious, though presented in the form of a joke. Castration recalled to him an Afrikaaner policeman whom he and two others had murdered recently in Adderly Street, late at night. The poor devil's testicles had been cut off with a rusty fret-saw and sent, in a parcel which was neatly addressed, to the Chief of Police. The *skollie* had finished the story when Rycliffe re-crossed the street.

'He is not there now,' Rycliffe said.

'Then, what?'

'Say for him, this. I will for him see, this afternoon. You understand?'

'In whatever place?'

'In my place.'

'Whatever time?'

'Five or six hours?'

'Pretty. One shall for him tell.'

'Good.' Rycliffe opened his car, but instead of leaving, sat in the kerbside seat, leaving the door ajar.

'What can you play?' he asked the *skollie*.

'What says the Doctor?'

'Can you small songs play?'

'Just so as the wind on the moon.'

'Play then, *What Does Your Pricker In My Primus Stove?*'

That the Doctor should ask for such an obscene song delighted the *skollies*. They laughed, and one of them offered Rycliffe a cigarette as a token of social acceptance.

When the *skollie* had sung six verses, Rycliffe said:

'Enough. Now I must away go, or I'll be back across the street.' He nodded towards the brothel, and the *skollies* chuckled again. 'Much thanks.'

He started the engine, and waving, drove away to complete his morning rounds.

Though he liked to be deep in the swim, Rycliffe did not look forward to the party in his house that night. Stale drunken conversations, the new dances, the inevitable games of cards, the absence of novelty dismayed. But fund-raising was a political duty.

After luncheon, he took his customary nap – half-an-hour on the sofa of his consulting-room; but this afternoon he was woken earlier, by a man whom his wife at once led into the consulting-room, with many gestures of deference. The man in any capital of Europe would not have drawn the slightest interest, for he was conspicuously ordinary. He was a small, plump man with a bald head and grave, square features. He was dressed soberly, rather like a working man on a Sunday outing, shoes so bright with polish they looked squeaky. His appearance was quite commonplace, but his manner wasn't. After a moment in his company, you were aware of a composure, a self-assurance, and an air of authority that were quite unusual.

Rycliffe was at first cross, but when he saw who the visitor was he thrust an anxious look behind a flamboyant welcome. The man examined Rycliffe quietly, patiently, steadily. At last, he shook his head and interrupted in a voice that at once shut Rycliffe up. 'Talk concretely, comrade!'

Rycliffe's manner instantly changed, he became serious and again his visitor listened, attentive, shutting his eyes every now and then by way of agreement, but scarcely otherwise altering an expression of grim taciturnity. Rycliffe talked mainly about Wollenhoven, watching his visitor's face intently for subtle changes.

Eventually the man said:

'And when is he coming?'

'Anytime now.'

It was almost five o'clock. They had been in the consulting-room almost the entire afternoon.

'Do you want to meet him?' Rycliffe asked, eagerly.

Humour flickered for the first time, briefly, in his visitor's grey eyes.

'I finished,' he said, 'with *lumpen* elements at *Tiflis*!'

He was referring to the bank robberies which the Bolshevik party had organised to raise funds.

Rycliffe laughed with exaggerated heartiness.

'But you approve?' he asked.

'We will see,' replied his impassive visitor, and with that he left.

That he had not yet done his afternoon rounds did not disturb Rycliffe. He preferred work to pile up. Patient and meticulous application dismayed a temperament which enjoyed hectic compressed activity, with grand slam solutions following long intervals of careless abandon. The afternoon rounds would now be put off longer, because Wollenhoven might any moment arrive; later a concentrated blitz would inspire a sense of triumph deep enough to sustain the entire party. Nevertheless, Gromeko's unexpected arrival plunged Rycliffe into a trough of uncertainty.

He had quarrelled the night before with his wife; consequently, he offered no help in the transformation of the house. Mrs Rycliffe, however, had grown accustomed to her husband's need of wider than domestic approval, which usually preceded marital quarrels, and was quite content. In a new starched apron, hair thrown up in a serpentine mass of coils, she was in her element. She had two *acolytes* – two plain girls, sisters in name, appearance and disposition – who appeared to revel in being bossed about, and hurried from room to room with missionary industry. While the men talked, they put up paper lanterns, balloons and shimmering coloured balls. The large dining-room was swept clean; the partition between it and the breakfast-room, removed; sandwiches were cut, bowls filled with

117

fruit, nuts, sweetmeats and savouries; the bookcases – 'Intellectuals,' Rycliffe would assert, 'are notorious book thieves' – were draped with sheets. The women ate as they worked. By half-past five, preparations were complete. Mrs Rycliffe rang up the local off-licence to make sure that the alcohol would be delivered on time.

At six o'clock, punctually, a man of medium height, as broad-chested as an ape, wearing a shabby brown suit and an ordinary felt hat, knocked at the front door and asked, in a toneless voice, for Dr Rycliffe. He had an impassive, unmarked face, and his eyes had the lustreless look often noticeable in the eyes of men – ageing politicians and policemen, for example – to whom life can present no fresh novelties. He waited on the doorstep indifferently, and though he was not above average height, he gave an impression of enormous build and suppressed power.

When Rycliffe arrived, he neither took off his hat nor made any effort to be sociable; he followed the Doctor into the consulting-room with the *gravitas* of a Roman legionary pursuing a course of civic duty.

Ten minutes later, when he and Rycliffe came out again, his manner hadn't altered. To the Doctor's final instruction he gave only blank, automaton attention; once when he spoke, his voice was tired and disinterested.

On the doorstep, Rycliffe put a hand on his shoulder, as if to drag from him a vestige of human feeling; but he might have appealed to granite: his disarming smile received the cold stare of dull, expressionless eyes.

The man seemed to be the embodiment of unadulterated will power. His arrival threw darker colours and shadows into the political spectrum of the Rycliffe group.

This was shortly after six o'clock. Less than four hours later, when Henry and Katherine arrived, the javelins of fate required only a few more furbishings to be ready for action . . .

It was a black night, cool with mists and crystal stars. As Henry's car mounted Upper Chester Road in Walmer Estate, the headlights streamed out, yellowing the ranks of other cars on both curbs.

'There!' Katherine pointed to a large, double-storied, wedge-shaped villa beyond a vacant lot on the left. Despite evidence of multitudes and festivity – figures and shadows traced in blazing windows, the criss-cross of conversations, the plangent wail of a saxophone above other instruments – the villa looked lonely, perched as it was thin-edge-up precariously between two vaults of darkness, two cities of tiny glittering lights – Cape Town in the vacant lot, and the sky overhead. For Henry, manifold activity seemed to expand the house: to add an impression of people trapped and panic-stricken, feverishly saving damned selves in a tottering blaze.

'We won't stay long,' Katherine said, but she was inordinately tense.

Henry agreed. He, too, had not quite recovered from the events of the afternoon; the death of the African, so unexpected after the innocuously entertaining concert, launched presentiments of more disorder, but he was determined not to be superstitious. It was, after all, Christmas Eve, and like Katherine he was afraid of missing something. Detachment would be selfish. Katherine justified their coming by claiming to want 'to see who was there', but she felt, rather as Henry did, that a phase of her life was to be sealed, and she was already preparing herself for the stiff, critical inner aloofness necessary for any glimpse of its fading splendours.

Mrs Rycliffe – tall in high heels, a green velvet figure – stepped out of a blur of smoke and wandering shapes, and clanked a metal box under their noses.

'Five shillings!' she said with a leer which intimated that any intention to get in free should immediately perish.

While Henry was paying, and hoping that Shaikh-Moosa's cheque would soon arrive, Mrs Rycliffe asked Katherine to lend a hand serving drinks at one of the bars. It was almost ten o'clock. Though the party had been in progress three hours, people were still sober.

Rycliffe's surgery was being used as a cloakroom and when they had relieved themselves of their coats, and Katherine had added a few last dabs of powder to her nose, they wandered into the crowded corridor.

A five-piece band was playing at one end of the long high-ceilinged dining-room. The atmosphere was blue with smoke. Christmas decorations fluttered and spilled over the heads of perspiring dancers.

They had two dances – a quickstep and a slow fox-trot – then Katherince disengaged herself and went to find out at which bar she should help. She had danced rather mechanically, casting her eyes frequently about the room as if to find somewhere assurance for inner unrest. Unsettled himself, Henry put her rather abrupt departure down to the events of the afternoon. He felt slightly more detached, and after buying a drink, wandered about the room, greeting old acquaintances, occasionally stopping for a chat and sometimes simply watching people, with his characteristic ironical rationality.

He was, in fact, doing exactly this when Pieter, looking fresh and excited, slapped him on the back.

'Hello!' Henry said, 'how'd you get here?'

'Doc tolt me.'

'Where's he? I haven't seen him anywhere.'

Pieter shrugged with majestic indifference. He buttressed the sole of one shoe, and his long slouching back, against the dining-room door.

'I tolt you, yes?' he said, thickly. 'This month, home I am going.'

'Home?'

'Yes. And Jessie, she kum wit me, too. Ve get marritt, soon.'

'Well,' Henry said. 'Well . . . congratulations!'

Pieter smiled awkwardly, shook hands, and glanced anxiously down the corridor.

'Yes. Tere, she is kuming.' He nodded with relief.

Jessie ambled self-consciously through the eddying throngs. Chin in, eyes dipped to make a quick final inspection of her small high bosom and her frock – saffron-coloured taffeta with black bows – she plucked at her shoulder straps, glanced down at the black high-heels which gave her carriage a certain mannequin elegance, then seeing she was being watched, blushed and delivered a bright, humble smile.

'See!' she said, flicking a tiny diamond engagement ring towards Henry. 'See?' Her arm turned a wide, gleeful circle which landed her insinuating for protection under Pieter's right arm. Out of this cover, she smiled again with happy, bright-eyed candour.

'We thought we saw your car,' she said.

'Yes,' Henry said, surprised she should be so volatile.

'We went to Froggy Pond.'

He remembered again the concert, the African, the tea-room proprietress; but decided, because they were so engrossed in their happiness, to be silent.

While they were talking, there was a small commotion at the front door. Mrs Rycliffe was refusing admission to a group of men who, though they were dressed up, looked like *skollies*. They were arguing with her.

Pieter and Jessie went to the door to watch, and a young man smirking behind rimless glasses touched Henry on the arm, and said:

'Third door on the right.'

'What?'

'That's right,' affirmed the youth. 'Third on the right.' He pointed. 'That's the room you want.'

'Is it? I see. Thanks.'

Thinking that perhaps Katherine had sent the fellow, Henry went to investigate and found himself in a room filled with hard-faced card-players. They sat around a large, round table under a bare electric bulb. A long trestle table bearing plates of sandwiches, snack-bowls, ash-trays and empty glasses stood against one wall; the rest of the furniture had been piled into a corner.

Annoyed, Henry turned to leave, only to be hailed from the table by a bold, mildly raddled voice.

'Hello, Professor. How are you?'

Without glasses, Rycliffe had been unrecognisable. He leaned his chair backwards on its hind legs and took a cigarette out of his mouth. Though he seemed unaware and behaved normally, the absence of glasses gave his face the wild, unsure look of an undergraduate.

'Well, Professor? How's tricks? These chaps are taking me to Queer Street.' He cast with mock indignation about the table. 'Especially that bastard there!'

Stewart, who was sporting a marvellous purple velvet stetson and an equally vital yellow tie, parted lips in a snarling smile. He turned to Rycliffe.

'What d'you expect, Yussouf? You should read Hoyle before you press luck against skill.'

'I hope you're going to make a donation from your blood earnings,' returned the Doctor.

'Like hell I am!'

Stewart pulled a comic face and the table chuckled.

'How's the little lady?'

Rycliffe brought down the front feet of his chair, collected a hand of cards, and looked back at Henry, his eyes glinting maliciously.

With attention focussed on his reply. Henry blinked to collect himself.

'Whom do you mean?'

'Mistress Katherine Margaret, of course. Have you another?'

Both he and Stewart were grinning as if they shared a secret.

'She's grown up now,' Henry said coldly, immediately aware the reply was as much in bad taste as Rycliffe's emphatic play upon words.

Rycliffe seemed to wince, but sprang at once back to battle. He shook his head gravely.

'You Durban chaps have no speed. No go. No gumption. By jove, in my day, the chaps had all the doings. When we fell for a gel, boy oh boy, we fell for her, got straight down to business – it was a snip! No hanky-panky stuff about it!'

Henry smiled tolerantly.

Rycliffe wagged his immature face again.

'Chaps are stone cold,' he mumbled and steered a new hand through the table litter.

When the room shifted again to the grim business of betting, Henry escaped and met Doc with a small company of young women coming down the corridor.

'Well, hello there, Henry boy!'

The girls were introduced as the four renowned Goodwin sisters; one of them was celebrating a birthday; another passionately confirmed this.

'It's her birthday!' she shrilled. 'Her very own b-b-birthday!'

Henry apologised for having been unaware.

'Many happy – '

'Oh, don't say that!' cut in the girl. 'That's what everybody, just everybody's been saying. Say something too, too heavenly mad.'

'Something too, too heavenly mad?'

'Thank you,' said the girl, gravely.

'Well done!' said Doc. And to the girl: 'Now, how 'bout a nice big birthday kiss for little Maurice?'

'How little is little Maurice?'

'Tiny. A midget!'

The girl pecked his head, reverently.

'A little squeeze now?'

The girl shook a pouting mouth decisively and pushed his chest away.

'Later,' she said, with a silly laugh, 'later, honeybunch.'

'Well, then!' Doc composed himself. 'Come along now,' he shouted to the party. 'Everybody in line now. Hands on hips. Right. Everybody right? Everybody breathe *in*!'

The girls formed a single file behind him, hands on one another's hips, and breathed in.

'Everybody breathe *out*!'

The formation solemnly obeyed.

'Right! *Acti*vate now. That's the stuff. *Pos*itive! One-two-three, *la conga*! One-two-three . . .'

The procession danced foolishly away, marking time whenever the corridor was overcrowded. A few people smiled indulgently: others shook prim, respectable heads. The girl who was last in the line looked faintly sheepish and tried, several times, to break away.

Moving towards the dining-room, Henry noticed an over-dressed girl in a green frock standing beside one of the draped bookcases of the corridor. The look on her face – the look of a cornered animal – startled him. She was staring wildly down the corridor. At first Henry thought she was staring at Doc, but when he followed the direction of her stare, at the same time recognising her as Madge, he realised that her gaze was fixed upon the Goodwin sister who was having a birthday. She stood alone, looking as if she was suppressing a frenzy of pain.

Henry checked an impulse to console her. It would be sacrilegious to interfere in Doc's private affairs. He moved quickly into the dining-room and joined the conversation which an old friend of his, a well-known Jewish barrister, was having with a remarkably beautiful, elegant and self-possessed woman who looked Malayan, yet was dressed in a sari.

The lawyer had been talking about the Palestine war, and the woman, with a charming chuckle, declared that she and her husband had just returned from a visit to Egypt.

She spoke in a light, champagne voice with a clear, neat English pronunciation, and glanced about the dining-room with an expression that was quick, lively, and missed nothing.

'You look like my youngest son,' she told Henry, with another well-bred, disarming chuckle. 'He's doing law too. At Durham. Dear me, how lovely it must be to be young – my God!'

She broke off with sudden alarm.

Yussouf Rycliffe, who had just entered the room, also looked as if he had seen a ghost.

'Aisha!'

'What rotten luck. It's Yussouf!'

'Aisha darling. What a surprise! How are you, my dearest one?'

'Frantically unhappy now. How are you, you scoundrel?' She turned to Sam Cohen, the barrister. 'You didn't tell me this bounder would be here.'

'It's his house,' Cohen muttered, crossly.

The woman giggled.

'It was a plot. Now I know. Yussouf, pet, give me a kiss and don't let your wife see. Where is she?'

She put out a cheek and Rycliffe kissed her lightly, with very gentle, old-fashioned grace.

'How's the Princess?' she asked.

'Well.'

'Do you see her often?'

'Sometimes,' he said.

'Love?'

Rycliffe seemed to wish to discontinue this esoteric conversation.

'How's your practice?'

'Oh, I'm not working, darling. We live quietly in Johannesburg.'

'Where's the hubby?'

'Business, darling,' the woman said. 'Don't be a bore.'

After a moment, she added crisply, 'He's coming to pick me up shortly, so don't get any ideas.'

'Dance with me, darling.'

'What! In front of all these people?' To Henry, she said, 'He used to be a *killer-diller*, that guy. Dance you off your feet,' and to Rycliffe, 'D'you remember the *Four Hundred*, darling?'

'I live only for those golden days.'

'We had fun.'

He led her away, protesting.

'Who is she?' Henry asked, quite overwhelmed. He felt as if he'd been dipped momentarily into another world.

'Don't you know?' Cohen smiled, urbanely. 'She's Aisha Rassool. Her husband's a rich businessman. She and Rycliffe did medicine together. A delightful woman. She plays cricket.'

'Who's the Princess?'

124

Cohen shrugged unconcernedly.

Rycliffe and the woman were speaking to the bandleader who was nodding. There was a *hugger-mugger* among the bandsmen.

Rycliffe and Mrs Rassool stood like silent statues, smiling wickedly into each other's eyes, a stance of readiness; then when the band struck up, they swept into a cyclone of arm and leg movements.

'Well, I'm damned. Look at that!' Henry cried.

Other people had stopped dancing to watch and crowded round. With authentic gestures, Rycliffe and his partner were doing the Charleston. Eventually Mrs Rassool had to give up. People clapped and made way for them.

'Jiminy Crickets,' said Mrs Rassool, breathless, flushed, but still smiling. 'I don't think I'll try that again.'

'You were heaven,' Rycliffe said.

'Was I, darling? Thank you.' she paused. 'And now, Sam, I must scoot.'

'Don't do a bunk. Stay a while,' Rycliffe urged. 'Have a drink.'

'Can't, my love. Bad for tum-tum. Gives Aisha colley-wobbles.'

'Just a spot?'

'No, my dear. I'm getting too rachetty for this sort of thing. Must go home and grow old gracefully. Ready, Sam?'

'Get your glad rags,' Rycliffe inserted. 'I'll bus you.'

'You!' Mrs Rassool laughed. 'I don't trust you.'

Rycliffe turned to Cohen.

'Are you still mulcting the poor?' he asked.

'Like you,' Cohen returned, 'yes!'

'Oh, dear, politics – how tiresome!' said Mrs Rassool. 'Do, for heaven's sake, come, Sam.'

She gave Henry a light, farewell pat on one cheek.

'Much love to the Princess,' she said to Rycliffe. 'I miss her terribly.'

'Why don't you visit, then?'

'I think I will. Chin-chin.'

Rycliffe chaperoned her and Cohen to the front door.

It was eleven o'clock. Henry went to look for Katherine but he couldn't find her, so he consoled himself with two whiskies at the bar, taking the second one onto the balcony at the back of the house.

The balcony overlooked Cape Town. Now and again, when the moon loomed free of clouds, an unearthly radiance silvered the face of Table Bay. A cool smell of night earth informed the darkness; faint breezes puffed veils of whitish mist across the Milky Way. Occasionally car engines starting up disrupted the tranquil, grigging crickets. Within the house the band was playing hit tunes of 1947 – *Slow Boat to China, Those Little White Lies, Laughing Samba, Too Many Irons in the Fire* . . .

The atmosphere induced in Henry nostalgia for a life savoured only in fragments. The balcony had a wooden seat which obscured any occupant from general view, and, being able to isolate himself in this way, restored to Henry the sense of privacy which had been a treasure of childhood. A staircase led down from the balcony to a large garden, darkened by trees and benches and clustered bushes. A few human forms wandered among the trees; occasionally a match lit up a brief face above one of the benches.

Henry thought, sentimentally, of Mrs Rassool: of her poignant, frail gaiety. She defined another aspect of Rycliffe's complex character: London; the 1920s; Piccadilly Circus with its lights and taxis and gay young things . . . the Flappers in cloche hats and long bead necklaces and quaint bosomless dresses. It seemed a less harsh world than his own, unsullied by dreary colour bars and atom bombs, and he felt happy for Rycliffe that he had seen better days. He sat for a long time in this state of brutish maudlin, sipping the whisky and watching the shifting patterns of flocculent cloud upon the night sky.

The band was playing *Too Many Irons in the Fire* a second time. A woman was singing:

> Too many irons in the fire,
> And there's too many hearts you desire.
> It's off for the old and it's on for the new
> You'll never know what it means to be true.
> And there's too many parties, and then,
> There'll be sadness and tears in the end.
> You'll never have a baby boon,
> You'll never spend a honeymoon,
> With too many irons in the fire.

The saxophone had begun to take a solo when Henry heard Katherine say:

'It's alright for you, but I just can't. I won't!'

Her tone was desperate and bitter: it paralysed Henry.

'Well, you know the alternative,' said a man.

'Well, I don't want that either!' Katherine almost shrieked.

'Okay, it's your deal, baby,' Stewart said. 'When you make up your mind, papa's waiting. I can't do more.'

They were coming up the staircase. Henry drew into the shadow of a pillar, not to embarrass both them and himself. His heart was galloping.

'Oh what a mess! I can't stand it!'

'For Christsake, keep your voice down!'

A silence.

'Does he know?'

'No, I haven't told him.'

'Well, you'd better wise him up. For a bright cookie you're bloody stupid. Shit. You're right. What a mess!'

'Look. I can't stand this. I'm going in.'

'Wait . . . Listen – '

'No. I'll see you later. Just let me be.'

Henry heard Katherine's footsteps hurrying away, then Stewart swearing tersely. He waited, aghast, sickened by the unknown, then he heard Stewart going down the stairs again into the garden. The band was still playing, but now the music nauseated. Now he understood why he had instinctively loathed Stewart: he sensed that he and Katherine were lovers and jealousy, like hot acid, immobilised him. He could not cry, feeling intense pain plunging through his loins. 'O God, how awful,' he whispered to himself. 'O God, I'm lost.'

He remained where he was for some time, bleeding inwardly, sweating; suddenly, there was a rumpus in the street in front of the villa. Fresh horror sprinted through him. Men were shouting; feet scampered; a woman screamed hysterically, in a voice eerie and cold with terror.

'*Donder hom, die wit vark!*' someone shrieked.

There were sounds of a scuffle, a crash of splintering glass and the thud of a body hitting the pavement.

'Come on, I'll take all of you, you bastards!'

It was Stewart's voice: another scuffle; then, the sound of running feet again.

In seconds Henry had forgotten his own lacerations and was running through the house. The band had stopped playing and people were gathered in a hush about the front door. Stewart, his face bleeding profusely from a gash across the forehead, was being escorted by Wollenhoven towards Rycliffe's surgery. Blood mangled his gleaming yellow tie.

A few minutes later two other casualties were carried in: Pieter and Jessie. Henry broke through a thick cordon to help the bearers.

People were talking all at once, indignantly decrying the fracas. There were several conflicting stories. One account was that a woman had button-holed Dr Lambert while he was leaving with a drunken brunette. She had caught the brunette by the hair, and having forced her to the pavement, had started to kick at her maniacally. When Doc had attempted to intervene, the *skollies* had set upon him.

Another rumour was that Councillor Holmes had sent a group of *skollies* to break up the party. Yet another was that a rival gang of *skollies* had got word that Wollenhoven was in the area and had come to murder him. Then there was the story that the attempt to break up the party had been inspired by Afrikaaner racialists. Lastly, it was said that Rycliffe was to blame, for having introduced a 'lumpen element.'

The story that seemed most plausible, and the one that made most sense to Henry, was that the gang of *skollies*, who had been turned away by Mrs Rycliffe, had returned in larger numbers. They had attempted to assault Mrs Rycliffe, but Pieter had sprung to her rescue. Seeing who he was, the *skollies* had at once transferred pent-up discontent upon him. It was then that Jessie screamed and then that Stewart, brandishing a chopper, had rushed into the street. For a few moments, Stewart had gone quite berserk and if Wollenhoven hadn't arrived and cracked him hard across the forehead with the butt of a revolver, he might have killed several people. It had, in effect, been the appearance of Wollenhoven that had broken up the fighting: his reputation had been enough. It was said that the windows of several cars had been splintered, and hearing this, Henry at once went to see if his car was damaged.

The car was unharmed, but when he opened a door he found, with just a brief moment of panic, that it was occupied. A woman – Madge – was crying in the darkness of the back seats.

'For heaven's sake, what is it?' he asked, recovering, closing the door and taking her hands. She was shaking; her green dress was torn in several places and her left cheek was puffed.

'Oh please . . . oh please . . .' But she could not stop shaking.

'Do you want me to take you home?' he asked.

'Yes!' she panted, gasping, 'Yes. Please!'

'Okay.' He got into the driver's seat, but she said, again gasping: 'My coat.'

She described the coat, her voice a wail. It was in Rycliffe's surgery.

'Please, hurry,' she said. 'I'm sick. I'm pregnant.'

Compassion stiffened Henry.

'Pregnant? Doc?'

She nodded, shaking her head distractedly.

'Wait here,' he said.

When he reached Rycliffe's surgery, people were leaving. Stewart's head had been bandaged and Pieter, still unconscious, had been taken to hospital. Henry found Madge's coat easily, and was about to leave with it when Katherine appeared.

'Oh there you are,' she said, urgently. 'I've been looking for you everywhere.'

'Have you?' he said coldly.

'What is it?' She went white.

'Please don't ask,' he said. 'It's private.'

She glanced at Madge's coat on his arm, and hesitated.

'Oh, tell me. Please tell me,' she said very desperately.

'Very well. If you must know. It's about a pregnancy. Anyway, you know damn well already.'

'O God! O God!' she said.

'Look, I must go,' he said. 'Phone me. If you like.'

Katherine, her lips compressed, said nothing. Her face was ashen. 'O God, Oh God, God! God! God!' she thought. 'She's told him! She told him!' Her fists were clenched. She watched him pass through the crowded doorway – a stiff, upright back, with an unturning of final condemnation, of irrevocable farewell. For a moment, agony almost annihilated consciousness; but she managed to turn, to walk stiffly, instinctively, with atavistic courage, towards the bathroom. But when she had locked the door, the strain was too unbearable; she sank to her knees on the floor, cold and bitter and furious, saying: 'O God! Oh God! how awful!' then dramatically, and aware of self-dramatisation, her hands clasped her belly, massaging it and now, remembering the child, she wept, remembering it was now,

129

irredeemably, lost, and she wept for it, for the young life she and it would never know, forgetting herself, weeping for the child, dissolving into oceans of mutilated love, into a future of nothing but despair.

She cried a long time, uncontrollably, then people began to test the doorknob, and to knock. She rose weakly, still crying, and with an effort, washed her face; but the sight, in the looking-glass, of swollen eyelids, returned the self-pity and the consciousness of tears running down her cheeks. The knocking continued, persistently, accompanied by voices. She washed her face several times, then she discovered, accidentally opening the cabinet behind the looking-glass, a pair of Rycliffe's sunglasses, and putting them on, walked through a barrage of indignation, looking through the darkened world for Stewart, ready to accept his offer.

Meanwhile, Henry was driving Madge to Newlands. The thought of going home had alarmed her, and she pleaded that he take her to his place, so that she could compose herself before facing her family. Henry had already begun to feel that, perhaps, he had been too brusque with Katherine, and resolved to return to her as soon as possible. He would make amends, take her to Froggy Pond, and there find out, conclusively, how he stood. He was in a tough, wilful mood.

When they reached Newlands, he led Madge to his bedroom, and helped her off with her coat. Her dress was rent in front and at the sides, disclosing a portrait of bulging hips and breasts. She was wearing paste earrings and costume jewellery which added to her voluptuous vulgarity. The room was characteristically neat and functional: a white coverlet and a brass bedstead; a simple, dark-brown mat thrown across the centre of the wooden floor; a writing desk piled high with books, papers, and writing utensils; crammed bookcases in between a bamboo wardrobe and an old-fashioned dressing table.

Calmer, Madge sat, with her torn dress on the bed, blinking half-drunkenly. There was an empty divan opposite her.

'Are you okay?' he asked, gently touching her left shoulder. 'Would you like a drink?'

She nodded, bemused.

While he went off to forage for a drink, she undressed herself, automatically, without thinking.

She was in her brassière when he returned; otherwise naked, she fingered the back loops, hopelessly.

'Oh, help me out,' she said, sullenly. He undid the straps, and at once launched the drop of her enormous breasts. He gave her the drink with condescending patience.

'You'd better get some rest,' he said, quietly.

She had grown tense and quiet.

'I'm high,' she said, in Afrikaans slang, 'help me,' but when he reached forward she threw one arm round his neck and drew him down, and for a moment they looked at one another.

'Don't you want me, *bokkie*?' she asked.

Henry smiled, compassionately.

'Of course I do, honey. But I can't. I'm not in love with you.'

The drink spilled in her outstretched hand, and she put it down on the bedside table.

'Good,' she said, in Afrikaans. 'Give me just a kiss then.'

He leant forward tolerantly but she clasped him in a fervent embrace, heaving fat sensual thighs and tumescent breasts. Henry pulled himself away, firmly and gently. He kissed her forehead.

'I'm sorry,' he apologised, and again leaned forward and kissed her remotely. 'Go to sleep.' He lifted the blankets, heaved her under them, and still sadly smiling, tucked her in. She pouted with discontent.

'Madge,' he said, firmly. 'I'm sorry. But you know it would be wrong. You're upset. I'll see you in the morning. We can see what can be done. Sleep well.' Again, he kissed her on the forehead, very kindly, then he rose and with a reassurance that she would not be disturbed, put on his coat and returned dutifully to Walmer Estate.

It was only when he reached the Rycliffe villa that the eroding foreknowledge began to work. Katherine was nowhere in evidence: a telegram of pain in the bloodstream. Mrs Rycliffe announced with a smirk that she had left half-an-hour ago with Stewart. Any comfort of fresh self-deception was sealed. In the dining-room, the remains of the party were telling bawdy stories. Only a brutal concentration of will power carried him to the back verandah, where he sat for some time, the wound so total and weakening that it cancelled all power of rational thought. Pride resisted every urge to follow them. Total rejection recommended total revenge: he did not wish to see or talk to anyone. With another effort of will he left the balcony, and rather than walk through the house – an open butt for pity – he reached the front gate via the garden. Here he could not avoid John Moodley and

Doc who were sitting in his car passing round a bottle of brandy. For some reason, instead of exasperation, the discovery stimulated a storm of hysterical scornful laughter, which would have angered Moodley and Doc if both of them were not at that stage of genial drunkenness which is insensitive. In fact they laughed with him and offered the bottle which he first refused, but later accepted. The alcohol had a quietening effect; he had another pull to drug a revival of the pain; then another; then he wasn't talking to Moodley who had rather puzzlingly disappeared, but to Doc who was regarding him impatiently, with exasperation. He had a faint recollection of movement; then black insentience again – until, in a half-darkened bedroom, which spun a bit, unsteadily, he opened his eyes, and seemed to distinguish shapes . . . two people . . . writhing naked on his own bed, a woman with huge buttocks raised against the chest of the man who was violently assailing her. The smell of wild roses in full bloom poured through the bedroom windows, as if it was a black crazy juice bleeding from the clustered thorns crushed into the soft, black flesh of the sky. Immediately, he thought, 'O God, hell!' and acids rose from his insides, and roared through his mouth; then he was senseless again.

CHAPTER 8

It was mid-morning when he woke. He was still in his own bedroom.
The door was wide open. He was lying on the divan opposite his bed,
which was a tumbled mess, and there was a sulphuric stench of half-
wet vomit caked to his cheeks. He rose at once, disgusted, and after a
thorough bath, cleaned out his room, opening all the windows, and
powdering the divan with crystals of lavatory deodorant. He was
thirsty and his senses blundered, like cannon thuds, at the back of his
head. He took several aspirins, and the water which washed them
down was like fresh alcohol, making him sick again, and giddy.
Katherine was still a flame of dull pain burning the floor of his heart.

Madge was next door, dressed in Doc's bath robe. She was
mending her dress with a needle and thread. She answered Henry's
polite greeting with a taunt that suggested his behaviour last night
could no longer hold him in public esteem. He ignored the malice;
she was merely defending herself. He offered her an opportunity to
unburden with a considerate enquiry after her health, but when she
was non-committal, he tacitly assumed that she and Doc had made
up, and deliberately refrained from any further interference in their
affairs. She, however, mistook courtesy for condescension, for an
attempt to reach superiority by freeing himself from desire, and thus
humiliating others; an attitude that infuriated her enough that she
decided not to tell him Katherine had telephoned twice during the
night, leaving an out-of-town number. In this malice she was
unaware of the torture she might have spared: in particular, his
inability to expel Katherine from his mind. He was alternately listless
and animated. It was a cold, showery, spiritless day: on the spur of
the moment, he drove out to Muizenberg, but wandering for over an
hour on the deserted beach, scarcely aware of the waves flushing up
white petticoats of foam, was no relief. He succeeded only in
drenching himself to the skin, at first a glad punishment, but later
unpleasant, because it brought on chills and nervous shivering. He
did, however, renew his determination not to lure fresh humiliation.

If Katherine had left freely, she must return freely. It was an excruciating decision to accept, but its prosecution was supported by years of self-discipline and self-denial. Anguish was not easy to cope with; it kept recurring, sometimes with a vehemence that challenged any desire to go on living, but now that he had resigned himself to despair, he felt slightly better. When he returned to Newlands, Madge had been taken home, and Doc was in the sitting-room, reading brochures about a new batch of medicines and drugs.

Henry was changing out of his sodden clothes, when the front door bell rang, and after a few palpitating moments of hope, Doc came to report that it was not Katherine but Shaikh-Moosa who had arrived. He was waiting with a 'hideous camp-follower' in the sitting-room.

'The man must be mad,' Doc decided, 'to employ a man so ugly!'

'He employs me,' returned Henry, with a shrug.

'Exactly.'

In the sitting-room, Shaikh-Moosa, dressed in a black suit, paced up and down the carpet, hands behind his back, expounding business lore to John Moodley's father. He was wearing a black fez and a thick black overcoat. It was still raining outside, and the winds were rising.

'– couple o'hundred pound would be 'nough,' he was saying, 'don't you think so, Mr Moodley?'

As usual, Mr Moodley assented.

'Ah, here is the man. How you keeping?' Shaikh-Moosa turned to Moodley. 'You know Mr Moodley, don't you . . . John Moodley's father?'

Moodley was studying the furniture with unconcealed distaste.

'We've met,' he muttered, looking unhappily at the tattered sofa beside the fireplace. 'You live here?'

'At the moment,' Henry confirmed.

Moodley snorted as if he expected lawyers to occupy less shabby quarters.

'Thing is this,' Shaikh-Moosa said, to recover Henry's attention. 'I wonder, there is one small favour you could do for me?' He paused, then added, 'By the way, a cheque is in the post. Very good job you did for me at Durban. Two hundred pounds it is. That is just for the expenses, you know.'

'That's very kind of you,' Henry offered cautiously.

Shaikh-Moosa waved a magnanimous hand.

'That is nothing. Don't think 'bout it,' he insisted, 'the rest we can settle later.'

He tilted his head in a typically Indian fashion, sideways, to underline the casuality. Henry nodded politely.

Shaikh-Moosa's overriding idea had skulked off somewhere between his lips and gold teeth. He made several ugly, sucking motions to dislodge it.

'What I'd like,' he at last intimated, 'is to meet Dr Rycliffe.'

Henry's surprise was so flagrant that Shaikh-Moosa hesitated. At last he had to justify the ambition.

'Thing is this,' he explained. 'People been telling me his politics – if you catch me? I want to find out a few things for myself. Do you follow me?'

Henry didn't. The explanation was a clumsy lie. But he nodded.

'I wonder – ' Shaikh-Moosa inquired, ' – could you take me now? My car is outside.'

The prospect of going to the Rycliffe villa aroused in Henry mixed interest. The role of go-between would excellently shield deeper motives, and yet to learn conclusively that Katherine was beyond recovery sent through him anticipation of fresh pain. An interview, however, between Shaikh-Moosa and Rycliffe was irresistible.

'I'll just get my jacket,' he said, after a moment.

'We not taking up your time?'

'You are. But it's a holiday.'

Shaikh-Moosa smiled uncertainly. Other employees showed greater deference.

In the car – a seven-seater, chauffeur-driven Packard – Shaikh-Moosa developed his new politics.

'Rycliffe is a communist,' he declared. 'Matter of fact, I'm bit of a communist myself. Wouldn't you say so, Mr Moodley?'

'Too true,' Mr Moodley agreed. 'Without the business, you would be the greatest of communists, Mr. Shaikh-Moosa.'

'No. No. Mr Moodley.' Shaikh-Moosa looked quite hurt. 'Not like that. Not in that way. It is because I am in the business that makes me a communist. All day long I am working for other people. Not for myself. *Myself*: I don't care tuppence about. And who profits? Who *benefits*: tell me *that*? Not me. In the nights I don't sleep worrying 'bout all these things. Too much headaches they are giving me. I am giving my *whole* life for other people. You get the point isn't it?'

Moodley, for once, was puzzled.

'Mr Naidoo understands.' Shaikh-Moosa was sitting next to the African chauffeur; he turned to Henry for sympathy.

Henry nodded glumly. He had the sense of being with a pack of lunatics.

'There is!' Shaikh-Moosa crowed, triumphantly. 'Mr Naidoo agrees with me. There is the point of view of a man of education. You can't go against that, Mr Moodley!'

As they neared the Rycliffe villa, Shaikh-Moosa began to show signs of unrest. On the doorstep he coughed several times, patting his chest ostentatiously; he fiddled with his diamond ring, turning the stone palmwards.

'Good thing not to brag, isn't it?' he whispered to Henry, looking for reassurance. 'Don't want him thinking wrong things – that I got too much money.'

The doorbell was answered by Mrs Rycliffe's sister, the slim, dainty Amina. She looked as if she had a hangover, and examined Shaikh-Moosa and Moodley distrustfully. Towards Henry, she was a shade less cold.

In his usual unpredictable fashion, Rycliffe had risen late and had converted afternoon to morning. He was now doing last night's calls and would be returning shortly for breakfast. Amina led the party into the dining-room and there left it to fend for itself. The shrouds had been taken off the bookcases, but many balloons and tinsel decorations still floated from the high ceiling; the floor had been swept superficially, but not waxed; one of the carpets hadn't been unrolled. A fug of stale beer, dead cigarettes, and dust clung to the room.

The party sat down, quietly. Shaikh-Moosa occasionally consulted his gold wrist-watch, his jaw hardening each time with exasperation. Moodley inspected the loaded bookshelves with awe. Conversation was desultory.

'I often thought of becoming a doctor,' Shaikh-Moosa announced after one long silence. He looked uncomfortable. 'Only one thing put me off, Mr Moodley.'

'What was that?' Moodley graciously asked.

'The studying part. Six years is a long time, Mr Moodley. Too long. Hundreds o'thousands o'pounds I could make in that time.'

'Too true,' Mr Moodley agreed, satisfied. 'Too long, it is. Far too long.'

Shaikh-Moosa had addressed his henchman perhaps because he was unsure what Henry's cold, introspective silence betokened.

There was another long, awkward pause.

'One time,' Shaikh-Moosa at last dilated, 'I bought some stethoscopes – seven gross from a firm going bankrupt. Cheap they were going. And you know what I did, Mr Moodley?'

Mr Moodley shook his head with rapt curiosity.

'I sold the whole lot 'cepting one. This one I kept for myself, and every now and then, sometimes, four to five times a day, even more sometimes, I would call my driver and listen to his heart.'

Moodley looked strongly impressed.

'A good feeling, that gave me,' Shaikh-Moosa confessed 'That fellow even asked me, one time, if I was a doctor.'

'Proverb: a doctor a day sends the chauffeur away,' Henry was tempted to suggest, but he desisted. Let Shaikh-Moosa stew in his own clownish concoctions. The man resembled elements of Dostoyevsky's *Karamazov* and Isherwood's *Mr Norris*. Sympathy had to be won at the price of buffoonery. In his own surroundings, the apocryphal story would have been entertaining; in the empty dining-room, like the man himself, it was out of place, and sensing this, Shaikh-Moosa grimaced at his watch, and lapsed again into unhappy silence.

At last, at two o'clock, Rycliffe returned. Instead of going to breakfast, he came straight into the dining-room.

'Wonderful car you got there, my dear fellow!' he told Shaikh-Moosa. He answered Henry's greeting with a brief nod. 'You must loan it to me one day. Give my patients an uplift. People are proud of their doctor, you know.'

A quick inspection of Moodley was enough for him to predict that a more balanced protein diet would totally miscarry. He turned to Shaikh-Moosa.

'Sit down, my friends. No ceremony, please.' He sat down himself, crossing arms and legs comfortably.

An unbelievably humble, almost pitiful, expression had settled into Shaikh-Moosa's face, and Rycliffe fixed on him, for a moment, a suspicious, measuring gaze.

'Looks like you had something of a party here,' Shaikh-Moosa observed, eyes glistening as if he had found an irresistible opening gambit.

Rycliffe waved a hand and the matter away.

'Don't think me rude.' Shaikh-Moosa hesitated. 'But could I ask you one thing?'

'Go right ahead, my dear fellow. No holds barred.'

'How much money you made?'

'In the party? Oh, twenty or twenty-five pounds, I don't really know.'

The information restored Shaikh-Moosa's self-confidence. He drew out his wallet and handed Rycliffe a cheque.

'I brought this,' he put out, with just a hint of discomfort, ' – for your election campaign.'

Rycliffe examined the cheque with an amused frown. Henry lit a cigarette, casually, to disguise intense interest in the bargain which, like the turn of the screw, would arrive, as it did in all Indian business deals, slowly, after perhaps another false hare, at the end.

'I been reading your paper – what's the name of it? I forget.'

'*The Flame*,' Henry assisted quietly.

'That's it. That's the name. *The Flame*. I should remember it. It reminded me of fire. Lovely paper. Warm like a fire. Lovely pieces of real political ideas, it has!' Shaikh-Moosa smiled at Rycliffe apologetically and lowered his voice. 'And I would like you to know this. Ever since I read your paper – what's the name again?'

'*The Flame*.'

'That's right. That's the right name. Ever since I read it – forgive me for being frank – I been on your side.'

Because Rycliffe was still musing over the cheque, Shaikh-Moosa continued. 'That is nothing,' he advanced. 'Nothing at all. Just an instalment, so to speak. You can put it in your paper. Only thing, don't print my name . . . an anonymous donor . . . I like to keep outside of the limelight.'

Rycliffe tossed the cheque with disinterest onto the coffee-table next to his chair, and smiled cynically.

'Now what do you want?' he asked. He seemed to be controlling a rising temper.

Shaikh-Moosa raised innocent eyebrows.

'Nothing at all . . . nothing,' he answered.

'Come off it,' Rycliffe said, sharply. 'You boys don't give money away like that. What's your game?'

Because Shaikh-Moosa continued to look offended, Rycliffe suddenly broke into classical Urdu. 'My grandfather, you know,' he said, 'was a big merchant. He wasn't a *buniah*, but he knew all the tricks. I went to school in India, moreover. So this kind of stuff won't wash.'

The purity of Rycliffe's Urdu astonished Shaikh-Moosa.

'That's right. That's right,' he agreed, 'let us talk the language of our forefathers.'

'Rot!' Rycliffe snapped back. 'You'll tell me what you want, or get the hell out of here!'

'Very hard you making things,' Shaikh-Moosa became his most unctuous self. 'Why be so hard? I'm not an educated man like yourself.' In ungrammatical South African Urdu, he said: 'I come to you, high sir, to make you a present and you treat me like an untouchable. Is this not an insult to our homeland?'

'Your homeland – not mine,' Rycliffe said in English. 'Drop this bloody chauvinism and come to the point!'

'I suppose,' Shaikh-Moosa tested in Urdu, 'it would be too much to ask the big Sahib to stay out of this election?'

'Out of the question!'

'Well, then. Perhaps this one small favour?'

'Speak up, man!'

'Nothing much. Just this.'

Shaikh-Moosa pulled a crumpled piece of paper from an overcoat pocket.

'This thing,' he offered the paper to Rycliffe.

It was a handbill advising District Six to form an organisation to protest militantly against any attempts of property owners to raise rents.

Shaikh-Moosa shook his head, grimly. 'Very much trouble a thing like this would cause.'

Henry took the handbill from Rycliffe and read it himself, reddening, but he controlled the spate of questions he wanted to ask. He wanted to know what the deal would be.

'Trouble for whom?' Rycliffe demanded.

'Trouble all round. Everyside. First there is the tenants, then the Council – the Cape Town City Council – even I would have trouble. But I'm not thinking 'bout myself. I was telling Mr Naidoo: like you,

I am a communist. Other people's welfare, *that's* the thing giving me most worries. If it wasn't for other people, I would be a happy man. Forgive me being so frank. But I have to speak the truth! Isn't that so, Mr Moodley?'

'Quite right,' confirmed Mr Moodley. 'Never a word of lies!'

Rycliffe bellowed with laughter.

'Oh God! Where did you chaps get this routine?' he asked.

'Routine? How is that?'

'All this bosh about frankness and truth?'

'But it is the truth,' Shaikh-Moosa asseverated with conviction.

Rycliffe heaved. 'Alright then, Professor. It's the truth. Now come to the point!' He glanced pointedly at his wrist-watch.

Faced with emergency, Shaikh-Moosa became astonishingly lucid. He was building an enormous housing estate in the Cape Flats; for this enterprise he had borrowed heavily from the banks which held his District Six properties as security; if the rents in District Six were raised, he would be able to pay back loan interest, and still have capital to complete the Cape Flats deal successfully.

Rycliffe interrupted.

'You mean you're going to build new houses for your tenants in District Six?' he asked.

Shaikh-Moosa paused to adjust to the idea.

'That's it!' he exclaimed fervently. 'Now you understanding me. For them. Even for some others, too.'

'What others?'

Shaikh-Moosa seemed stumped.

'Any others,' he suggested, 'needing a house for themself.' Then brightly, 'The squatters, for example. These people without no homes, at the moment.'

'And the rents?'

'Less than what they are now paying!'

Rycliffe was thoughtful. Either he was taking Shaikh-Moosa at his word or, more likely, he was looking for a loophole through which, without losing face, he could go back on the earlier uncompromising stand, and perhaps even insert a few terms of his own.

'Let's have it all again,' he said. 'So we've no misunderstanding.'

Shaikh-Moosa recapitulated the scheme, adding this time that it would be only in three months' time that he could start on the project; he was still short of some capital.

'I see,' Rycliffe concluded, 'so, in the meantime, you don't want a fuss about rents in the Council Election?'

'Very well you are putting it,' agreed Shaikh-Moosa.

'And what if I don't agree?'

'Then there is no new houses!'

'What about Holmes?'

'Ah!' invited Shaikh-Moosa. 'Now we are getting somewhere. I could see to it that Councillor Holmes wouldn't be standing. Then you could win hands down!'

Even Rycliffe was astonished. 'What! He wouldn't run at all?'

Shaikh-Moosa shut his eyes, modestly.

'These matters, all,' he offered quietly, 'can be arranged.'

'I don't understand.'

'Alright,' Shaikh-Moosa explained, patiently. 'See it like this. This way. There is the housing 'state in the Cape Flats. Now who would be the contractor?'

'Holmes?'

'The same man.'

'How do I know you're not lying?'

'There is the plans. I could show them in my office.'

Rycliffe ruminated. He picked up the cheque and studied it again.

'The first instalment?' he asked.

'After the election, the rest.'

'I'd like to see the plans.'

'Come to my office. Now! This minute, if you like!'

Rycliffe was about to rise, but Henry said:

'Just a minute!'

Shaikh-Moosa looked at Henry with exasperation.

'So you're Fylfot Holdings?' Henry asked coldly.

'I have some shares.'

'A controlling interest?'

Shaikh-Moosa rose impatiently.

'These things we can discuss another time,' he said. He turned from the small fry to the hooked big fish, and smiled. 'Time is getting short.'

'Like bloody hell it is!' Henry blurted. He was furious.

'What is that? You speaking to me?' Shaikh-Moosa was also furious.

'I damn well am!'

'Now, now chaps. Easy. No tempers,' Rycliffe tried to intervene.

'Just stay out of this a minute,' Henry acidly advised.

'Look here, my boy,' Shaikh-Moosa began; but Henry cut him short.

'Don't *my boy* me,' he shouted. 'Talk that way to your lickspittle over there.' Henry pointed to the amazed Moodley. Shaikh-Moosa's face had purpled; his fists were clenched, and he might have brawled if they weren't in Rycliffe's house.

'Let's get a few things straight,' Henry continued, with icy self-control. 'If this deal goes through, you can be damn well sure I'll blow the gaff!'

Quite dramatically, Shaikh-Moosa turned cordial.

'Wait a minute,' he smiled magnanimously. 'We all losing our heads. Come way with us by my office, Mr Naidoo. Come and see the plans for yourself.'

'No!' Henry said, with equal courtesy, but firmly. 'I've heard quite enough. Not one of you have had the decency to consult anyone in District Six. You all talk as if the people there were . . . were just . . . just objects to be moved about at whim.'

'But they would never agree,' argued Shaikh-Moosa sweetly. 'Take it from me, Mr Naidoo. The people in District Six got no sense. Anything they want they try to get without plans. Everything spur of the moment; reckless, like that. That is their way. No long-term plans. They breed like rabbits.'

'That may be,' replied Henry more coldly. 'But why don't you show them a little courtesy. Show *them* the plan? If it was in their interests, they might agree.'

Shaikh-Moosa shook his head.

'I couldn't take the chance,' he said.

Rycliffe, who had been following each speaker attentively, now sided with Shaikh-Moosa.

'My dear fellow,' he told Henry, 'you don't know the first thing about politics. What did Lenin say? "Never trust the masses!" They need leadership. They're fickle, too hotheaded, too spontaneous!'

'That's right,' Shaikh-Moosa supported. '*There* was a great man – Lenin! Great truth he was talking.'

'I'm sorry,' Henry said. 'You people do what you must. But you can count me out. I'm going home now.'

'Perhaps, we could give you a lift?' Shaikh-Moosa offered.

'No, thanks,' Henry said. 'I'll catch the bus.'

Shaikh-Moosa flexed the muscles of his jaw impatiently.

'As you like, Mr Naidoo. I'll be getting in contact with you.'

'That won't be necessary,' Henry replied. 'Just pay your bills!' And with that, he marched out of the room. When he reached the front door, he heard Rycliffe mutter confidentially to Shaikh-Moosa:

'Don't worry, old chap. Let him cool off. I'll bring him round. Patience, my dear fellow. Patience is a great virtue. Little things for little people!'

When he reached the town centre, instead of going home, Henry caught the Sea Point bus.

◇

I was entertaining guests when he arrived, and though surprised, delighted to see him. He looked like a shipwrecked mariner – haggard, exhausted, red-eyed. When he heard I had guests he was disappointed, but thin lines of courtesy sketched themselves on his face and manner.

'I'm sorry,' he apologised. I had a sense of keeping him from leaving at once: of holding him on a tenuous leash. He asked if he could wait in the bedroom: he didn't want to meet any people.

'Of course,' I said, 'surely.'

Half-an-hour later my guests left, and I found him fast asleep, sprawled across my bed. I shut the door quietly, and left him there. When he woke, he complained of a headache, and after a few aspirins, he had coffee; then we talked. I offered him a drink, but he wouldn't touch a drop. He explained Shaikh-Moosa's newest ambitions, and characteristically, sought approval for his actions; by the clarity and certainty with which he expressed himself I suspected that it was not this settled matter he had come to see me about. In private affairs he was always circumspect; he seemed to prefer to discuss himself in the third person, as if he was a philosophical problem. The only interesting part of this conversation touched on areas of doubt. What would be the most effective and ethical action that the Tenant's Association might take? We agreed that because the Organisation, as it was presently constituted, was insufficiently representative, it might be advisable to issue invitations to all organisations likely to be interested. A meeting in which certain minimum principles might find agreement should be arranged. The next stage would be a mass meeting with speakers proposing a definite course of action. We drew up a list of organisations to invite, and people to contact and Henry, to his credit, was in favour of excluding no one, not even the Rycliffe group, Holmes, or the Communist Party. 'The issue,' he argued, 'crosses party lines!' We also drew up an agenda for the first meeting, and discussed the structure of the Executive which should come out of this meeting. Our decisions were tentative, but out of experience, we both agreed that some firm proposals ought to be offered to the attending delegates. We discussed finance, and after we had talked away most matters to mutual agreement, Henry at last allowed himself to have a drink.

Perhaps it was the bedroom that lent an air of intimacy to our exchanges, perhaps the intensity of Henry's feelings, but I soon found myself privy to regions of sensibility and interest hitherto always tucked behind his horizon. I was rather touched that he should make of me a confidant, and I was determined, come what may, to do my utmost to honour his confidence. He began the confessional by asking with characteristic circumlocution, after my wife, Yvonne.

'You are lucky,' he concluded, 'at least you love her, and in her turn, she dotes on you. I'm sorry I haven't been to see her recently.'

She was improving, I assured him; she had asked after him, yesterday.

'Give her my love,' he said, 'and I'll try to visit her soon.'

Then suddenly, for no reason at all, he began to cry. I had never found him in this condition before, and I was both surprised and embarrassed. He blurted out something about being in love. For some time he rambled on about the condition and never mentioned Katherine by name. When eventually he did, I was even more amazed.

'Katherine Holmes!' I exclaimed.

'That's right! Do you know her?'

There must have been an element of superiority in my smile, for he at once responded:

'Oh, hell. Not you, too.'

I understood him at once, and shook my head.

'No, Henry,' I explained. 'It's not like that. Wait a sec.' From my bureau I brought out a family album with pictures of Katherine and Yvonne, as teenagers, dressed in tennis shorts, posing arms around each other's shoulders.

'We grew up together,' I said.

He seemed reassured.

'I'm sorry,' he said. Then he explained what he understood to be her relationship with Gordon Stewart. He also presented a detailed account of Rycliffe's Christmas Eve party, and when he had concluded, I did not know what to think.

His need for reassurance was so urgent that for a moment I hesitated telling him what I really thought. He was, after all, one of my best friends. Should I lie? For a while, I waffled, but seeing that he did not believe me, I said with conviction:

'Kath has changed. Things have happened to her. She isn't as pure as she used to be. She's changed.' From his account, I was furious with her, as exasperated as he; she had again immersed herself in the spiritual drains from which I had already once released her; she seemed beyond redemption. I advised him to forget her.

For a long while he was silent.

'It's difficult,' he said in a tortured voice. 'Adrian, it's impossible!'

'But you must try,' I comforted platitudinously. 'Be a man. Think of the Tenant's Association!'

He was brave, but with the courage of despair.

'Yes,' he decided. 'Yes. One must not think of oneself!'

I did not see him again for a few days, but I gathered from rumours that he had thrown himself into the Tenant's Association with an ardour that aroused suspicion even among those – like Mr Parsons – who were immediately associated with him. He was a poor public speaker, having none of Rycliffe's flamboyant turn of phrase, or Holmes' quiet reassuring vacuity, but his sincerity drew dividends. He talked and talked, and visited every threatened house in District Six, and he held not one, but three meetings of the Tenant's Association. Within an incredibly short time, by undeviating will, he collected around himself a small, fervent crew of followers so minatory that even Rycliffe began to bend calloused ears. What lubricated these fanatical engines is worth considering.

CHAPTER 9

By unstinted application, as I have said, Henry started a tide of public sympathy; in the first swell a person I have mentioned already, 'the young man, Abu' cast in with him. What induced Abu to break ranks is not quite clear. It was Henry's opinion that Abu had been drifting from his uncle for some while: that he had been keeping a steady lookout for another flag. No doubt, independence and revenge were among Abu's motives. Nevertheless, it is surprising that Henry should lay such mean charges – opportunism and treachery. Did he himself feel he had violated a traditional pact? Did he transfer his own guilt to Abu? The diary makes strange reading. Why should Henry refuse to Abu the scrupulous self-determination he so hand-somely awards himself? From my own meetings with Abu, I suspect that Henry shared some of Shaikh-Moosa's and Rycliffe's cold-blooded suspicion of people less gifted than themselves. Perhaps this was partly why he proclaimed such intense allegiance to the commonsense of the common man, why also the proclamation was a sacrifice. It was almost as if he wilfully fostered convictions against another knowledge, against despair always a few heart throbs away. Certainly Abu's intimations supplied most welcome ballast.

Rationality now received a thorough drubbing, the rationality which had misinterpreted the Desai deal, and which now stirred currents of self-reproach. Here was the region of character which the stream of life had left dry, his Achilles' heel; from reason, the compass swung round to the other extreme. Henry learnt that throughout Desai's visit, Shaikh-Moosa had been in the next room, listening in on microphones, and in this way had been able to operate a bear. This was why Shaikh-Moosa had needed a solicitor so urgently. He had paid Desai in Uralco shares: in coin, that is, of a company in which he himself held a controlling interest. By appropriate tele-phone calls, he had first arranged a bulk buying of shares, and later, when Desai's properties had become his own, a bulk selling so that within a few days, all Uralco shares had become valueless. Then, of course, when the distressed and ruined Desai had thrown himself upon the Great Man's mercy, quite bountifully he had bought back the wretched fool's shares, 'for a few pence', and had at once set about, with fresh bulk purchases, re-establishing confidence in Uralco. In this way he had gleaned Desai's flats, and, a fat fortune.

But this deal was only part of a much larger operation, and it was I who first had wind of it. One of my cousins was, at that time, the private secretary to a high-ranking member of the Opposition Shadow Cabinet. According to my cousin's wife (a woman of almost limitless self-importance who revelled in being in the know) the Nationalists, when they came to power (and it was generally accepted that they would win the General Elections in 1948) might implement two closely associated schemes. The scheme which had strongest support was one in keeping with their policy of *Apartheid*. Under this scheme, the entire population of District Six would be evacuated to the Cape Flats and the evacuated area would, after slum clearance, be converted into an exclusively European residential district. The second, and more far-reaching, scheme involved the possible manufacture of nuclear weapons at an experimental factory to be set up in the Cape Flats. Opposition thinkers believed that overdependence on gold was industrial suicide; that uranium should become a supplementary mainstay; and therefore, that if the Cape Flats could be turned into a Coloured and Malay dormitory, not only would the people – moved there – help to erect a nuclear factory, that is, the Opposition's new economic insurance policy, but they would also supply a stable pool of cheap, unskilled labour.

What lent credence to the scheme was the steady traffic of South African atomic scientists to and from Europe. The newspapers of the time were filled with accounts of these visits. The scientists were despatched mainly to raise foreign loans, and to explain that South African deposits were richer than those in Katanga, and that since the commodity was scarce, by simple supply and demand, few shareholdings could match its dividend promise.

How Shaikh-Moosa tumbled to these plans adds another remarkable depth to these conspiracies.

The Government of India, as a diplomatic reply to the treatment of Indians in South Africa, was arranging to place an embargo on jute traffic to South Africa. Since this would bring much of South African secondary industry to a stand-still, the government had secretly been

147

looking for ways – without abandoning cheap labour: the base of its racial policies – of evading the ban. Now, because Shaikh-Moosa also ran most of the trade in spices from the East, he had the kind of contacts most at a premium. He had himself proposed to ship the valuable gunny sacks from Goa via Portugal and Mozambique. Increased transportation costs would of course, send up the price of jute, but at least, essential South African supplies would not dry up. According to Abu, this was just another of several interrelated operations which Shaikh-Moosa was elaborating, and it put him in direct touch with the highest policy-makers of the Nationalist Party. No sooner did he learn what might take place than he began machinations of his own. He floated Uralco, a company to finance commerce and mining of uranium. This was the long-term plan in which the ruin of Desai, the depopulation of District Six, and the jute traffic were details. Soon Uralco began to attract foreign capital – mainly American and West German. Traditionalist Britain wavered; there were a few London buyers, but in the main, satisfaction with gold remained steady; semi-officially, City of London brokers doubted the ability of the Afrikaaner Nationalists to keep gold and the rest of the country economically and politically stable.

Shaikh-Moosa was, therefore, selling skins before killing the bear – a shrewd, but also a hazardous enterprise. What scandalised Henry most were the ramifications. Shaikh-Moosa seemed to be part of a power craze that was tidily swallowing all that stood in its way. In Henry's view, Shaikh-Moosa was drastically reducing the power of others to choose: a fact that reinforced his own determination to launch the Tenant's Association successfully.

Having now quite thrown overboard most earlier ambitions, he entered seas swirling with wildest rumours; currents of opinion, speculation, and fact ran to and fro, now making, now dispersing, sense. Only the most uncompromising will could steer an even, pre-charted course.

There was, first of all, the amazing suggestion that Rycliffe had abdicated his intention of standing as a candidate in the District Six Election; that he was urging his followers to support Holmes! There must have been some truth in the story; *The Flame* dropped hints that Rycliffe would be speaking at one of Holmes' first meetings. This possibility was of so much local interest that it was decided to postpone the third meeting of the Tenant's Association until Rycliffe's public position had been clarified.

The meeting was held in the same hall in which the Christmas Eve concert had taken place.

A large audience packed the hall. Several groups of *skollies* lounged against the walls near the platform. The long vertical windows were draped with black material. Above wooden rafters, the tile framework of the roof was visible.

Henry arrived early and managed to find a seat at the back. Several people greeted him. By now he had become *au fait* with the different factions in Cape politics. A small supercilious group of Communists sat languidly in one corner; the *Flame* group, Rycliffe's own supporters, were rather more strategically distributed, they sat in twos and threes quite far apart from each other, except for a large youth contingent, which was huddled in seats to Henry's left; then there was a group of elder people, mainly teachers; Holmes' election committee, who seemed impatient for the meeting to begin – they sat near Henry, and not far from the delegation from the Tenant's Association, which included Old Mr Parsons, his talkative nephew, Jonathan December, and Jessie's father.

On the platform were four men: the Chairman, a mild man who was President of a Teachers' Association; Holmes' agent, a thin, voluble, commonplace man named Hendricks, who had once acquired a certain renown as a cricketer and who now ran several Christian youth clubs; Holmes himself, and, sitting apart, wearing dark glasses, Yussouf Rycliffe.

Hendricks spoke first. He listed Holmes' achievements and presented the vague, universal platform on which Holmes stood. The audience listened patiently, rather in the way people listen to door-to-door salesmen. Then Holmes, wearing a three-piece grey suit, the chain of his fob-watch across his waistcoat, was introduced by the Chairman. He delivered an impression far more self-assured and clear than the one Henry had privately received. But the main attraction was Rycliffe. When he rose he was given a standing ovation from all but the small group of communists in front. His flamboyance captivated the audience but he said nothing. He spoke generally about the time having arrived for people 'to identify their struggle for rights with the general liberatory struggle throughout Africa', and of how it was growing impossible for people 'to escape their political obligations'. His phrasing and manner were arresting, and he again drew the strongest applause. What was puzzling to Henry was that Rycliffe did not openly support Holmes; he did not even mention the election! It became clear now that the most significant part of the meeting would be question time.

The first question was for Hendricks. It concerned his youth clubs and was quickly answered. A few practical questions were addressed to Holmes, mostly about the location of bus stops, about sewerage, and about rates. Jonathan December wanted to speak, but could not catch the attention of the Chairman who now asked if there were any questions for Dr Rycliffe. The first question plunged the meeting into a silent hush. The questioner was a person whom Henry had never seen before, a woman, who asked directly whether Dr Rycliffe was or wasn't supporting Councillor Holmes, also whether the Doctor intended to stand as a candidate himself. Rycliffe waffled for a few moments, again talking generally about 'the national liberatory struggle going on throughout Africa', and was in the midst of his histrionic evasion when the heels of two events followed hard upon each other.

First, the woman, rising angrily, interrupted him: she demanded plain answers; then, while she was rephrasing her questions, a folded note reached the dais and was passed, by the Chairman, to Rycliffe. Turning round Henry noticed a small, plump bald-headed European standing in the back doorway of the hall. At first guess, Henry took the man for a plain-clothes detective – the man had such a self-composed, official stance – but then, behind Wollenhoven's bulky shoulders, and with a sudden sea-sick swoop which mixed panic and jealousy, he saw Stewart. Stewart was talking urgently to the small, inscrutable man. Henry suddenly wanted to leave; by mere presence, Stewart plundered his composure.

While Rycliffe read the note the audience shifted restlessly. For a moment he looked confused, and glanced at Stewart who nodded vigorously. The small, bald-headed man merely blinked his eyelids once.

A buzz of irritation rose from the audience. Someone shouted, 'Go on, get on with it!' and there were murmurs of agreement.

Like a high priest about to deliver benediction, Rycliffe put out both hands.

'My friends!' he proclaimed. 'My friends!' He waited dramatically for total attention. 'I was invited here to speak. But no one said about what. I was supposed to speak in favour of Albert Holmes.' The audience seemed to converge attention on the abrupt jerking round of Holmes' face. 'But I cannot.' Holmes' body went stiff: eyes terrified, yet fascinated like snake prey. Rycliffe did not even glance in his direction. 'I cannot. Not because I have anything against Albert, personally. No, my friends, on the personal level, we are old friends. But on the political level, we are enemies. Politically we part from one another, and today, we must grow even farther apart. For today, my friends, it has become clear to me that I should offer myself to you as an alternative candidate – '

In the tumult that greeted this pronouncement, hats were thrown into the air; the din was so deafening that Rycliffe could not continue.

He used the uproar to tear the note into small shreds and to deposit it in a coat pocket.

It was now that the real trouble started. Holmes rose, and shouted some words but was drowned in another crescendo of shouting. The *skollies* who had been lounging against the walls went into action, but before they could reach the stage, the younger members of the *Flame* group, led by Wollenhoven, who materialised beyond the footlights, rose together and linked arms forming a double phalanx between the *skollies* and the stage. There were a few light skirmishes, then a general *mêlée*; bottles and chairs flew, women shrieked, people surged towards the exits.

Henry found himself carried in the stampede towards a side exit. In the street, mass fighting was in progress; people were dispersing in several directions. Henry felt someone clasp him by the arm; he turned to retaliate, but it was Old Man Parsons, who said, 'Come . . . quick! . . . with me!' He led Henry down a side alley to the dirty backyard of a small ramshackle house surrounded on all sides by a high, brown, wooden fence. In the house were three other members of the Tenant's Association, and presently they were joined by eight more. Only one member had been injured in the fracas, and couldn't attend. All wanted to discuss the meeting, but Mr Parsons brought them to order. Now that Rycliffe's stand was clear, he said, they had to decide what to do themselves.

The impromptu meeting lasted several hours. Henry sat quietly in a corner of the small, crowded, drab parlour, listening to the others, and feeling like someone who has been jolted awake from an all-commanding dream. Gradually, he pulled himself together, and began to make rapid notes on the back of an envelope. When he had quite settled his views, he waited for an opening and made a series of practical proposals.

With two exceptions, Mr Parsons and a tailor by the name of Karim Ismail, none present had any first-hand political experience. At the first meeting, they had been modest and attentive to Mr Parsons and, more particularly, to Henry, whose professional qualifications gave his every recommendation an authoritative ring. But at the next meeting, finding that their own views were not merely welcome, but actually signified that what they proposed could be written into the principles and future activities of the Association, they soon lost their lack of self-assurance and at once a feeling of cohesion and personal responsibility began to prevail. What Henry proposed was therefore received critically. Ismail was first to point out the extravagances. In principle, Henry was right, a broadsheet exposing Shaikh-Moosa, Holmes and Rycliffe ought to be printed and distributed; but Ismail wondered whether such a tactic was premature. He knew Rycliffe himself, had played cricket with him, and had in fact cut several suits for him; he did not agree with Rycliffe's socialistic views, but opined that, unlike Holmes, Rycliffe was 'a man of the people' and therefore ought to be given an opportunity to declare himself more specifically. The rest of the meeting concurred with this view, and it was left to Henry to draft a letter of special invitation to Dr Rycliffe to attend the Delegates' meeting the next day, to be held in the lounge of the Stakesby-Lewis Hotel. The final agenda of this Delegates' meeting was drawn up, and after a short financial report and an appeal for contributions, the gathering broke up.

When he returned home, Henry was groggy with words, yet his mind would not rest and kept turning to the events of the evening, and to future problems of the Tenant's Association. Doc was not at home, but a bottle of his whisky stood in the living-room, and Henry had a few glasses, hoping that the whisky would have anaesthetic effects: that he would be able to get to sleep easily. The whisky induced a feeling of loneliness. After a few more glasses which were meant to wipe away this feeling, he went to the kitchen where a particular sight gored him. He had been training himself to ration certain kinds of introspection. Doc had, as usual, forgotten to clear away the remains of his supper, and a half-eaten bunch of grapes lay on a plate on the draining-board. At once the image pounced – Katherine, in a red headscarf and blue dress, appearing in his office suddenly, her eyes at once gay and vulnerable, offering the brown paper bag and saying almost apologetically, laughing, 'I brought you these 'cos it's my birthday!' He heard her voice again as if she had actually spoken and it sent a flaw of pain through him 'Oh Heavens!' he said to himself, audibly, 'heavens!' He took up the grapes as if they were part of his own body – a vital organ, perhaps – surgically removed, and stared at them as if they were not quite real: as if he could not quite understand their significance. Perhaps it was the void, perhaps the whisky, but suddenly he started to cry. It was only the second time in a long while he had allowed himself to do so, and he felt curtains were being drawn very finally across a portion of his life.

The meeting the next evening drew a bumper attendance. Henry had spent the morning drafting the letter to Rycliffe and clearing away routine legal problems. Shaikh-Moosa's expenses cheque had arrived and been cashed, but so far, the main bill had brought no response. It was rumoured that the Great Man had left town. Henry decided to wait a week before sending a reminder. Meanwhile, he was financially out of the red, so he was able to use the afternoon preparing for the meeting, without any further pangs of conscience.

The preparation proved to be a waste of time; the meeting assumed a logic of its own, but produced no spectacular results. Action was a general desire which clipped wings of debate. A new Executive was elected; a monster meeting, properly advertised, followed by a demonstration, was to be arranged by the Executive, and was to take place immediately after New Year's Day celebrations, on the Parade – the huge square carpark which stood in front of the City Hall. Henry was elected Organising Secretary of the new Executive. The best satisfaction to be drawn from the meeting was that the Tenant's Association now spoke for a wider, more representative public.

The meeting took place in the lounge of the hostel, and might just as well have been held in the living-room in Newlands, for it shared with similar rooms all over the world – men's prisons, school dormitories, YMCA common rooms – that peculiar neutered emptiness and impermanence which invests an atmosphere when the sexes are segregated. Rycliffe did not turn up, nor did the Communist Party, but several older socialists of another generation – the generation of the purges – did. These latter were a curious medley of humanitarians and independents who serve causes only as long as they don't smack of regimentation. Among them were two souls with whom Henry was later to make deeper acquaintance. Though unmarried, the two lived in a small low-rental house in Mowbray. Indeed, they had lived together over thirty years, and from a glance, anyone could see that their temperaments were eminently suited to each other. They seemed to be bound by those ties of affection and mutual respect often found in common law marriages. The old man was still on the vigorous side of seventy; he had a large head, large hands, and large bones; his hair was grey; and he had the friendly, innocent eyes of a young boy. He wore clumsy boots and clothes of the kind that can be bought in street markets. He had come to South Africa early in the century, from a village in Yorkshire, and he still retained intact that warm broad dialect of northern England. He had been responsible for the foundation of several Trade Unions and, indeed, the Communist Party in which he had long been a prominent member until the Party came under Moscow control. Thereafter, with many others, he had been purged and had gradually weaned himself towards views akin to a kind of Tolstoyan pacifism. He worked as a cabinet maker, spent his leisure wood-carving and selling socialist tracts which he composed and printed himself, and was known, in the African townships, affectionately as 'the old man with the boots.' He and Miss Martha lived frugally, gave most of their lean earnings to the poor and kept a vertitable zoo of stray animals – several dogs, cats, goats, two horses, and even a monkey – which they had collected over the years. Whereas Mr Percy, as he was called, was characteristically large-boned, quiet and slow, Miss Martha was lean, active, and quick. She had the small, intelligent eyes of a bird, and a face with the fine bones and complexion of people often found in religious orders. Indeed, till the age of thirty-five, she had been a nun, but had renounced the veil. She had been trained as a midwife, and because she now gave her service free or for a pittance to the poor, she was still, though almost sixty, in demand.

The old man had been elected unanimously Chairman of the new Executive, and because the office called for immediate consultation, he and Henry were invited, after the meeting, to the room which Mr Parsons rented in the hostel. The small company was not in the room half-an-hour when news of the first of several tragedies reached them. They had settled publicity for the monster meeting and the order of speakers, when Ismail, the tailor, burst in with the news that Jonathan December, Mr Parsons' nephew, had been found badly beaten up in a nearby back alley. There was nothing that could be done; an ambulance had already carted the unfortunate young man away. It was eleven o'clock now, but it was decided at once to hold an Executive meeting to discuss this new development.

It was quite clear that the assault had not been accidental. Before adjourning to Mr Parsons' room, Henry had lent Jonathan his car and, because it was a cold wet night, his raincoat as well. The idea had been that Jonathan would go home and smuggle a bottle of whisky into the hostel when he returned. But he had no sooner returned than he had been set upon by a small gang of *skollies*, who had dragged him into an alley and there delivered the beating that had knocked him senseless and bleeding onto wet cobblestones. The whisky bottle, his purse, and the keys to Henry's car, having been left intact, were circumstances that supported pre-meditation, and the next day, when Jonathan was slightly recovered, he confirmed that the *skollies* – one of whom he recognised as Drama Johnny, a member of Wollenhoven's gang – had mistaken him for Henry, and had repeatedly warned him to 'mind his own business.'

Several members of the Executive, which had been assembled with impressive despatch, favoured the formation of a vigilante group of local toughs to deal with any further threat of violence, but both Henry and Mr Percy, who were strongly opposed to any form of strongarm protection, eventually carried the argument. All agreed that a broadsheet, tersely setting out the machinations of Shaikh-Moosa, Rycliffe and Holmes should be circulated, and the meeting broke up with Henry, Mr Percy and Miss Martha leaving together to write and print the proposed broadsheet.

It was four o'clock when Henry got to bed that night, and because he rose late and did not reach his office 'till early afternoon the next day, he was quite unprepared for the series of events and rumours which were following hard and thick upon one another.

His first suprise was a long-distance telephone call from Paarl. Elizabeth wanted the news of the 'beating-up' of last night confirmed.

When he had fully related the incident, she asked after Katherine: a question put with such courtesy that Henry could not cut her short. In a slightly choked voice, he answered that the had been rather too busy to see Katherine, then quickly switched the conversation.

Shortly afterwards, word arrived that Shaikh-Moosa had not merely fled town, but had sold all his District Six properties. Fylfot Holdings, it was claimed, now belonged to a firm of Afrikaaner Nationalists who were assembling an armed mob of *ducktails* or European hooligans to move in if any demonstration against rent increases occurred.

Yet another rumour concerned Shaikh-Moosa. In one report, he was supposed to have shot himself; in another, to have been shot in Johannesburg by *ducktails* employed by the Nationalists; and when the question, 'Which Nationalists?' was asked, the reply, 'Afrikaaner of course!' was delivered with such certainty that it satisfied no one. Later on, Henry heard another story. It was now 'quite positively' suggested that an African had assassinated Shaikh-Moosa and that this African, a vagrant, had made several previous unsuccessful attempts upon the Great Man's life. Henry heard the crowning tale when he went for afternoon coffee. He bumped into one of Rycliffe's followers who insisted that, far from being dead, Shaikh-Moosa had decamped to an island off the coast of South-West Africa which he had recently bought. He had taken with him shiploads of goods with which to set up a trading station. In Henry's opinion this particular tale 'just about took the biscuit'; in his diary, he reports, 'Capitalism becoming Imperialism. Only the Rycliffe people could have dreamt up *that* one!'

Direct enquiries at the office of Fylfot Holdings were unrewarding; the man in charge would say nothing; it was like trying to fix shadows with pins.

Meanwhile, late in the afternoon, higher up in Hanover Street three events, which Henry was never to hear about, took place.

The first concerned Gordon Stewart. At half-past four, wearing nondescript clothes and a particularly taut expression, and carrying a small, heavy suitcase, he arrived at the side door of a certain dilapidated tenement house. Having rapped a distinctive tattoo on the knocker, he was admitted by a grimy-toothed hag who led him through a room, bare except for a few tables – used after midnight as a gambling den – into a smaller back-room which seethed with the smells of sweat and stale marihuana smoke and cheap alcohol. He received here a stony greeting from five men who had arrived earlier and now sat waiting without exchanging any but a few necessary remarks.

The other two events concerned Yussouf Rycliffe. While Stewart was meeting his assistants, Rycliffe was visited by a man who, answering to the name of Gromeko, gained instant admission to his surgery. This meeting was rather shorter than Stewart's, and indeed, much shorter than the one which took place a few hours later, when Rycliffe's nurse was putting up the blinds in the waiting room, having just let out the last patient. This time the nurse did not need a name, but recognised the woman with pleasure and surprise and told her that the doctor was still in the consulting-room. The woman thanked her graciously and passed through the waiting-room with an air of someone thoroughly accustomed to her surroundings. Before she opened the consulting-room door, however, she paused and her expression of calm momentarily deserted her. Her hands trembled slightly, and a look of fear glazed her eyes.

When she at last entered the room, the same look of a shocked, hunted animal was repeated in Rycliffe's eyes. He had taken off his surgical coat and had been lying on the couch, resting, after an arduous day. Now he half-rose and said in a choked voice, 'Oh God, Oh God! Not you!' Then, he slumped back onto the couch, this time to a sitting position, and buried his face in his hands like a small boy weeping.

Elizabeth Peters sat down in the chair behind his desk, and took off her gloves with exaggerated calm. Then she laid her handbag on the desk, crossed fingers under chin, elbows on the desk, like someone praying, and contemplated Rycliffe whose face was still buried in his hands. His collar was unbuttoned, his tie askew, his shirt-sleeves clumsily rolled to the elbows.

After a long silence, as if from the depths of a grave, Rycliffe groaned, and without looking up, asked her what she wanted.

Elizabeth, too, had difficulty speaking; her voice was unusually rusty.

''Sain,' she said, boldly, calling him by a pet name; his second Christian name was Hoosain. 'Have I ever asked you for anything?'

Rycliffe neither replied nor looked up.

''Sain?' Elizabeth repeated, more gently. 'Just two things.'

Again Rycliffe waited; and again Elizabeth found speech difficult.

'First,' she at last heaved, and hawked nervously, 'I want . . . I want to know where Katherine is.' Her voice was low, yet it was streaked with hysteria.

Now, Rycliffe looked up, eyes bloodshot and startled.

'I don't know,' he said, almost as a whimper. 'Honest Injun! I really don't know, my dear.'

Elizabeth explained. Katherine had been missing since Christmas Eve, five days now; no one had seen or heard from her; even her father was growing anxious. Rycliffe seemed surprised. He promised to make enquiries; then he asked for the second point of her mission. Again, Elizabeth was hesitant.

'I don't want you wrongly accused,' she said at last, 'but all I've heard isn't very pretty. Tell me, 'Sain, is it your people who beat up that young man last night?'

Again Rycliffe looked up, calmer now.

'Tell me. I won't hold it against you.'

Rycliffe did not answer.

'I won't hold it against you,' Elizabeth repeated, 'but if it is your people who're responsible, I want you to call them off!'

Rycliffe grimaced, shut one fist, and pounded it in the air.

'Have you read the broadsheet?' he asked at last.

Elizabeth nodded.

'Well, how can I do that?' he demanded with suppressed, yet plaintive bitterness, 'I'm fighting for my life, my darling!'

Elizabeth looked at him scornfully, then calmly opened her handbag and extracted a small bundle of papers wrapped in a rubber band, which she held up for examination.

'You know what these are?' she asked grimly.

The papers possessed enough horror to drive all blood from Rycliffe's sullen face.

'I think they belong to you.' She dropped them quietly on the desk. 'Just a gesture,' she said.

'I'll pay,' Rycliffe announced, still aghast. 'Ready cash!'

'Ye Gods!' Elizabeth replied, with sad contempt. 'Money! You!'

Rycliffe now looked thoroughly wretched.

'Oh, now. Not *you*. Not *you*, 'Sain! *Money!*'

Each word was the stab of a dagger.

'And I used to think you were a *gentleman*: that you had a sense of *honour*. Whee! How the mighty have fallen. The language of bankers and traders. And to *me*, 'Sain, to me! Years of love – flushed down the scuppers! No, you take them now. They're yours after all, my darling . . .' Emotion momentarily strangled her voice. ' – have them free, gratis, for nothing! Have them. For old time's sake. I don't want anything.'

She rose, but Rycliffe was too stunned to see her out.

After long brooding, he went to his desk and untied the bundle. It consisted of a large number of pawn tickets, all descriptions of women's jewellery, the title-deeds to two properties, now made out in his name, and a scrap of paper which, though it was no more than a hospital bill, sent tears into his eyes. Now he remembered London, a visit to the Derby which had furnished the cash that had freed him from the panic that he might be struck off the medical rolls, the cash which had sent 'The Princess' to a certain grimy street in Lambeth, two months pregnant, and when she returned, empty of fruit, a person no longer capable of love – not, at least, for him. He laid the scraps of memory, like playing cards in a game of patience, on the desk and, for a long time, considered them. At last, he folded them into an envelope, which he sealed and addressed to Elizabeth. Then, he picked up the telephone and made two calls – one to Gromeko, the other to Wollenhoven.

It was only much later that night that the news became public that Yussouf Rycliffe had withdrawn from the Election, and that the *Flame* group advised people in District Six to boycott the forthcoming election.

CHAPTER 10

During the two days before the monster meeting on the Parade, Henry's office was a cluttered whirlpool; faces, names, dates, instructions spun endlessly in and out, recurring at different levels of certainty and unsureness, circulating like tags or emblems or even more material manifestations of uncertain natural forces which were winding with fury to a preordained climax. The days resembled the alternating clarity and chaos that precedes a complex lawsuit, presaging now success, now a trial so vague and hopeless as not to warrant launching. Among the steadiest helpers was Jessie who anchored to Henry's typewriter with the tenacity of a barnacle; she stayed long after the others left. Pieter had postponed his departure for a few days, so, to replace the anxiety of waiting, Jessie had thrown herself consummately into her uncle's affairs. During those two days, Henry's admiration for her increased; she was unobtrusive, gentle, careful, industrious; in many ways, rather like his mother, and as he grew to know her better, his trust grew, and soon she became, during his more sombre, less buoyant moods, another trustee of intimate disclosures. It was, in fact, to her that he unburdened himself about Katherine, and from her that he drew the most generous solace. It was, indeed, from her that he eventually found out what had happened to Katherine, but that was only a few days later when he had been released from gaol. In the meantime, District Six was moodily quiet. Even New Year's Day, that year, had less dash and colour and spectacle than usual. An atmosphere of unreality crept into festivities. An international beverage firm had paid for the Coon costumes, and the men pranced through the dull, drizzly streets, rather like technicolour ghosts.

Although preparations for the meeting moved forward apace, pushed from within, attempts – inspired mainly by Henry – were made to negotiate a private settlement. A deputation was sent to the Mayor asking for laws clearly outlining the rights of tenants and also that rents be fixed by graduated scale. But the Mayor was busy and failed to acknowledge the gravity of the situation; he confessed that 'his hands were tied' until the Municipal Elections were over, and enjoined the deputation to do the absurd, that is, to 'have a word with Councillor Holmes'. The deputation came away with the impression that it was composed of a collection of cranks – a feeling which strengthened the general desire to draw attention by a show of collective power.

Another deputation was sent to the offices of Fylfot Holdings but met with less success. The man there confirmed the obvious, namely, that he had no authority to speak for the company: he would not say that the rents were going up, nor would he comment on the rumour that the company had been recently sold. It was Abu's belief that this story was just another of his uncle's manoeuvres, that even if the directors had changed names, his uncle was more than likely to be lurking in the shadows, preparing another volte-face. Since this view supported the general impressions of Shaikh-Moosa's cunning, it was accepted.

Attempts were also made to rouse support among the *Flame* group, but here the revelations of the broadsheet had quite shut out chances of a rapprochement. The *Flame* group was divided from within. The majority held that it was no function of a revolutionary party to be concerned in municipal politics; the party should 'overthrow capitalism and the entire system of Government which supported it'. Participation in elections, therefore, could amount to 'no more than bargains with the *Herrenvolk*, and would be class, historical, and revolutionary treachery, nothing short of a sell out, a trading-in of all that the group stood for and had fought for,' or as Rycliffe now dramatically announced, 'a compromise, my friends, black and distasteful!' Until recently, this majority had been only a faction. The earlier view, the one advocated by Rycliffe, had garnered force from Bolshevik representation in the Duma or, again as Rycliffe had put it, 'the need for strong, uncompromising, articulate representatives in these *Herrenvolk* institutions, in the democratic facade . . . the need for another forum in which to propagate socialist and revolutionary ideas, to represent the interests of the International Proletariat!' Like all well-read Marxists, Rycliffe could always shift Marx and Lenin and Trotsky to his own purposes, could always find an objective argument to support subjective intuition. The opposition of his erstwhile chief, Gromeko, had been disquieting; the disclosures of the Tenant's Association and the conflicting rumours about Shaikh-Moosa's disappearance had eroded confidence further; Elizabeth's final appeal had merely strengthened his desire 'to play politics from a distance,' not to endanger his popularity and equivocal social position any further. Hence the boycott line. But there remained some within the group still annexed to the older view, and others, like Benjamin Michaels who, for mixed motives, favoured support of the Tenant's Association.

While Gromeko was a first generation Marxist, and Rycliffe a second, Michaels belonged to the third generation. His opposition to Rycliffe sprang from his being 'the next in line in the leadership struggle', hence, he tended in principle to contest whatever position Rycliffe assumed, and he knew that to gain a following, he had to prove himself in active politics. He suspected that Rycliffe's refusal to associate with the Tenant's Association was akin to Holmes': Rycliffe stood to lose. Michaels, by contrast, had nothing to lose; he contended that if a political group attempted to 'keep its own hands idealistically clean,' it would not merely lose popular support but 'the relevance of an ideology to concrete political situations.' Michaels also saw that Rycliffe's withdrawal from the election left a gap, and he was sharp enough to sense that if Holmes shied away from the Tenant's Association, his popularity would completely end. Among the Executive of the Tenant's Association, moreover, there was no one either competent or sufficiently interested to oppose Holmes. Michaels, therefore, put himself at once at the disposal of the Tenant's Association and because, like so many of the *Flame* group, he was a practised orator, he was billed as one of the chief speaking attractions.

Rycliffe's reaction to his former associate's 'careerism' or, as he said, 'ratting on the movement', was to bring out a special edition of *The Flame* which, without mentioning Michaels by name, suggested that 'there were quislings everywhere' and that, as Trotsky had so clearly pointed out, 'bourgeois-democratic politics were merely a facade which rationalised the most iniquitous property relations!'

Within all these giddy cross-currents, Henry had difficulty settling his own convictions. Was he standing on those principles of natural rights he advocated so fervently, or merely attempting to exorcise the ghost of Katherine, throwing himself headlong into work which rescued him from thought and pain? The words of one of his favourite poets kept recurring, 'the busy are the loveless'; he felt he was becoming a mouthpiece for preconceived ideas, and had difficulty squaring this feeling with his belief in responsible choice.

The turn out at the meeting was large, but not 'phenomenal'. The newspapers put attendance at between three and four thousand. It was a mild summer afternoon. Car owners had difficulty finding parking space. The vast square opposite the City Hall was jammed; a raised platform faced the Central Railway Station, so that guest speakers could see, beyond the crowd and over the station walls, Peninsula trains arriving and leaving. On the fringes of the crowd, men with baskets sold peanuts, sweetmeats and pamphlets. When it was four o'clock by the Railway clock, the march was about to begin; pigeons and other birds fluttered from the roof of the new Post Office building to the dome of the City Hall; around the platform, banners with slogans were being undraped, and a few militants who held up placards bearing slogans were getting into line.

Except for Michaels and Mr Percy, the speakers had been poor. Henry had been only competent: he had been obviously tense and had repeated himself excessively. Though it was he who had been chosen to lead the march to the buildings of Parliament, it was Michaels, tall and cold, but compelling, with rimless glasses glinting on a hard aquiline face, who, as the newspapers were later to say, 'got the people moving'. And yet when the first detachments of police arrived it was Michaels who disappeared, and Henry who was among the first arrests.

The marchers had barely reached Adderly Street when the explosions were heard; within minutes there was chaos. Earlier, only a single Maria with one constable and two bored, dapper plain-clothes men supervising a wire recording, had stood near the platform; but once the meeting started to move, more and more police vans began to arrive, so that when the procession was within sight of the Public Library, the entrance to the Gardens had been cordoned off, and at that moment the bombs went off. Panic was general: a flailing of arms and truncheons and people rushing in several directions. Half-an-hour later Adderly Street had been completely cleared, and several arrests made.

Fortunately for Henry he was detained one night only. He was released on bail, but charged to appear for trial in six days' time. His night in gaol was, as he writes in his diary, 'a kind of puzzle, a mixture

163

of disbelief and gradual despair'. He felt as if he had become a pawn of alien forces and had difficulty adjusting to the bleak, ugliness of the cell. In his last diary, he records that it took him some time to understand imprisonment:

I look at the walls to corroborate this suspicion, to reassure myself that I am celibate, cannot open doors at will, that I can see the world only through a rusty, barred grating. Now I know how Africans feel: their unabating confinement. The atmosphere smells like a men's hostel: too many unwashed bodies in close, airless confinement, a dank underground smell of rotting blankets and harsh chemical antiseptics. Food tastes neutral. I sit on a rough horsehair blanket not quite believing that I am alive. I lie down on a hard straw mattress which rustles, and am conscious of sensations – of the coarseness of the mattress, of my body, of the unreality of my thoughts. I try to sleep. It is dark. Occasional footsteps and voices and clanging cell doors. Whenever I wake up my limbs are numb, and the side I have been lying on is cramped. I scarcely believe I have been asleep, but soon doze off again, knowing full well I shall wake again, soon, with the same nauseating disbelief, the same wretched exhaustion around the eyes.

Initially his consciousness and attentions were superficial. He was struck by the confinement of his cell and the capacity of his mind to journey wherever it chose. He was equally impressed by the absence of meaning in his thought. Now that he had time, there was no justification for not thinking. There was no more reason for having to be practical. And yet he couldn't think constructively.

God, he writes, in his diaries, *has not assembled a cosmic plot that can be unsealed by reason. Life is not a legal birthday. There is no logic between what has been – the past – and what might be – the future. South Africa has spawned in me a past without a future. South Africa has eclipsed all practical dreams.*

Perhaps this is why – in gaol – I was unable to focus my thinking. There were no native patterns. Memory supplanted thinking. I tried hard to impress webs of purpose over the random events of my life. But logic evaded me like the loss of true liberty in that cell.

What absorbed me more totally were images, and sometimes, the most excruciating memories.

Two memories produced my mother.

164

When I tried to think of my childhood – and what had made me – I recalled instead Zululand. As a boy I used to listen to the Zulu women: their dark, liquid voices. I used to watch them, distant at their songs, babies lashed to their backs, as they walked in slow dignity along the shale-shining gorges of that magnificent summer countryside – valleys of rolling caneland, green and yellow under torrid sun, knolls of dry open veldt with aloes, wattles, and thorntrees bristling above dense nests of subtropical jungle.

Who am I?

My first memory is of the bare, earth yard of a large plantation in which a great, scraggy turkey – or is it a moorhen? – brilliantly feathered, swaggers among motley smaller fowl. The out-houses are white walled and jigsawed with cracks, plaster peeling, waved tin roofs, a silent sputter of silver-blue in the noon sun. In one of them – a single raftered room; cold at night and in the rainy season; airy in summer – our family cooked, ate and slept.

Once, when I was seventeen, visiting a country friend, I re-experienced quite unexpectedly the atmosphere of that out-house room – a Proustian sensation . . . the calling, tightening, irrecoverable reunion of smell and place. A hurricane lantern, suspended from a rafter, was lit and out of the diffused light, impregnated with the confusing smells of cow-dung – or mist, as it was called – of the bare hardened floor, of paraffin and the richer resins of wood-smoke arose an original floor, wood and charcoal fire-red in its surround of greyish ash, grate of black bricks, large iron cauldron smoking with curry, brass bedsteads (a new acquisition), packing cases which served as tables and clothes chests, and then . . . most poignantly of all, image blown awake through heart's whimpering muscles, tragic swoop of belly and loins . . . knowledge of profound love . . . mother, young again, so tragically young, her sari of coarse white gauze, and she pounding and rolling spices out on the intagliated hollow of a lead-coloured, stone mortar.

That memory recalled others. I remembered at once how father used to leave home in the half-light of early morning – the cocks would not have crowed yet – in a summer sky still a distant curtain behind fresh darkness. But mother would have lit the primus stove – or primus, as everyone called it – strong tea in the billy-can would be brewing, and father – a man of medium build, young, hair still tousled – wearing long-legged white underpants which served as pyjamas, would be climbing into a pair of soiled trousers that reached only to the shins where they frayed and snarled. He would pass around the plump post of waist a strip of cord or even a string of an old tie so that the trousers, which were too large, might never inconveniently descend to subvert that quality of character about which he was most particularly sensitive – his dignity.

My parents would follow this morning ritual wordlessly, rather as if they were parts of a universal clock which denied natural alternatives. An Indian woman of our class and mother's generation treated a husband as if he incorporated deity. Moreover, mother had a reticent disposition – a feature which pleased her husband, himself not a man of many words.

Father would do his shaving in a shard of looking-glass pinned to the plaster above one of the beds. After breakfast – warmed-up dahl and chaparties and strong orange-coloured tea – a red muffler tucked into his collarless shirt, hair black and stiff with cheap sticky brillantine, he would set off for the sugar mills not to reappear before dark of evening.

One day he came home early, with a large green lorry which smelt pleasantly of diesel oil and sheep. Our possessions were herded into the rear, and away we went – driving hard all night until, in gelid light of dawn, we came to a broad slow river spanned by a wonderful steel bridge. A settlement of a dozen or so wood-an'-iron houses clustered anxiously around a trading store at the foot of a low green spur.

This was Umgeni, now a suburb of Durban, where the rest of my childhood was spent.

That was one memory; the other was more excruciating.

Even today I invariably think of her as she appears in the only photograph I have. She is dressed in a wrapper, the sari of the poor. A woman of below medium height. She stands in front of a fading mango tree. A shawl or orni, decorated with a braid of flowers, shuts off her hair except for a grey-black strip across the temples. Although she looks patient, one detects in her stance an element of guilt as if she should be elsewhere, fetching water perhaps, on her head, from the trading store tap, or cleaning the household brassware which she polished so assiduously.

When I showed Katherine this 'snap' – which is what she called it, surprised that I should keep it and other treasures padlocked in a suit-case under my bed – she exclaimed unexpectedly, 'But she's beautiful! Exquisite! You have her cheekbones and her eyes – so soft and gentle and round.'

At the time the comment was embarrassing because I very seldom think or bother about how I look. Now it is strange, not just because it belongs to a beautiful, painful, irredeemable shared past but rather because, as I told Adrian recently, 'Beautiful or ugly are words you don't use about people you have lived with a long time: people you're used to.'

I remember traits of character better – the gravity, the gentle silence, above all: the unobtrusive resourcefulness.

Indeed it was this final trait remembered, which produced the most unexpected pain. Is that true? Or was it the memory of her – on the back verandah, crying – that resurrected her resourcefulness?

After the sugar mills, my father drifted restlessly from one job to another. He was not home for long spells, and often only represented himself in an irregular flow of registered letters.

Not until I met Guriah was I made aware of how low – how close to the crucifixions of poverty – the funds of our household sometimes reached.

Of course neither of my parents ever gave so much as a hint of straitened circumstances. Theirs was a generation which was stoic, which never confided in children.

It is only now, when I look back, that I can guess what had happened. At the time I took her ingenuity for granted.

When our circumstances were most reduced, she would 'dump' me on a neighbour, or when I was older, simply leave our small, three-roomed bungalow in my charge, and off she'd go to ply her services as a washer-woman among the European rich of Durban North.

A week or so before I unexpectedly came across her on the back porch, she'd made a wicker basket and gone house to house hawking the tomatoes and carrots, runner beans, paw-paws, grenadellas and custard-apples which she'd grown in the back garden.

It was a shock to find her crying. On her lap was the handkerchief in which she used to knot coins, wrapped in paper notes, and as she stared at its emptiness, fingers twisting and untwisting the already crumpled linen, tears ran down her otherwise expressionless cheeks. In her face was the look I was later so often to encounter in Katherine's – a look of total vulnerability.

I never did find out what had happened, whether she had been cheated by her European clients, or more simply whether the money had been lost or stolen. What was clear was that she had been trying so hard to make ends meet, and now she was exhausted.

Equally painful for Henry was what he learned – again by accident – about his father. In gaol, he remembered his father as an old man with a grey thinning pate: a man who ate alone, slept alone, and sat in a special cane chair on the wooden back verandah.

There – his diaries record – *he sat, an old man, shoes and socks removed, trousers rolled, like someone at the seaside, tired blood running blue down varicosed legs which a wrinkled hand periodically and reflectively massaged. The porch stood on brick stilts – a gap of about two to three feet between floorboards and ground. He sat for hours, there, in that chair, scarcely moving, recuperating from goodness alone knew what economic debauchery; dreaming, while noisy fowls scuttling from roosts under the house fed in the slashed netted mud, and gusts of weak wind rattled bright green tears of rain out of the thorny mutangula hedges. He would fall asleep, sometimes, head dropped to one shoulder, mouth snoring open; other times, he would sit motionless, forehead puckered, blood-shot eyes baffled by the Burman Bush – a hill overlooking the backyard – as if fate had inducted him into a species of minor chieftainship, had left him there, stripped of all faculties except that of impotent observation. Each year brought fresh changes to the Burman Bush; each year, my father slept less and less, as if the ravage to which he was a witness represented a process within himself, as if forsaking the Bush he had expediently abandoned territory of self that now lay beyond will and choice and quite definitely beyond check, relief, or repair.*

The early diaries treat his father first with awe, later with scorn and fear. What, later still, reversed this strange distaste was Henry's encounter with a man called Guriah.

The encounter took place on Grey Street, the appositely named main artery of Durban Indian commerce. It was on Shaikh-Moosa's behalf that Henry had returned to Durban, and the best account of the accidental meeting is in a letter to Katherine – a letter never sent.

Katherine, dearest Katherine, (the letter begins)

Since my last letter I have, by pure accident, come across an overwhelming piece of information. It concerns my father. I cannot tell you how ashamed I feel. You will remember I always believed him a rather stupid man. Till now the conduct of his last year always seemed beneath contempt. I even blamed that last year for my mother's death! Fancy going to work for those Grey Street swine! No excuse.

Now I realise what a fool, what a callous, unthinking ingrate I am!

I cannot go into detail at the moment, but, as you know, the thought of being back in Durban, of somehow having lost you somewhere in transit, made me more than a bit miserable. I'd done most of what I'd come to clear up. (I was wrong, incidentally: Desai's flats are straightforward real estate – no strings attached.

I'm having to revise feelings on several scores!) I had just left a pot of flowers on my mother's grave when I met Guriah. Funny isn't it, sometimes, when you're thinking of a person, someone else mentions that person? Perhaps that's why we've coined the phrase, 'Speak of the devil'. I was going down Grey Street, thinking about my father, not feeling much, just thinking of him in that last year when he got tangled up with the big warehouses, when quite by accident, I met his old crony, Guriah. The man was quite delighted to see me (he recognised me at once, so I can't have changed that much, after all!) He was so pleased, he took me to coffee in a small, new tea-room next to the 'Royal' bioscope, or rather next to where the 'Royal' used to stand. (I remember the 'Royal' well. As children, we used to call it 'The Imperial' because we had a curious idea that 'Royal' and 'Imperial' were identical words; perhaps we wanted to show how smart we could be!)

Well, after a lot of conventional twaddle about how different I looked now, how I'd grown, etc., Guriah asked what it felt like to be back. I was in a black mood. Durban, and particularly the Grey Street area, gave me a sense of being contaminated. Perhaps this was a reflex of guilt for having taken on this assignment. I wanted to rid myself of the bad taste Grey Street left in the mouth, to free myself in an assertion of scorn and superiority. But the bloody thing backfired! I let poor Guriah have a piece of my mind, and he listened patiently – poor fellow – frowning. I happened to include my father in the reckless diatribe. He had been one of my father's closest friends. It was clear that his feelings were hurt. I tried to make amends. I offered him another coffee. He refused. I tried a dozen moves to get the pain out of his face. Anything to salve conscience, to apologise for rudeness. Things became sticky. Though I wanted to leave, somehow I couldn't, and he sat looking at me, cold, frowning, also unable to move. I was the boy who had made good, returning to his home-town, what a prodigal, what an ass! so full of airs and self-importance! For a while, he went on looking at me, speechless, his face a tight mask of pain and censure. Finally, he said quietly, very firmly (as if he had long wondered whether I deserved the comforts of human speech) 'You're wrong! Quite wrong! You don't know the first thing about it!'

My first instinct was to bluster back, but – what was it? The certainty of his tone? The impression that he spoke not merely out of loyalty to my father? – something stopped me. Then he let me have it – straight from the shoulder. He was angry, furious in fact, and justly so. And when I'd heard him out, I didn't know what to say. The damage was done. I'd shot my bolt. Now there was nothing for it but to bear the pain of stupidity, to eat humble pie.

What he told me was a revelation, and I still can't get over it.

Can you imagine? The reason my father got mixed up with the Grey Street shysters was on my account! I couldn't at first believe it, but gradually dimly remembered facts began to fit together. Error was like the brand of hot steel: I reddened with shame.

I told you, remember, of how after father's funeral, mother had said that a trust had been set up to put me through University. Like father, she was matter of fact and never explained costs. (And I used to condemn him for leaving me so little, for forcing me to eke out my pittance with extraneous earnings!)

The whole thing puts his degradation in a new light. After our final interview – about a year before his death – he had said, vaguely, but now I know, deliberately, (his altruism was almost boundless!) that he would manage something towards my University expenses. He was so imprecise that I remember thinking that he found the affair an encumbrance and that he was not going to do much about it. Very good, I thought, I'll just have to go it alone, thank you for nothing, and I'll know where true obligations lie. Foolishness! From Guriah's report, the business of putting me through University became an obsession. He told no one, but he began to stint himself outrageously. He cut down on food, stopped smoking, forced himself to make do with one suit and pawned the rest. He was fond of going, once a week, to 'bioscope' – a childish thing, he was addicted to cowboy films (probably where he learnt his morality) – but he stopped going altogether. Guriah says that at his death, his friends clubbed together to buy him a pair of shoes so that he might be buried as he had wanted, fully dressed, or as he himself had said, 'respectable'! A piece of absurdity, really, for what does it matter how one is buried? – little things like this haunt. Can you imagine what shoes mean to a commercial traveller? At his death, his own were quite rent, he used to fill them with newspaper, and to preserve that unaltering dignity that was characteristic, he used to blacken the paper where it showed through the sole. But his friends knew. Some had already begun to shun him because he had become something of a scrounge; others because his breath stank – he had refused to go to a doctor. Everything that might cost money was strictly avoided.

My education had become a religion. Money wasn't being saved fast enough. In desperation he turned to the big warehouses – the abyss.

I wonder if you can understand what this means? There are certain houses which commission men won't touch. They peddle black market stuff – pornography, drugs, stolen goods, that sort of thing. Profits are high, but the work is dangerous. Guriah wouldn't say so, but he dropped strong hints that Shaikh-Moosa was the ace of this greasy deck, but this angle is far from clear. The point is that it was this kind of thing that must have broken the old man. Once involved, there was no 'out' (as the Americans say) – they had tabs on him, could threaten blackmail. This way, they halved commissions and could goad him to greater applications. It became like a speed wobble on a motor-bike: no way out but faster; and faster he went. His health was in bad repair, and pretty soon he went under. Guriah describes how after his first stroke, he became delirious and kept wildly, urgently repeating – 'My son, my son! I must do something for the boy. My love child!' (I translate the words crudely from the original Hindi: *Duniah* means 'the world'. Literally, the expression he used, *duniah ke unda ney hai beta*, means 'no where in world a boy-child'.)

After the second stroke he went for two days into the coma from which he never recovered.

When I think of it now I realize what it must all have meant to a man of his gentle, kindly temperament. He was really an alien to Grey Street; the place must have maimed the heart of his self-respect. He was really a peasant, with a feudal sense of honour; he acted out of the purest kind of love. He never gave in, he saw the business through. Funny, isn't it? Upon little, half-educated, honourable men like him, the great commercial houses grew fat, and yet when he died they turned their backs to rule off, then close another page of their ledgers. Guriah told me that his firm refused to pay mother three months' arrears in salary on the grounds that, if he had taken orders from others, he couldn't have properly completed their work!

But the final irony is that in that last year, hearing of his goings on, or rather being forced to hear, I had grown to detest him. I was very proud. The eyes of chance aquaintances kept repeating: 'See, that's Naidoo's boy – Commission Naidoo!' I loathed him. I loathed his having brought the family to this; I rejoiced over the dereliction his person was assuming – a just retribution for economic lechery.

So now you see me in my true colours: a faceless insect, shorn of pretences. I don't know whether I can bear to send this letter.

He never did.

During his night in prison, Henry slept fitfully. On one occasion, he woke with a premonition of evil. He woke, and quite inexplicably found his heart beating so rapidly that his first thought was death: was he about to die? Fear sprinted through him, intensifying the volume and speed of his heart. The cell was filled with that coldness that precedes dawn. Shuddering, he wrapped the coarse blanket about aching limbs, but the unreasonable panic would not diminish.

It was then – he told me the next day – that he wondered whether the images and memories that had overcrowded his immediate consciousness were presages of doom: that telescoping of history which is supposed to precede the arrival of death. A passage in the work of the German philosopher, Hegel, began to recur exasperatingly in his mind.

The passage was exasperating not just because it was unremitting, but – more importantly – because it was singularly devoid of meaning.

'Damned silly,' he told me hours later, when he was released, 'when the owl of Minerva spreads its wings, one is supposed to gain special knowledge. All I had were a series of disconnected memories.'

We were sitting in his Hanover Street office. The prison authorities had not allowed visitors, so we were only able to meet when I'd heard of his release.

'So you're a very famous person now!' was the greeting I gave him. 'You're in all the papers.'

His unshaven face released a brief smile of self-deprecating irony.

I wanted to give him the warning which had despatched me so urgently to his office. It had been too private to be relayed over the phone. Instead, I let him talk, which is what he seemed to prefer to do.

172

'Yes,' he murmured with another self-defensive smile, 'I've thought a lot about that recently – fame!'

It was ironical, he confessed, that he had once wanted so desperately to merge himself with the Cape, to belong here in Cape Town, and now that he belonged, he felt lethargic and disoriented. Commitment was producing too many obligations. His life was no longer his own.

He frowned suddenly as if an idea – like a shaft of sunshine – had escaped through the clouded sky of his face.

'Adrian,' he said with equal suddenness, leaning forward and taking one of my hands. 'Do me a favour, please?'

I waited for the vulnerable look of appeal to die in his eyes. When it did, it endured in the affection with which he held my hand.

'Look after my papers, please, my diaries, letters . . .'

'Of course,' I agreed, giving his hand a reassuring squeeze.

'It's not too much trouble?'

I shook my head, and continued to hold his hand.

'Is it the owl of Minerva?' I asked with a light grin, thinking about our earlier discussion.

'In part,' he admitted, 'but I wanted you to read in my diaries about how I felt when I arrived here – in the Cape, that is.'

I hesitated. Then – because the moment seemed right – I told him what had brought me to his office. I delivered what my cousin had not exaggerated: namely that there was a conspiracy to break the Tenant's Association, and that a team of hooligans had been hired to do the job.

'Get out,' I advised him. 'Get out now, while you can.'

He smiled sadly and in a tone of matching sadness, said:

'Thank you.' Before withdrawing his own, he gave my hand a final squeeze. 'I'll think about it.'

When I heard what happened later I searched his diaries, and came across the passage that, I think, he had referred to:

The moment, he writes, I set foot in Cape Town I had an unsettling premonition that I had crossed a Rubicon, but it was only after the death of my parents that I knew I could never return to Durban. Only someone brought up in a cramped intellectual backwater like Durban can truly appreciate the relief and excitement which accompanied those first years in the Cape. It was like the renaissance one might experience travelling out of a long, very dark railway-

tunnel and coming suddenly into a country of flowers and sunlight, meadows, valleys and streams. That was the effect of the Hex River valley; only, instead of flowers and meadows, there were acres of vineyard, horizon to horizon, deciduous orchards and blue gums and silvery willows shivering and glistening against cezanne-coloured landscapes and skies. For a while, I longed for the magical safety of familiar darkness; but soon impressions rearranged their shelves; and before I had fully grasped what had happened, my destiny had taken fresh direction.

At first, I was confused. But gradually the scales lifted. Durban became a cesspool of commercial lechery. I knew the poorer districts of Cape Town were squalid; but there is a kind of liveliness to old seaport slums that makes surburban respectability, by contrast, cadaverous. The streets of Cape Town were live with colour, sound, people: somehow gaiety, independence, a sense of belonging and identity had not yet been banished by the harsher realities of South Africa: by absurd racialism and materialistic vulgarity. Cape Town seemed to lie – a golden island of sanity, a pre-diluvial paradise – outside the 'Iron Curtain' of more general South African despotism. Traditional liberalism still made it possible for an outsider like me, an Indian, a Hindu moreover in a predominantly Cape Coloured and Malay community, to retain some human dignity, even if the right to sit anywhere in a bus, or to elect a fellow 'Non-White' to a Municipal Council was no more than a privilege reluctantly granted and daily threatened. The liberty of the Cape bemused me. I recognised, for the first time, my kinship in spirit with other under-trodden South Africans, in fact, with the under-trodden throughout the world. A little liberty creates this kind of awareness; and I discovered, too, that this liberty was insufficient, that what I hankered after was freedom of a more positive kind, one coupled with equality and responsibility, but if these latter were still remote, I would settle for the modicum I had, which is all just another way of saying that I now knew where exile should stop.

From this passage, and from a letter Katherine so generously sent, it became clear where his obligations would settle: also what he would do. He had principles to represent: personal courage was not at stake: he was not in a ritual bullfight.

He was still in this state of suspended rehabilitation when Mr Parsons and two other members of the Tenant's Association arrived with the news that the campaign had entered a new phase. The Executive wished to dissociate itself from the violence of the day before, and had printed a vast quantity of leaflets to this effect. These leaflets were being distributed by members who were keeping a round-the-clock vigil on the steps of the City Hall. Henry was asked to relieve a man who had done duty already for almost fourteen hours. The vigil was to be sedulously non-violent; only passive resistance, the Executive had decided, could win public approval for the campaign; and anyone who volunteered a stint of duty had to promise not to react to the most searching provocation. Henry could not refuse. The new tactic agreed with his principles which included the notion that once one had entered a contract it was a most sacred duty not to break it.

When, however, he reached the City Hall, some of his resolution defected. There were five others keeping watch and morale was low. One was a young boy, who felt foolish, standing with a banner before what he took to be hostile public inspection. Two others had been on duty all day and were anxious to be relieved; they kept going off for unaccounted coffee breaks. The old man was positively scared; some ruffians had been round earlier, and finding that whatever they did, produced not the slightest retaliation, had spent over half-an-hour ridiculing the campaigners and had threatened to return later, when the streets were more quiet. Lastly there was a short, fat woman, a gossip, who had already got on everyone's nerves, and who never stopped telling everyone how altruistic she was. When she wasn't bragging, she was retailing stories about her domestic routine when and how she did her washing, where she shopped, what the family ate at breakfast, and so on. Henry's arrival rallied the vigil, even if he himself had begun to believe the cause was hopeless. He felt, however, that he ought to set an example, and he was in the process of putting heart back into the others when Jessie turned up.

She had just come from Somerset West and was quivering with news. She had seen Katherine, indeed had had a long chat with her, and drew Henry aside to give him a spirited account of the interview. Henry's feelings ran amok; nausea flushed his loins; he listened defensively: he looked as if he expected to be physically assaulted.

Katherine was in Somerset West Hospital. She was convalescing but still looked bloomlessly ill. 'You wouldn't recognise her,' Jessie said, 'I didn't at first!' Drained of colour, her face was like an old part of a city, bleak, gaunt, desolate; it was mottled with yellow, and the black of her hair deepened the cavities of spiritless eyes. She had lost weight; she spoke in weak, flagging spurts, her voice an off-key whisper: a song of damaged notes.

The sight of Jessie had upset her; according to the nurses, she cried whenever she was alone, but put on a brave face when anyone was in the room. She ate little, and spent hours staring into space, even though she had a fair collection of books and magazines. She received neither visitors nor correspondence, and rarely spoke. In the last day her condition had improved enough for her, with help, to sit propped up against a pile of cushions – the position in which Jessie had found her.

When their eyes had met, Katherine had dropped hers away, and had not looked up for a long time, emotion twitching at the corners of mouth and jaw. Against Jessie's surprise and delight, she had kept her head lowered, her eyes expressionlessly fixed on the folds of the blankets. Only when Jessie had begun to relate recent political events did her interest prick up; and when she began to receive an account of Henry's reaction to her disappearance, she raised her face for the first time, startled.

The look of intense disbelief in Katherine's sunken eyes stopped Jessie's narrative; to Jessie's surprise Katherine had begun to cry. The crying had frightened Jessie. It had been accompanied by no facial movements, no convulsive sobbing of the throat. It had been almost as if a mechanical doll were being mulcted; only the pallid eyelids had moved, and mysterious tears had swelled in the empty eyes, brimming over and then stealing in steady unwiped courses down her cheeks, dripping eventually onto her pale-blue, muslin nightgown.

Jessie had spent over two hours with Katherine, and had won Katherine's confidence only after having repeatedly affirmed that Henry had not taken up with Madge. Indeed, Katherine had only opened up when she heard that Madge and Doc were getting married that very afternoon, and when Jessie explained what had actually taken place after the Christmas Eve party. 'But,' Katherine had protested, 'Madge isn't pregnant. She told me she's been wearing a diaphragm ever since she was sixteen . . .' She had broken off pained by sudden understanding. 'Now I see!' she had said, and then had explained how, on the day when they had gone to the hairdresser's together, because her spirits had been unusually low, she had told Madge she was pregnant, that Stewart had offered to pay for an

176

abortion, but that being so much in love with Henry she was uncertain what Henry's reaction would be; she had been unwilling to spoil her present tenuous happiness. Crying again, she had begged Jessie, in a harsh whisper, to tell Henry everything and to ask him, if he could forgive her, to come to see her as soon as possible. The mere thought of him hurt, she felt utterly lost, but if he could not come, she could forgive him, for now she saw how hurtful her own conduct had been. She had been so sure that if he had known she was carrying Stewart's child he would, in disgust, have left her. That had been another mistake, the result of the night when she and Stewart had been disturbed in the back of a car.

Jessie's revelations, instead of pitching Henry into an ecstasy of excitement, as she had expected, seemed, on the contrary, to spread over him a disturbing stillness. But this was only because she had never come across a temperament like his in a state of crisis.

In crisis, he writes in his diary, *whereas others panic and bustle, I grow strangely still. I have noticed this odd behaviour frequently. I become pure minded, detached, rational, cold, withdrawn, but all the while, inside, I am a tempest, a hot theatre of conflicting emotions, the still eye in the centre of the hurricane.*

After a long silence, he asked, laconically, if she was going to Somerset West again; and when she replied that she had only gone to the hospital to apologise for no longer being able to train there, he was silent again.

'Could you do me a favour though,' he asked at last, 'a special one?' And when she nodded, he continued, 'could you take her a letter. I'll write it now. If you come back in an hour it should be ready.'

'I'll go tonight,' she said, and was surprised to find herself enclosed, suddenly, by his arms and hugged with passionate gratitude. She wanted to cry.

There was no writing paper, so Henry used the backs of several leaflets for his letter, and while he was writing, Mr Percy, who had also been released from gaol, and Miss Martha, arrived to relieve two of the others. Their presence encouraged Henry to make off to his office to complete his letter under less distracting conditions. When he returned, it was already dusk; the traffic peak was over; the sun, glinting over the buildings, exaggerated the emptiness of the streets, and Jessie was waiting. He gave her the letter and thanked her again, this time with a full kiss on the mouth. In that moment, he was unaware that by despatching her, he inadvertently destroyed a chance of happiness, that Pieter, not finding her at home, would sail on his own that night for Holland, and that two days later, grief-stricken, she would commit suicide and her anonymous, young, sea-bloated body would be washed up on the dirty, oil-stained sands of Woodstock Beach. He knew neither that, nor that within a few hours he would himself be dead. But, at least, in his own case, he did receive a second warning.

The warning came at ten o'clock. He was talking to Mr Percy when the boy with the banner came to tell him that there was a man around the corner who wanted to speak to him. The man was alone in a large, seven-seater Packard. Henry thought at once of Shaikh-Moosa, but when he reached the car, he found John Moodley, puffing impatiently on a cigarette, in the driver's seat.

'See here, maart,' Moodley said, cutting short Henry's greeting. 'I came out of my way to see you here, and I'm going to Jo'burg tonight. Lemme just tell you one thing. Get out quick. Get out, maart, 'fore the ructions start. Doan ask me how I know. I know.'

'What d'you mean?' Henry asked. He was standing on the pavement. John started up the engine.

'Look!' he said, 'we been old friends, school-mates, okay? I done my duty. Take my advice. I can't stop and talk. I done my duty. Vam, kid. Cut a line quick. Twenty minutes from now, you gonna get the ructions! They gonna moor you!'

Moodley did not wait to gather Henry's response. He drove off; leaving Henry uncertain whether the caveat was another of Shaikh-Moosa's ruses. Now that Katherine again quivered upon immediate horizons, Henry was aware that if he kept his vigil it might – at best – mean being as cruelly thrashed as Johnathan December had been. More likely, given the curtain of violence spreading across South African political life, it might mean the end of everything – Katherine, his career, life itself . . .

Henry wavered.

He remembered the letter he had just sent Katherine: in particular the reference to the man who had taught him Jurisprudence, a man who was perhaps the most crucial leaven of character in his life. He remembered his response at Kalk Bay to Gordon Stewart, and earlier, how he had wanted to retaliate after having been smacked at Sea Point. Then he remembered his mother's counsel: the comforts of re-birth that she preached.

For a few moments fear again sprinted through him; courage failed. Across the Parade, under the streetlights, he saw a contingent of *ducktails*, with clubs and bicycle chains, moving in his direction. Now the Owl of Minerva swooped through his loins and with rising despair, he knew there was no turning back.

Moodley's warning was sound. The ructions arrived earlier than expected. In fact, they had already started when Henry got to the steps of the City Hall. A band of white hooligans were assaulting Miss Martha, calling her 'a whore' and a '*kaffirboetjie*,' and Mr Parsons was blocking their passage, and they had already begun to flail him with *sjamboks* and bicycle chains. The old man's face was a gush of blood, but he stood his ground, quiet and resolute, saying with simple dignity, 'don't do that, sonny, stop that, have a little pity.' Henry's first impulse was to save himself, but the sight of the old man being murdered was more than he could bear. He lost his sense and rushed, with fists flying, among the most immediate assailants. At once the *ducktails* turned on him. Less than a minute later he was lying on the pavement with a bicycle chain slashed several inches through the skull, his blood spurting in several directions. When the police arrived the *ducktails* had vanished, and Henry Naidoo was dead.

I need not say what became of the Tenant's Association. Like most political campaigns of that period it failed, and its casualties in personal suffering and disaster still seem to outweigh its positive achievements, moral or otherwise. Human life is not a problem in physics that can be accurately measured. Let me say only a few words about the others that have appeared in this narrative.

I met Gordon Stewart shortly before I left South Africa myself. My wife, Yvonne, who had been dying of cancer in Groote Schuur, had released me from all final ties with my homeland; even teaching at Cape Town University had become quite impossible; and I saw no prospect within the country of any change; my hopes had begun to focus on the world outside, and perhaps, in self-preservation, perhaps from common sense, I decided that my frail personal resources might be more effective in the struggle for South African freedom abroad.

I did not, and still do not, agree with Stewart's views, but I had no reason to share Henry's aversion for the man, so when I received, by messenger, an invitation to visit him in Hanover Street, where he lived in hiding, I went at once. He had changed greatly since our last meeting; his manner was more sullen and abrupt; his face was harder, colder; his hair, perhaps from months of underground life, had sallowed; and his short body was scarred in several places. He had, in fact, lost two fingers on one hand, while manufacturing home-made hand grenades – It was, of course, he who had blown up the police vans during the Tenant's Association demonstration – He asked me, tersely, whether, since I was leaving the country, I would establish contacts for him in North Africa, and when I refused, told me I was a fool and a shame to the International Anarchist Movement. We parted on bitter terms.

As for Rycliffe, he died shortly after being replaced by Benjamin Michaels as the leader of the *Flame* group. Michaels, of course, opposed Holmes in the Municipal Elections, and won, as Katherine later put it, 'hands down'.

Madge deserted Doc not long after their shotgun marriage. Frederic and Elizabeth and their children are now living in Britain, where Frederic enjoys modest renown as a 'Third World' composer. Mr Percy and Miss Martha have also returned to Britain, but the Great Man is now in the United States, where he has become a senior arms-broker in the tragic wars against impoverished Central Americans. His Cape Flats deal came to nothing and he managed to unload Uralco before its prospects were doomed. Senator Goodbrand, who had refused to support Holmes in the Municipal Election, now holds a Chair in Race Relations in a Cambridge College where he can safely utter the most insurrectionary solutions to the South African dilemma and drink vintage port twice a week.

My roll call would be complete but for one person who, as I write, is still capable of making my hand tremble. The day before I left South Africa my lawyer, AK Blum, telephoned to say that he would be sending someone with Henry's effects to the ship. Blum had a penchant for mysteries, but because I was in a hurry to tie up last-minute, loose ends, I preferred not to join his elaborate guessing games. It did not seem necessary to know whom he was sending.

That he was disappointed I could tell from the way he needed to satisfy his own curiosity.

'Okay,' he said, after an uncomfortable silence, 'you tell me something.'

I waited tolerantly.

He waffled a few moments – as he was wont – then he asked point-blank when I had decided to leave South Africa. Had the police intrusions been the cause?

'Yes,' I admitted, 'but not entirely.' I saw them, I explained, as very catalytic aspects of my general fate. Before them, I had postponed my date of departure twice.

When he realised that I was in no mood for the sort of long-winded discussions he relished, he hinted that I was in for a surprise.

'A pleasant surprise?' I asked so as not to be too ungracious.

'Wait and see!'

I did not give his messenger a second thought – until she arrived, and then I was overwhelmed. The last time I'd seen Katherine was way before Henry's death.

I was shocked. In not more than a year she had become an old woman. She had shrivelled like a branch that has been lopped off the main trunk. The operation in Somerset West, she delicately explained, had upset her hormone balance; yet behind rouge and powder and grotesquerie of fashionable clothes, a vestige of her former glamour remained. The eyes were still beautiful, alert but now more vulnerable; and while talking to her, for a moment I experienced some of the promise Henry had once detected in her; for a moment I lost my head: I begged her to come with me, to share my cabin, my life . . . But she smiled, sadly, her face desolate as a city street late at night, all expression stolen from it and said in a voice that I shall never forget, 'Darling Adrian, you are silly! Do you think you can ever forget me? Don't be sentimental. There's a pet. You know I can't leave Stewart now. I don't love him. Nor will I ever, but he stuck by me when it mattered, and I must serve my country and the empty future which is his. Henry would have understood.'

Henry, indeed, did understand. A year later, when Katherine heard that I was writing this book, she sent me by registered post, among other documents, a photostat of Henry's last letter to her.

The letter is long and passionate and rambling, and that part of it on which I close is only a scrap.

181

Dearest Katherine, (it begins)

Jessie's revelations have sent me into a muddled heaven of joy and pain. You are a silly fool! How could you possibly have imagined that I would have thought ill of your pregnancy? What a silly abominable pride you have! How is it possible to tell you that I love you more than myself, more than anything else in the world? . . .

Please forgive me for not coming to you now. The decision excruciates, but like you, I must not violate obligations. Forget all the Marxist claptrap about history. Remember that it is always human rights that finally count. What I am doing now and what I might die doing, my love, is for you . . . for you and for others . . . for the future. To come to see you would be self-indulgence . . . What could we say? . . . What could we do? . . . While you lie in your hospital bed, drained of blood and life? If I can get away, of course I'll come, but right now, it's impossible. From now on we have lost a very important value, liberty of choice; we are pawns now; the final fragmentation has begun; like our African colleagues, we can no longer live as settled families and communities; from now on the sexes must live apart, pulverised by the omniscient state, the rebels hiding, like Stewart, in the shadows, exiles from everything human . . .

You will see that I have lost faith in pacifist answers. There is no morality left but that of the tiger: brute force. That is why Stewart is our obscene and tragic salvation. If I die, choose him, choose blood and violence and pain. What a horrible future for our country! . . .

I see now what the point of my life was. I wanted justice. That is why I became a lawyer. I believed in justice within a tradition of law. But now that justice is no longer possible, it must be found by methods outside the law, by men not like myself, men trained not to be squeamish about violence and murder and brutality, men like Lenin, criminal saviours, cultural barbarians with wills of steel . . . I am played out, I belong to softer times . . . I would never make the grade . . . I am like Rycliffe, in a way, who has ditched us with his election boycott; now we have no thugs to protect us; we are quite defenceless.

Perhaps you will see now why I can't come to you, my love. I am

182

going to try to play a role in which I have no training, but, whatever happens, I cannot now opt out. Let me explain. At University, we had a lecturer – one of the finest men I've ever known – who used to say, over and over, in his lectures on Jurisprudence, 'Promise-keeping and truth-telling are, perhaps, the most final social values. Without them, no society can function.' He was a thin, intense, rational Welshman, and he would repeat this belief so frequently that it has become for me a kind of catechism. What sort of life could I possibly represent if I deserted these people now? I was not cut out to be a leader, but these people depend on me. No matter how foolish it seems, how tempting and easy the retreat, I must return the loyalty they seek. Let them betray rather than I betray them. Promise-keeping! . . .

You ask me to forgive you. Of course I do. But what is there to forgive? It is I, really, who should be seeking your forgiveness, being unable to give you the means with which to make life viable. I know now what my obtuseness failed to recognise: there is for me only one kind of true love, and that is responsible compassion. I hope you can forgive me . . .

Stay with Stewart: only he can resurrect the life we might have had. I will come to you as soon as I am free . . .

GLOSSARY

Boks   Lover/one who is eager (slang)
Bokkies   Term of endearment for boy/girlfriend or lover (colloq)
Braaivleis   Barbeque/grilling meat on coals
Buniah   Grain merchant or shop keeper (Hindu)
Dingaan's Day   Day of the Covenant. It celebrates the Africaaners' victory over the Zulus in Natal. They made a covenant with God that should they win the battle they would build a Church and keep the day sacred. Dingaan was the Zulu king at the time.
Dwaal   Daze/day dream (Afrikaans, colloq)
Ghalas   Liking something very much (slang)
Herrenvolk   God's people
Jorl   To go out on a spree/have fun/party
Kaffirboetjie   Someone who is sympathetic towards blacks (derog). Literally translated from Afrikaans as Kaffir brother.
Jasgiin-Bah   Gaol (slang)
Meshugenah   Crazy (Hebrew)
Narghiles   Oriental tobacco pipe, similar to a hookah
Platteland   Country districts/rural areas
Pondokkies   Hut/shack (Afrikaans)
Skollies   Petty criminal, hooligan (Cape, colloq)
Sjambok   A stout rhinoceros or hippopotamus hide whip
Tiekkie-Draai   Fast dance when couples turn round and round on one spot
Veldtschoene   'hide shoe' (lit), type of rough suede ankle boot or shoe
Voortrekker   'to pull forward' (lit). The *voortrekkers* were the pioneers who emigrated from the Cape to escape British rule